THE

MADDENING

Book 2 in The Muladach Series

MELISSA PLANTZ

FIRE and GRACE
Publishing, LLC

Melissa Plantz
FIRE and GRACE Publishing, LLC
fireandgracepublishing.com

Printed in the United States of America
First Printing 2021
First Edition 2021

ISBN: 978-1-7354248-0-4

10 9 8 7 6 5 4 3 2 1

Cover Design by VC Book Cover Design

For my children

and grandchildren

PROLOGUE

The dinging of the doorbell interrupted Maren. She winced as she stood.

Alec moved quickly to her side. "Do you want me to get the door?"

"Yes, that would help," she answered as Alec headed for the front door. "I forget I can't just jump up right now," she grumbled to me as she slowly made her way to the front door.

I watched as Alec opened the door wider for Maren. An old priest and another man dressed in blue jeans and a wool coat stood on her porch.

"Father Mahon! Stephen! This is a surprise. You normally call."

"Yes, but I wanted to check on you face-to-face. The discharge nurse told us you'd already left," the older priest said in a New York accent.

"Please, come in. I want to introduce you to someone." Maren and Alec moved away from the door to let the men inside. She motioned for me to come closer.

"This is Gerald Reynolds' daughter, Ainsley."

The priest removed his black hat and shook my hand. "Ainsley, I knew your father well," he said. He was no taller than me, with white hair that stuck out in tufts from the side of his head. "I see you're wearing his amulet. Maren told us how you bravely stood against the demons and their host. Thank you for using your gift to serve."

"Thank you, but to be honest, I didn't know about any of this until recently. My father kept it hidden from his family." I stared into the older man's kind eyes. He reminded me of someone's grandfather – the type who might sit down and launch into a story at any moment.

The younger dark-haired man stretched out his hand. "Hi, I'm Stephen Reeves. I pastor a small church in West Virginia, just north of Charleston. I was with your dad on a number of investigations," he said, with a twang that matched Maren's.

"Maren told me that he didn't do a lot of them after I was born." Stephen looked as if he might be around Dad's age.

"Not like he used to," he answered and gave me a sly grin as if he and Dad shared an inside joke.

Maren touched the priest's arm. "And this is Alec Graham, the detective who helped Ainsley. He saved her life."

Father Mahon turned and shook Alec's hand as he narrowed his eyes as if observing something in Alec's face. "Thank you. You remind me a little of Gerald. You have a commanding presence about you."

"Thank you, Father Mahon. It's a pleasure to meet you both." Alec nodded at Stephen.

Maren motioned for the men to sit, and I offered the priest a bottle of water. When he refused, Maren enticed him with a cup of coffee which he heartily accepted.

"Stephen, you still take yours the same? Half and half and sugar?" she asked.

"Oh, you know I do, Mare. I'll come help you." He quickly pulled his coat off and left the room with Maren. He wasn't what I pictured a pastor to look like. I'd always seen preachers in suits on Easter Sunday, but Stephen wore jeans and a black sweater with long sleeves that he'd pushed up to his elbows, showing off a tattoo sleeve. Was it only on his forearm like Alec's, or was it full length? From the giggles coming from the kitchen, it sounded like Stephen and Maren went way back. Alec and I smiled at each other. Why couldn't we sneak into another room and giggle like that?

"I'm so glad that both of you are here at this time," the older gentleman said as he reached for my hand.

I wasn't sure what to do, but the man patted the top of my hand while he spoke. "Seeing you here is not only a bonus but a sign from The Almighty. You've been chosen to continue Gerald's work here on earth. To scatter the demons and deliver the people from evil."

I slowly slipped my hand away from Father Mahon as I glanced up at Alec, who'd turned to face the patio doors. "I'm sorry, Father, but that's not who I am. Trust me, before this, I didn't believe in much. Our family only went to church on Easter Sunday. I've seen things now, but I don't know much about the Christian faith. For all that my father helped you, he kept us in the dark. I'm definitely a believer now, but my involvement in all of this supernatural stuff ended when the Muladach vanished."

"The Muladach?" Father Mahon looked confused.

Maren carried his cup of hot coffee into the living room and carefully handed it to the priest. His hands shook slightly as he set it on the coffee table.

"The Muladach is the term coined by someone else who saw the demons," Maren said as she slipped into her chair. "They tried to influence him first, but it only served to drive him to madness."

"Ah, Muladach," he repeated. "It has been a while since I've heard that word. What an odd term to use to describe them. Yet fitting. Madness, sadness, sorrow. All things the demons bring into the world under the veil of humanity. However, the demons may have vanished for a time, but they will return. How many did you see?"

"Two," I answered.

"Just two?" Stephen asked as he emerged from the kitchen with a large mug in his hand. He stood beside Maren's chair and gave me that inside joke smile again.

The priest chuckled. "My dear girl, there are far more than two in this plane. As a matter of fact, there is, right now, an entire cluster of demons, probably a dozen, at an old plantation home in South Carolina. They are mimicking the sound of children and attracting those who tout themselves as paranormal investigators. There have already been two deaths associated with these "ghosts.""

Alec and I exchanged glances. "I mean no disrespect, but that sounds more like a movie or a book than real life, Father," Alec replied.

"Every good story is rooted in truth, Mr. Graham," Father Mahon answered.

"As a pastor, I believed in the supernatural from the get-go, as God Himself is supernatural," Stephen said to Alec. "However, my belief leveled up when I became involved in this with Gerald. The demons are real. The warfare is real. And people are dying every day because either they are influenced or totally possessed by them. Murders, suicides, mass killings. Of course, some people are to blame, sick people. But, others, you will see, are under an influence."

"Detective Graham, if I were to tell you that you were the only one who could save someone from certain death, what would you do?" Father Mahon asked Alec.

Alec frowned. "I'd learn everything I could about the situation and act accordingly."

"You would risk your life to save the life of another person?"

"Yes," Alec answered. He held the older man's gaze steadily as he crossed the room to stand beside me. "That's why I do what I do."

Father Mahon nodded and then turned to me. "That is what makes up every fiber of Mr. Graham's being. His job is to protect others. But Mr. Graham cannot see the demons. He cannot hear them. That gift was given to you. Yet, the two of you were brought together in such an unlikely and dramatic way. The Seer and the Protector. So, I ask you, Ainsley, what if I were to tell you that *you* were the only one who could save someone from certain death, what would you do?"

I lowered my eyes as Alec placed his hand on my shoulder and gave it a reassuring squeeze.

"I'm not Catholic."

"Neither was your father," the priest answered. "Or Stephen. This isn't about Catholics or Protestants or Jews. Our organization includes many members of different denominations. This is about trusting in God, Your Father who knows your needs, and stopping an insidious evil before more innocent people lose their lives. Saving people like your friend Molly."

I reached up and gripped Alec's hand on my shoulder.

The Seer and the Protector.

"What would you have me do to continue my father's work?" I asked, knowing full-well a trip to South Carolina was in our near future, and I still had no idea how to explain any of this to Mom.

CHAPTER ONE

"Can I talk to you for a minute?" Alec's green eyes bore into mine as he motioned towards Maren's front door. My psychology teacher, counselor, and a secret friend of my father's, Miss Maren Bell, nodded from her recliner that it was okay to leave this impromptu meeting.

I followed Alec out the front door and to his SUV parked across from the townhouse. He was quiet for a long while as he rested his hands on the hood of the truck, the crisp breeze ruffling the top of his messy yet perfect brown hair.

Finally, he spoke. "Ainsley, I think you should carefully consider what these people are saying. You don't know any of them. That priest and that preacher just came out of nowhere and handed you praise about your father. There has to be a reason why Gerald Reynolds never so much as hinted to you about any of this. You can't seriously consider traveling to South Carolina to an old house to rid it of its so-called ghosts?"

I'd never seen Alec so agitated. Of course, I'd only known Detective Alec Graham for two weeks, but we'd become close. So close that he'd almost lost his job because he'd befriended his almost eighteen-year-old witness in a murder case. We managed to survive the confrontation with a murderer as well as the vicious rumors by my classmates. Alec was still on suspension and we'd spent the last few days talking about officially becoming a couple after my birthday in six weeks.

"You know what they're saying is true," I said as I placed my hand over his. The warmth from his hand felt comforting despite the cold metal from the SUV hood and the North Carolina Fall air. "Alec, you know it was the demons that influenced the murderer to take those lives. They are the real reason people are dead. Father Mahon and Stephen helped my father send the demons back to Hell. If there is an old plantation house in South Carolina that is 'haunted' with demons mimicking children and killing paranormal investigators, I can't *not* go. I'm the only one who can sense them. According to Father Mahon, I'm the Seer."

At that, Alec placed his hands on my shoulders. I hoped he would pull me in for a hug, but instead, he leaned down to look me straight in the eye. "Mahon also said I was your Protector. There is no way I'm letting you go to South Carolina alone. Or, even with these people."

I pulled away and took a step backward. "You can't stop me from going, Alec. You're just my friend."

Alec raised an eyebrow.

"Okay, maybe something a little more than a friend, but you are not my parent."

He didn't budge. "And what *will* you tell your mom? Stella Reynolds isn't exactly going to authorize you to travel out of state. Especially after what happened in Charlotte," he lowered his voice, "and to Molly."

I bit my lip. He was right. When my father died two years ago, my mother had become a suffocating presence over my younger brother and me. She'd gone through her own personal Hell when she found out that I'd become friends with the homicide detective investigating the case. But, she'd really been afraid when she found out I'd confronted the killer to save my friends, and now my BFF laid in a coma in the hospital only minutes away from where I stood.

"Ainsley," Alec said as he stepped closer. He tilted my chin up, forcing my gaze to meet his. "Could it be that you think you'll feel closer to your father by working with the people he knew? That somehow, by finishing your father's work, maybe you are bringing him back to life?"

I swallowed hard. "The priest asked you that if you knew you were the only person to save others, would you do it? You answered yes. This is no different. I don't know how to tell Mom. Not yet. But, I have to find a way before other people die because of the Muladach. My father trusted these people."

Alec searched my eyes, and I hoped he could see how committed I was to this. Someone had coined the demons as "Muladach" because they led their victims to sorrow and madness - and almost always death. Whatever people wanted to call them, I could see and hear them, and now I knew how to stop them.

Kind of.

I was still thinking about the Muladach when Alec leaned down and kissed me. It was a gentle kiss like he wasn't sure if he should have just then. When he leaned back, he smiled as he sighed.

"I guess we need to find the best way to get you to that old house," he said.

"We? Are you coming?"

"I'm not going to let you go without me. I don't think I can go one day, one hour, one minute without you now."

"Hm. What about work?"

"I'm still on suspension, remember?" He wrapped a long lock of my blonde hair around his finger. "I need to make sure you are safe this time," he whispered as he bent down to kiss me again.

Just as Alec's lips touched mine, I heard Maren's voice ring out, "Come on, you two! We have more to discuss."

~ ~ ~

The white-haired priest remained seated on Maren's plush couch when Alec and I slipped back in the front door. Stephen Reeves, the preacher from West Virginia and apparently, a very good friend of Maren's, was leaning against the wall drinking his coffee. Maren made her way back to her chair, slightly holding her side at the location of her stitches – a wound she'd received when she'd saved my life.

"So, have you decided to pick up where Gerry left off?" Maren asked. I hated it when she called my father Gerry instead of Gerald. No one ever called him that except her.

"I think so," I said as I took a deep breath. "But, I'm not sure how to explain any of it to Mom. Getting her permission for a trip out of the state is a longshot."

"I think I may have a solution to that," Maren said. "There is a group of students who have volunteered as part of their Community Service hours to work with an organization building a house not far from the estate that needs investigating. I could add you to the group. They leave in about a week. You would stay with them at the hotel, but I could excuse you to run errands or work on another project for me. Maybe we could say it is for the college experience."

"If Ainsley is going to South Carolina, then I'm going too. Someone has to have her back, Maren." Alec picked up his bottle of water and took a drink.

"That could work." Stephen set his cup on the coffee table. "I'm going down, and you can ride with me. We'll need to get motel rooms."

"I'd rather stay in whatever hotel Ainsley is going to be in," Alec answered.

"Well," Maren said as she bit her lower lip. "The money for the trip has already been taken. I'll check with Mr. Clendenin, but if all of the hotel rooms in our reserved block are gone, Ainsley will have to get her own room. Ainsley, can you afford to stay at a hotel?"

I lowered my head as I studied my black boots. Finances were tight, and Mom kept a close eye on our expenses. I hadn't even started the after-school job at The Locklyn Gym yet because of the traumatic events in Charlotte.

"Um," I started.

"I'll pay for it," Alec said quickly. "I'll get *separate* rooms," he added when everyone stared at him.

Maren nodded. "Okay, then it's settled. I'll call Mr. Clendenin tomorrow morning.

CHAPTER TWO

B ut there was no reason for Maren to call Mr. Clendenin, as I soon found out upon entering the small foyer to my own split-level home I shared with my mother and nine-year-old brother, Benjamin. My school's Vice-Principal was standing in the dining room dressed in jeans and a polo, calmly talking to my mother. He'd covered his mostly bald head with a ballcap, and I could barely make out the white hair that peppered at his temples.

"Ainsley, I was just going to text you and see when you were coming home," Mom announced as I dropped my purse on the table.

"Ainsley, how are you doing? I came to check in on Stella and you," Mr. Clendenin said as he studied my face. Nick Clendenin and my mother had gone to school together in our small town of Locklyn, situated at the halfway point between Charlotte and Holden Beach. I hadn't realized they'd become closer friends since all of this started with the Muladach.

Not until now.

"I'm fine," I said as Mr. Clendenin narrowed his eyes as if trying to decipher if I was telling the truth. After everything that had happened at the school and with Alec, I didn't blame him. "Molly is doing a bit better. They're going to try to decrease the oxygen from the ventilator to see if she will breathe more on her own."

"Good, good to hear," he said as we stared awkwardly at each other from across the table. "I plan to reach out to Sora and Nikki tomorrow," he added, referring to Molly's parents.

"How is Ms. Bell?" Mom asked.

"She's doing much better," I said with relief as I walked around Mr. Clendenin and into the kitchen to get a bottle of water. I leaned on the island counter that separated the kitchen from the dining room and watched my Vice-Principal as he smiled at my mother. She was smiling back in a way I hadn't seen in a long time. With their guards down, maybe now was the best time to bring up Maren's idea.

"Mom, Ms. Bell suggested that maybe I take a break from everything and let it all settle down. You know, with school and Molly. She mentioned a community service project for a group of seniors in South Carolina that I could attend. But, I would need your permission soon because they leave in a week."

Mom frowned and glanced over at Mr. Clendenin. "I don't know, Ainsley. I'm a little wary about you going so far away after what happened."

Mr. Clendenin walked over and rubbed his hand over Mom's arm. "Actually, Stella, that trip is well chaperoned. Maren Bell is going to try to go if she feels up to it. This might be perfect timing. It'll give Ainsley a chance to hang out with people her own age - and away from other influences."

Other influences? Did he mean Alec? I watched as Mom's neat blonde brows knitted together.

"I don't know…how much does it cost?"

"Ms. Bell said if the hotel block of rooms is full that I will have to get my own room at the same hotel. Alec offered to pay for it for the duration."

"Alec offered to pay?!" Mom asked, her voice rising. "Why? I just mean, I'm surprised he would want you to leave."

I took a long drink of my water and forced my beating heart to quiet down. Finally, I shrugged. "I believe Alec wants what's best for me like you do. Maybe some time apart would be good. I mean, a lot has happened."

Mom nodded, and I noticed she'd fixed her thick blonde hair into waves around her face instead of her usual top bun. Had she been expecting Mr. Clendenin to come over? I studied the two of them. Had something developed while I was caught up in the Artist case and Alec?

Mr. Clendenin rubbed his hand down Mom's arm once more and winked when she looked up at him. "The hotel block is full, but I could call Maren and confirm she is going to go. She could make sure Ainsley's room is at least near the block of rooms. Honestly, this trip might do your daughter some good, plus she'd be helping a worthy cause." He looked over at me and smiled.

I wasn't sure what to make of this new development and decided I would ask Mom about it later. "Please, Mom? I'll stay safe," I promised and hoped I could keep my promise this time.

"Okay. Get me the information about it from the school and the permission forms. But, you have to give me your word you will stay with the chaperones and other adults."

I smiled. "Absolutely."

~ ~ ~

After I left the VP and Mom in the living room, I made my way to my bedroom. Mom said Ben was staying the night at his friend Gavin's house, which made me suspicious that she and Nick - could I call him that now? - had planned a stay-at-home date.

When I heard them put a movie on and turn the surround sound up, I called Alec.

"Mom said I could go, but she doesn't know you are going to be there."

"I hate lying to your mother, Ainsley. If she finds out later that I was even near the South Carolina border, it's going to cause problems for us in the future," he answered. I imagined him kicked back across his bed with his eyes shut.

"If she knows that you plan to be in the vicinity, she's not going to let me go. After my birthday, it won't matter." I heard a crash in the background, and Alec growl. Apparently, he was not kicked back on the bed like I was. "What is going on?"

"I was grilling steak and dropped a plate on the kitchen floor. It hit just right and shattered everywhere. I need to get off and clean this up. When you find out about the hotel room situation, let me know so I can set it up."

"Are you sure, Alec? I mean, it's just that you're on unpaid leave, and I feel like I'm spending your money. Money that you might need later."

"Ainsley, you don't know anything about my finances. It's fine. Trust me."

When I didn't answer, Alec sighed. "I'm sorry. I don't mean to snap. I think the last few days have worn me down. Try to get some rest, and I'll talk to you tomorrow. Okay?"

"Sure. Good night, Alec."

I didn't know why, but his words left an unsettling feeling behind. We weren't an official couple, so his finances were none of my business, but to have him say it like that bothered me. I decided to Google average salaries for homicide detectives in North Carolina.

I was sorely disappointed.

~ ~ ~

I woke up the next morning wanting to call Molly and ask her advice about Alec - and the Mr. Clendenin situation. Then I remembered that Molly was still in the hospital. Instead, I decided to get dressed and visit her. After I showered and dressed in a pair of distressed jeans, a rose gold sweater, and boots, I blew my hair out and applied my makeup. Ever since I'd cut back on fast food, my face seemed to be going through a detox. I did my best to cover the offending pimples on my chin. Good grief, I could expel a demon apparently, but get slain by my own hormones. When I finally felt like I had it together, I opened the door and made my way to the kitchen.

I had just passed through the kitchen doorway when what I'd seen registered in my brain. I poked my head around the doorframe. My mother lay asleep on the couch with her head resting on Mr. Clendenin's shoulder. He was sitting upright with his chin dropped only inches from his chest. The television was still on. They'd fallen asleep watching a movie.

I knew Ben wasn't home, but I still didn't know what to do about the sleeping adults. I continued into the kitchen and started making as much noise as possible as I made my coffee, hoping to wake Mom. Finally, I heard her voice carry into the kitchen. She sounded embarrassed.

"Ainsley, I didn't expect you up so early," she said from the doorway a few seconds later.

"I'm going to the hospital to sit with Molly for a while," I answered, staring hard at the Keurig as it whirred to life.

"Okay. Well, I'm going to brush my teeth. I'll be right back." She hurried down the hall.

This was awkward.

"Good morning, Ainsley," Mr. Clendenin said from the other side of the island. He turned his cap around and motioned toward my coffee, his dark eyes watching me. "Would you care to make me a cup?"

"Sure, Mr. Clendenin," I said as I mentally noted that, no, *this* was the most awkward moment of my entire life. As I placed a mug in the tray for his coffee, I finally asked, "So, do I refer to you as Mr. Clendenin while you are here? I mean, I guess while you are dating my mother?"

He took a deep breath and then let it out loudly. "Um, I guess you should call me Nick when we're out of school. Your mother and I have been friends for years. We all went to school together; Stella, Gerald, Sora Hiroto, and me."

"It's…awkward."

"Why? Because your mother might be getting into an interracial relationship?"

"No. It's awkward because you are my Vice-Principal and the one we all fear will find some fault and send us to the office. Except we're not at school."

Mr. Clendenin - Nick - nodded as he laughed. "I see. I'm not your VP right now. I'm your Mom's friend. As for my relationship with Stella, it's complicated."

I handed him the filled mug and motioned toward the stevia packets, but he shook his head. "So, you don't know if you are dating or not?" I asked, trying to understand.

"Again, it's complicated. From what I've heard, I think you have a grasp on complicated relationships."

I frowned. "Are you referring to Alec and me?" I took a sip of my still too hot coffee. Nick nodded.

"I know we didn't handle ourselves as we should have, but he's a good guy. I know where I stand with him."

"Do you?" Nick asked with a slight frown. "He's older than you, by what? Maybe six years? Eight years? That's eight years of life experiences that you don't know anything about yet. But I think you know that. You should trust your God-given intuition over what people say or do."

I shifted. I didn't like this line of questioning, maybe because I'd already asked myself the same questions.

"Do you want me to make breakfast?" Mom asked as she came into the kitchen. She'd pulled her hair up, and I could tell she'd freshened her makeup.

"Actually, Stella, why don't you let me take you two out for breakfast?" Nick asked as he stood up from the stool.

"That's okay. You two go and have fun. I'm going to the hospital for a while," I said as I poured my coffee into a travel mug. I would have to get used to this new relationship in extremely small doses.

CHAPTER THREE

Nick Clendenin and Mom dropped me off in front of the hospital. They'd decided that since Ben was staying at Gavin's for the whole day, then the two lovebirds would make a day of it and head to the beach. Mom wanted to go to Holden, but Nick talked her into Sunset Beach instead. It'd only taken Mom twenty minutes to shower, dress, and pack a tote.

I was happy for her. For the first time in a long time, Mom seemed happy. It wasn't with Dad, but Dad wasn't coming back anytime soon as much as our hearts ached for him.

Mrs. Hiroto was coming out of Molly's room when I arrived. "Oh, I see you've brought your comforter," she quipped as she pointed to my large coffee thermos.

"Never leave home without it. How is she?"

"She's doing better. She started stirring on her own and is responding to questions by turning her head and groaning. Her eyes are still closed, but you can tell she is trying to open them. I imagine she thinks she is dreaming."

I smiled. Molly was a fighter, and she would pull through this. She had to. "Can I see her?"

"Of course, Ainsley. Oh, how is Alec?"

Nikki Hiroto and Alec had worked together on The Artist case as she was the lead forensics investigator. "He's doing well. His back is healing, but it's scarring around the edges." I shivered as I remembered what the serial killer had been doing to Alec when I arrived on the scene.

"I'm glad he's alright. Tell him to call me sometime and fill me in on what's going on. I miss seeing his face at the station when I stop in. I'm going down to the cafeteria. Do you need anything?"

I shook my head and watched as Mrs. Hiroto left in the elevator. Molly's room was a small private room with at least a dozen vases of flowers to make the room appear cheery. I sat down on the side of her bed, careful not to disturb the many wires snaking out from under her blanket. The ventilator was gone, thank God.

"Hey, Girl," I said as I played with a lock of Molly's smooth dark hair. "You need to wake up soon. I miss you, and there is so much happening that I need to tell you. Alec, for one, then a weird development with Mr. Clendenin, and of course, we need to talk about Elijah." I stopped there. If she could hear me, perhaps dredging up her memories of Elijah and the events in Charlotte wasn't the best thing for her subconscious.

I leaned closer to Molly's face. "I have to leave for South Carolina soon, but I'll keep tabs on you while I'm gone. The minute you wake up and are alert, I'll come home. I promise, Mol."

Molly didn't answer me. Her eyelids moved back and forth as if she was dreaming. I prayed that whatever she was seeing was beautiful and enlightening. I couldn't imagine being trapped in a semi-awake state and not knowing what was real and what wasn't. I swept the hair from her face, an act she'd done to me on countless occasions, and then planted a light kiss on Molly's forehead. She needed to wake up soon.

Someone cleared their throat behind me, and I turned to see Alec standing in the doorway. "Hey," he said quietly. "I figured you were here. I need to talk to you about yesterday."

I moved off the bed and went to stand in front of him. He smelled divine as usual with that rich woodsy scent. "We can talk at my house if you'd like. Mom's on a date all day, and Ben's at a friend's house."

Alec frowned as if he wasn't sure about my offer.

"We could pick up a pizza. I skipped breakfast and haven't had lunch yet. Plus, I would like to jump on the research for this place in South Carolina we're going to see next week."

Finally, he smiled at me. "We can do that. I just don't want your mother to assume the worst if she walks in."

"We'll stay in the living room. I promise."

~ ~ ~

Alec carried the large pepperoni pizza into the kitchen and set it on the counter. I grabbed us each a bottle of water from the refrigerator as I watched him take off his black leather jacket and hang it on the back of a dining room chair. Watching him do simple daily activities always made my heart beat faster. He filled out his tight tee shirt with little effort. Well, there was some effort. I'd seen him workout at the gym.

I retrieved two plates from the cabinet and tossed a slice on each, and then joined Alec in the living room. "Just a second, and I'll grab my laptop from the bedroom." I hurried down the hall to my room.

When I returned, Alec was seated on the floor in front of the square coffee table. He watched me as I set the laptop in the middle of the table and then dropped down carefully near him, crossing my legs and pushing a stray hair away from my eyes. I could feel the heat moving up into my cheeks. Any time Alec looked at me like that, I melted, and it took every ounce of dignity to keep myself upright.

"Do you remember the name of this place?" I asked.

"The Ashbury Estate. It used to be a small plantation before the Civil War. Afterward, it was used briefly as a hospital, then a tuberculosis treatment clinic. I think it was a temporary school for a while when a new grade school was being built in town. Someone bought the house and made it a private residence for around twenty years or so. But it's been empty for decades now."

"Oh. You've already researched it then," I said, a bit disappointed. I'd looked forward to us discovering the Ashbury Estate's secrets together. Alec studied my face, and I realized he hadn't touched his food yet.

"No. It's in Mire Marsh. I grew up ten minutes down the road from it," he answered.

"You're from there? Why didn't you say something sooner?"

He took a deep breath and let it out slowly while he played with a lock of my hair. "I haven't told you much about my childhood or my past in general. I came to Locklyn for a fresh start, and it seems like I keep getting pulled back. The Ashbury Estate is near Rich Branch Road, where I grew up, in the little town of Mire Marsh, just north of Parris Island. That's where I graduated from Marine Basic. I was disappointed they didn't send me to San Diego." He smiled. "There's always been rumors about Ashbury, not just with the military, but the older locals, some of which had been inside when it was a school."

I opened my computer and powered it on. I had so many questions for Alec. What was his childhood like? What about his parents? He never mentioned them. He never talked about his family at all.

"What are you thinking?" he asked as he took a drink of his water.

I sat up to type in the YouTube search bar before settling back down to answer him. "You know everything there is to know about me. You know about my family, my parents, my friends. I don't know anything about you except what you just told me. So, while we're in the area, will you take me to see where you grew up?"

Alec frowned, but it disappeared as quickly as it had formed across his rugged features. "Of course. Anywhere you want to go."

I pulled the Ashbury Estate up, and we searched through news reports of the deaths of two paranormal investigators linked to the site. One of the most viewed videos was a segment from a popular ghost hunting show. I had seen the show in the past, but not this episode. The host of the television show, Kyle Drekr, was a handsome guy in his mid-twenties with blond-highlighted hair and a superior attitude that made him sometimes a little hard to watch, at least in my opinion.

The segment started with Kyle standing in front of a large abandoned white mansion in a colonial style with several white pillars surrounding the front porch and balcony. He thumbed over his shoulder at the house.

"The Ashbury Estate," Kyle said. "First, a plantation about half the size of its neighbors that housed a dozen or so people and later a makeshift hospital during and after the Civil War. The Ashbury burned in 1916 when a fire started under mysterious circumstances and was rebuilt by the descendants of the original owners in 1918. The downstairs of the home was converted into a clinic when tuberculosis swept through the area."

"The Ashbury has seen her better days. During the 1950s, it was a temporary school with plenty of acreage for the children to run and play during recess. After the new elementary school opened, the family sold the home to Isabella Ivers, a retired businesswoman. She made Ashbury her personal residence but maintained the historical significance of such a beautiful place. Rumors spread like wildfire that the older woman saw visions within the house and heard children playing on the many balconies. But, she refused to leave the house she'd made her home."

The camera zoomed in on Kyle's face. "However, Ms. Ivers passed away more than twenty years ago, and rumors of the Ashbury's past and its secrets made this home one of the most haunted and horrific houses we've ever investigated."

The next segment showed Kyle and his team inside the house investigating sounds they'd heard on the home's second floor. When this was filmed, there was furniture in the home with a film of dust on each piece. As I watched Kyle round a corner, a loud bang startled not only the television crew but me as I jumped out of my skin.

Alec laughed.

"That didn't scare you?" I asked, clearly perplexed as I paused the video. "If I had your gun, I would've drawn it."

"And that's why you don't have it," he answered with a grin on his face.

"Where is your gun? I've noticed you haven't worn it the last few days."

"It's in the safe at home. I decided to lock it up while I'm on suspension after I got it back from the police department in Charlotte. Speaking of guns," he leaned back onto his elbows and stretched out on the carpet. "I heard a story that the lady who owned the house kept an entire bedroom full of guns because she thought she could fight the ghosts haunting the house. Someone told me that she fired more than sixty shots one night off her back porch."

"She was firing at ghosts? Or what she thought were ghosts?"

"I guess. But I've been thinking about that story. What if she could see them like you can? What if she knew they were demons but didn't know how to expel them?"

"Hm. Maybe. Poor woman. No one would have believed her. Too bad she didn't know Dad, or she could have called him to fight for her."

Suddenly, a loud crash sounded through the house. Alec jumped up and grabbed my arms, shoving me behind him.

"What was that?" I whispered.

"Stay here," he commanded as he picked up a marble candleholder from the end table and moved silently down the hallway, carefully stopping to check out the bathroom, then Ben's room. He glanced at Mom's open bedroom door. Then Alec stopped in front of my room. I'd left the door open when I'd come out with my laptop, but I could see that someone or something had shut the door. I motioned to Alec that it should be open.

I slowly crept down the hall toward Alec as he turned the knob and pushed the door open. He went in first, and I waited, but after a full minute of no sound, I snuck a peek. Alec was standing by my bed, holding a broken picture frame, the frame that held my father's picture.

He looked at me. "There's no one here. This was on the floor. I swear it looks like someone threw it against the wall."

He was right. There was glass shattered on the carpet along the baseboard, probably ten feet from my nightstand where the frame belonged. I took the frame from Alec and carefully slid out the picture of Dad and me at the pier, and placed the broken plastic in the trashcan by my dresser.

"What happened then?" I asked.

"Maybe the wind blew in." He glanced at my closed windows. He and I both knew that wasn't plausible, and his confused expression betrayed his words.

"I don't feel any demonic energy. Do you think maybe it was because we were watching those creepy videos about Ashbury?"

Alec looked down at me and smiled. "That it creeped us both out, so now we imagine things?"

I shrugged. "There's no one here, so maybe."

Alec set the candle holder on my nightstand and stuffed his hands in the pockets of his jeans before studying my room. My cheeks grew red as I realized he'd been in my bathroom just minutes before looking for an intruder – my bathroom where I air-dried my best bras.

As if sensing my embarrassment, Alec smiled. "I like your room. It's larger than I expected," he said before frowning at my twin-size bed. "Even if your bed is smaller than I imagined."

"Not all of us can afford to have a king-size bed," I retorted as I retreated from the room.

But Alec was right on my heels in the hall, and he grabbed my wrist, turning me to face him. He wrapped his hands around my waist and looked me in the eyes, his face inches from mine. "Since when have you seen *my* bed?" he breathed.

My heart caught in my throat. "The time before last when I was in your house. You left your bedroom door open." When he didn't answer, I summoned my courage. "Since when have you imagined the size of *my* bed?"

Alec pulled me closer, his breath on my face. The warmth emanating through his shirt felt comforting. Holding him was like holding onto a brick wall where at any moment, I might crumble under his weight. His green eyes revealed that battle once again raging there. He wanted to kiss me. Not just a passing kiss as we'd become accustomed to in private. I swallowed hard as my heart threatened to burst through my chest.

Alec touched my cheek with his nose as if waiting to see if I would protest and then tightened his grip around my waist as he lifted me easily. I felt the solid wall behind me for only a moment before Alec's lips crashed over mine. I clung to him. He was real. Flesh and blood. My protector. I wrapped my arms around his neck and pulled his head even closer.

Alec lowered me slowly, but we didn't stop. After a dizzying few minutes, I vaguely became aware of Mom's laughter. She was coming through the front door. Alec moved away from me like he was on fire and slipped down the hall and into the kitchen.

I quickly gathered my thoughts and smoothed my hair with my sweaty palms. Hopefully, my lip gloss wasn't too smudged. How much longer would we have to hide how much we adored each other? I needed to slow my breathing before I hyperventilated especially, before facing my mother and my Vice-Principal.

~   ~   ~

If either Mom or Nick had any inclination that Alec and I had kissed only moments before they came into the house, neither one let on. I met them at the top of the stairs as I casually went into the living room to retrieve our plates.

"Hi, Honey," Mom said. "I saw Alec's truck outside. Is he here?"

Alec came out of the kitchen and into the dining area with another bottle of water. "Hello, Stella," he answered. "Ainsley and I were just watching

Paranormal Houses on the computer. Do you want to watch it with us?" I couldn't believe how casual he sounded. How could he stay so calm when everyone in the room could probably hear my heart?

"Ah, you must be the famous Alec I've heard so much about," Nick said as he held his hand out to Alec. But as Alec shook his, Nick continued, "Or, should I say infamous?"

"And you are?" Alec asked with a slight tilt to his head. He was still smiling, but I could tell he was beginning to fake it.

Mom dropped her tote onto the loveseat before coming over to run her hand over Nick's back. "Alec, this is Nick Clendenin. He's the Vice-Principal at Ainsley's school. He and I, and Gerald, graduated in the same class."

"I see," Alec said.

"Yes, I recognize you from the pictures on my phone," Nick continued.

Geesh. Could this get any more awkward? I fought the urge to groan out loud.

"Pictures?"

I decided now was the best time for me to step in. "You remember, the ones that I told you that girl from school took? Why don't we finish watching Paranormal

Houses?" I asked and smiled up at Alec, hoping he would get the hint that I could tell him more about the pictures later. I'd never actually gone into detail about them with him.

"Sure," he said as he took another sip of his water. I gave Mom a look as I took the plates into the kitchen and deposited them onto the counter. Mom followed me into the room and rolled her eyes. So she did think Nick's comments were ridiculous. Neither one of us could say anything without both men hearing us with the partially open floor plan.

"Bet you could use a Dr. Pepper right about now, huh?" Mom asked.

I wasn't a drinking girl, but if this awkwardness continued, I would need something stronger than Dr. Pepper.

CHAPTER FOUR

The following Monday, I waited in Room 310 to meet with the group going to the little town of Mire Marsh. Instead of our regular first-period class, we were allowed to gather for details and introductions. Only nine students, including me, were going on this trip. Apparently, not everyone needed or wanted community service hours building houses in another state so close to Halloween.

I wished Molly was going with me. She was starting to wake up and respond to commands, but she was nowhere near ready to hold conversations yet. My friend Bronwyn had taken an excused sabbatical from in-person classes and transitioned to virtual learning for the time being. I didn't blame her. She'd suffered a loss during the Artist's reign of terror. With my two closest friends gone, school felt lonely now.

"So, if Ms. Bell's not going on the trip, who is going to chaperone?" A girl I'd seen before but didn't know her name asked.

A boy answered. "Who knows? Maybe we'll be on our own. I mean, we are seniors. How much trouble do they think we're going to get into?"

Listening to other students pipe in made me realize just how wrapped up I'd been in my own life since Dad died two years ago. I didn't know any of these kids' names yet recognized them from other classes.

"What about you?" The blond boy asked. "Do you think they should cancel it if Ms. Bell can't go?"

But before I could answer him, his eyes grew wide. "Wait a minute. You're the girl that was at Queens University when they caught that serial killer. You're Ainsley Reynolds."

I pressed my lips together to keep from letting him see me grimace. The other students got quiet. "Yes," I answered, "I was there."

Thankfully, before the boy could ask another question, Nick - er, Mr. Clendenin - walked into the room with another man. Upon closer inspection, I realized the other man was none other than Kyle Drekr, the host from the television show Alec and I had watched last night. What in the world was he doing here?

"Good morning, Group. It's good to see your bright faces this glorious and chilly morning," Nick said as he looked about the room at the nine of us.

The blond boy mumbled something under his breath.

"What was that, Ethan?" Nick asked.

"I said you're in a good mood this morning," Ethan piped up. The other students snickered.

Nick smiled before turning around to his guest. Man, I hoped he wasn't in a good mood because he'd spent the last few days with my mom. Or, maybe I should be happy about that. It was so strange.

"Some of you might recognize this young man, but for those that don't, this is Kyle Drekr. Kyle hosts an international television show, but he helps organizations like Serenity build houses for people in his spare time. He's agreed to go with you to South Carolina for this project."

The students nodded, and a couple of girls giggled. Kyle placed a small satchel down on the floor before sitting down on the desk in the front of the room to address us. He took his time removing his wool coat, and I had a feeling that was for the benefit of the female students in the class. He definitely lifted heavy weights. "Hi, guys. So that you know, Ms. Bell will be riding along with us on this trip, but she won't work on-site as much as she has in the past since she is still recovering. That's another reason I agreed to work with Maren," Kyle Drekr said as he looked directly at me. "I'm here to make sure things get sorted out and sent back to where they belong."

What on earth?

When the group remained silent, he added, "I mean returning the tools and equipment."

A girl in the front row raised her hand. "Will you be staying in the same hotel block as the rest of us?"

Kyle grinned. "Absolutely. But as I assured Mr. Clendenin, this is a professional volunteer project. As such, we expect you to maintain professionalism as the future generation of successful Locklyn High School students. Sadly, there will be no fraternizing allowed. In any capacity."

The girl made a pouty face that almost made me laugh.

"Well, Kyle, if you've got this under control, I'm going to slip out. Stop by my office before you leave," Nick said as he made his way to the classroom door.

"Thank you, Sir," Kyle answered.

I thought about texting Maren about this change in our plans. Would Kyle's camera crew be there too, or just him?

"Maren, or as you call her, Ms. Bell, sent the final paperwork for you to have your parents sign. If you can, please have them back to Mr. Clendenin tomorrow, so I can let her know. As soon as I give you a copy, you may go on to your next class." Kyle pulled out a manila envelope and a pen from his bag.

I watched as he stopped at each student to ask their name. Then he would write something, I assumed their name on the paper, and then hand the permission slip to them. One by one, he stopped; Ethan, Gabe, Izzy, Jay, Everly, and her twin sister Waverly, Jamal, and Freya. I wasn't seated near the back of our small group, but it seemed that Kyle gave each student their paper and waited for them to leave before moving to the next person.

Eventually, Kyle and I were the only ones left in the classroom.

"Ainsley, right?"

"Yes. How did you know?"

Instead of handing me a paper, he sat down in the empty desk beside me and rolled the paper up. "Maren told me you were coming as a last-minute addition."

I nodded. Of course, she had. His pale blue eyes carefully studied me until I felt the heat rising into my cheeks. "Do you have my paperwork?" I asked.

Kyle glanced over at the closed classroom door before turning to look at me again. He pulled his tee-shirt away from his neck as if he suddenly needed to breathe.

"I worked with your father on a few cases when I was first starting," he said in a low voice as if he were afraid someone might burst into the room.

"You're with them? With Father Mahon and Stephen?"

"And Maren, and others. I work with the organization Malus Navis. I've been to the Ashbury Estate, and it's no joke. Two investigators died in that house. I thank God it wasn't anyone from my crew, but I'm hesitant to go back. I heard about what you did with that small demon cluster in Charlotte. You're going to need help. I can help you at Ashbury." He ran his hand through his thick hair as if he'd just unloaded a pressing but reluctant confession.

"So, you're not going with us to build houses?"

"That part is true. I do volunteer to build houses in my spare time. However, I can't let Gerald's daughter go and fight a dozen demons on her own."

"I won't be on my own," I said.

"Oh, that's right. Your detective friend is riding down with Stephen," he said it with such disdain that I grimaced inside.

"Stephen and Maren will both be there. You don't have to feel like you're babysitting me, Mr. Drekr," I said as I stood. I held my hand open for the papers he still held rolled up in his grip.

But Kyle didn't rise or back away. He didn't hand me the roll of papers either. "Sit down, Ainsley. We're not through."

I gritted my teeth. After a brief hesitation, I sat down again. "Only because you worked with my father and you asked me so nicely."

Kyle rolled his eyes. "Look, I can tell that you and I are going to butt heads. Your dad was headstrong too. But unlike your dad, you don't know what you are getting yourself into." He leaned forward, closer to my desk. "You think because you bound a couple of demons once that you can take on more. They're more clever than you realize. It's never the same scenario twice."

"And you know how to expel them? Then why didn't you when you were there before?" I challenged.

Kyle rested his elbows on his knees and pressed his steepled hands up to his mouth as if he needed to summon the patience to deal with me. I very much disliked Kyle Drekr.

"I can feel the supernatural shift in the atmosphere when something is near. It's why I'm good at picking the right locations for my show. I can sometimes hear them, very faintly, but I'm not a full-fledged Seer. I don't have as much of the gift as you do. I can do more with a Seer present. When I worked with your dad, he used my gift for protection."

"Are you saying my father used you as his Protector?"

"Several years ago, yes."

"Did he always have a Protector with him?"

"No. Sometimes he went by himself. He was alone on his last mission," Kyle answered as he stared at me hard. "I know that Maren and Stephen make all of this demon-busting stuff sound sexy and intriguing, but your dad knew better. No one is putting their lives more at risk than the Seer."

"Yet, he went anyway. He left his family when other people begged him to help," I said, standing again, a rage filling my belly. "I'm going on this trip. If you want to come, then I can't stop you, but don't try to talk me out of it. I already gave them my word." I held my hand out.

Kyle slowly stood, towering over my five-foot-six-inch self by at least eight inches or more. His broad chest blocked out what I could see of the classroom. He thrust the paperwork at my chest. "Do what you want, Reynolds," he growled as he turned. "You seem to do the opposite of what your father would want anyway."

"What's that supposed to mean?" I demanded as I watched Kyle walk to the front of the classroom to retrieve his coat and satchel. He didn't answer me until he'd opened the classroom door. Then he turned to face me as I stood rigidly at my desk.

"Your father would be disappointed to know that you are following in his footsteps. He'd also be livid if he knew you were involved with a twenty-six-year-old cop."

And with that, Kyle Drekr left me standing in the classroom alone.

CHAPTER FIVE

I pushed my two travel bags and backpack onto the bus seat and maneuvered my body around them to the window. Maren had reserved a school bus for our group to travel to South Carolina. Thankfully, there was plenty of room for each student to take their own row plus have extra space between us. Maren boarded the bus with Kyle behind her carrying her bags as well as his. His Highness must have decided to join us on the actual riding in the bus.

I didn't know why I was still angry at Kyle for his words. Perhaps because deep down, I wondered the same thing. Was I doing the right thing helping Maren's organization? Would Dad have really been opposed to me seeing Alec? Part of me already knew the answer to that last question. I'd been Daddy's Little Girl. There was no way he would have allowed me anywhere near Detective Alec Graham.

If I were honest with myself, I knew Dad would have shot Alec in the face after he'd caught wind of the first rumor about us.

Off in my own little world, I hadn't noticed that Kyle stopped at my seat. "You all right, Reynolds? Last chance to change your mind."

Startled, I looked up at him. He wore a black hoodie and black jeans with a matching beanie on his head. His blue eyes searched mine.

"I'm fine. Thanks," I mumbled. Kyle opened his mouth to say more, but one of the twins saddled up to him in the narrow walkway.

"Hi, Mr. Drekr. Are you riding on our bus?"

I observed what I felt was a fake smile appear on Kyle's face before he turned to address the girl. "I sure am. Now, which one are you? Waverly or Everly?"

"I'm Waverly," she answered. "I'm the pretty one."

I couldn't help but laugh out loud. The twins were identical in every way except for their clothes. Waverly dressed in tighter-than-tight skinny jeans and short skirts that were probably prohibited district-wide. The other one, Everly, dressed more like me. Flattering, but comfortable. I would rather wear Converse than five-inch heels any day.

Waverly turned to look at me as I worked to stifle my giggle. "What are you doing here, Ainsley? Did your cop boyfriend remember to sign your permission slip?"

I took the verbal hit with a smile and a nod. Students were still making comments about the rumors they'd heard about me. However, none of them knew how close Alec and I were.

"Waverly, why don't you get settled before we leave?" Kyle asked her with a smirk on his face. She pointed to her seat to let him know which one was hers. He nodded and winked as if they shared a secret.

I refused to gag.

He turned back to me. "I take it you get a lot of those comments?" he asked just barely above a whisper.

I shrugged. "People can say what they want. None of them know the truth."

Studying my face again, Kyle answered. "I do."

"You only know what someone else has told you," I retorted.

When other students started boarding the bus, Kyle moved back up front to sit near Maren. I pulled my phone from my back pocket to text Mom that I was safely onboard and waiting for the remainder of the group so we could leave. I reminded her to call me when Molly was fully awake. I had no intention of breaking my promise to Mol.

I started to text Alec but then glanced back up at Kyle, who had moved to sit on Maren's bus seat, and was listening intently to something she was saying to him. I didn't like the doubts that Kyle was planting in my head about my relationship with Alec.

Finally, I pulled up Alec's name. **Hey, I'm onboard. Waiting for the others so we can leave. You were able to get my room reserved, right?**

Alec: **Yes. Your room is around the corner and down the hall a bit from the others. I'm already on the road with Stephen. Stephen wants to know if Drekr is behaving himself?**

Crap. I hadn't told Alec everything Kyle had said Monday morning. I'd only relayed that the television host was coming along because he was a member of the organization and had worked with Dad. I prayed that our conversation about Dad's disappointments was only between us.

Me: **He's made at least one girl swoon**; I started to type out then deleted it. That didn't sound right, although I meant Waverly. **He's talking with Maren, so I think so.**

Alec: **Missing you already. I'll see you at the hotel.**

I swallowed. Surely, Alec knew he couldn't let the group see him with me.

Me: **Where is your room located?**

Alec: **Wouldn't you like to know?**

Me: **Alec.**

I waited while the little bubbles moved on the screen, indicating that Alec was typing. I glanced over at Waverly, who was whispering something to her sister. They both looked at me and then giggled.

Alec: **I got a double room for Stephen and me. It has an adjoining door that leads to your room. This way, we can all meet together to discuss Ashbury without anyone suspecting anything. Plus, our rooms are very close to the exit stairwell. I'll talk to you when we get there. I'm going to message Maren about the rooms.**

I tapped my foot on the seat in front of me. I was sort-of sharing a hotel room with Alec. Well, if you forgot about the metal doors separating our rooms and the fact that Stephen was going to be there.

Maren must have received Alec's message because she turned in her seat and nodded. I smiled back until Kyle scowled at me. I'd almost forgotten about Kyle. He would be at any meetings about Ashbury, so obviously, he and Alec would have to work together.

I had a feeling that the demons weren't the only vicious snarling I was going to hear at Ashbury.

~ ~ ~

After about three hours on the road, the group decided to stop for lunch at a family-owned restaurant. I was thankful that Mom had given me the second debit card to her bank account since mine was almost empty. She'd added me to hers when Dad passed, but I wasn't allowed to use it unless it was an emergency.

The restaurant was excellent and well decorated with a beach theme which I truly appreciated. We were still about an hour and a half from the hotel, but we would only be a short drive to the local beaches once there.

I scooted onto a chair between Freya and Ethan and looked over the menu. I was too nervous to eat, but I figured I would feel dizzy later if I didn't order something. After Dad died, I'd turned to eating whatever, whenever I wanted. I'd packed on about twenty pounds, but for the last month, I'd found a balance. I'd lost around ten of that excess so far, and it resulted in more of an hourglass shape, which I secretly loved to emphasize now.

After the server came by and took our order for the eleven of us plus the bus driver, Waverly launched into a dozen questions for Kyle about his show. I zoned out listening to him brag about the places they'd investigated. Mostly because I felt that he rigged his shows for ratings. There was no way that he ran across paranormal activity at every single location.

My cell vibrated in my back pocket, and I retrieved it to read a message from Alec: **We're almost to the hotel.**

Me: **We stopped to eat. I'll see you soon.**

"You're Ainsley, right?" Freya asked as she took a sip of her tea.

"Yes," I answered. I'd had classes with her before, but we'd never spoken.

"I'm Freya Montgomery. I think we had English together last year."

When I nodded, Freya asked, "I heard about Molly. How is she?"

"She's doing better. She's starting to wake up. My mom is going to let me know when Molly's strong enough for visitors. If it's while I'm here, then I'll need to find a way back to Locklyn to visit for a few hours."

"Absolutely," Freya agreed.

"Where are you going?" Kyle asked. Was he not just entertaining the table with his ghost stories?

"When Molly Hiroto wakes up, I need to return to Locklyn for a few hours to visit her."

Kyle glanced at Maren, but the Psych teacher only smiled. "Of course, we are all worried about Molly...and you plan to return after your visit."

The others in the group nodded. Molly was pretty extroverted and, thus, popular. Most people liked her.

"Maybe we can send her flowers or something," Jamal said.

"That sounds great," Everly agreed. Everyone in the group nodded.

I text Mom that I might need to pull some money out to contribute to the pot for Molly's flowers.

"So, are you planning to do any ghost hunting while you're near Parris Island?" Izzy asked Kyle.

"If so, I want to tag along," Gabe added.

Kyle laughed with what I was sure was his fake made-for-TV laugh. "Not this time. I may have to run a few errands for future locations, but no actual investigations."

The group gave a collective groan but perked up when two servers arrived with food. People continued to ask Kyle questions about his paranormal investigations and the things he'd seen that he was more than happy to share. I caught Maren watching me, but she only smiled. She and I hadn't had a chance to talk lately since the trip started. Maybe after we got settled at the hotel, I could catch her alone.

After I ate a cranberry salad and a roll with honey, I absentmindedly played with Dad's amulet around my neck while I listened to Kyle drone on about his adventures. At the same time, the other students oohed and aahed. They had no idea about the real demons in this realm.

As we were boarding the bus to take off again, Kyle brushed by me. "Listen, as we get closer to Ashbury, you're going to feel them. Maybe even hear them. You can't let on."

"What do you mean?"

"You're about to see a whole lotta crazy stuff. But you need to keep the crazy to yourself." He walked past me and got on the bus.

CHAPTER SIX

I realized what Kyle was talking about when we arrived at the hotel. It was late in the afternoon as we gathered our bags and climbed off the bus. The group gathered around Maren for further instructions. As I stood there, I heard *them* – the now-all-too-familiar sound of the Muladach. As I studied the outside of the large hotel, the building itself rippled at the same time that I heard an audible growl, so close I could feel them. Menacing, moving, not exactly here, but close. I somehow knew that if I ripped away the veil separating the realms, I could see them, touch them.

I steadied myself as I pushed my heels into the blacktop of the parking lot and let out an involuntarily gasp. The energy sent a surge up my spine and into my head. I used to think my blood sugar was dipping too low when I felt dizzy. Now I knew, thanks to Father Mahon and Stephen, it was my body reacting to the manifestation of demonic energy.

Suddenly, I heard Kyle's hot-tempered whisper in my ear. "Get it together, Reynolds. You don't hear *anything*."

I looked up at him. I knew my eyes had to be as wide as saucers. Could he hear them? How much of this gift did we share?

He glared at me through slits before nodding toward the group. Waverly and Ethan had stopped talking when they'd heard me gasp. Kyle casually moved closer to Maren. As the group made its way to the entrance, Freya dropped back to where I was slowly maneuvering my steps.

"Are you all right? You look like you saw a ghost back there."

"I'm fine. Thanks. Must've been all the talk back at the restaurant."

Freya nodded, but she didn't look convinced. Thankfully, she sped up and joined the others at the customer service desk. After Maren sorted the rooms, then it was my turn. "I'm here for a room reserved for Ainsley Reynolds," I said as I handed the petite brunette behind the counter my ID.

The clerk took my identification and read something on her computer before handing me a key card. "Here you go, Miss. It's Room 220. If you need anything, just let us know."

"Are you not staying with us?" Ethan asked when he overheard the clerk.

"No, I was an add-on, and the hotel block was full."

"Oh, Miss," the clerk shouted after I'd turned away from her. "Do you want the receipt, or should we just email it to Mr. Graham?"

I felt my face redden as I turned to the counter. "You can just give it to me."

"Oh, okay then. We'll print it out for you upon check out."

Really? Couldn't you have brought that up then? I wanted to say it. Instead, I nodded my head as I turned on my heel only to see Kyle smirking at me from the middle of the corridor with the rest of the group waiting to ride up the elevator to the second floor. But then I saw a much better smile further behind him. Alec stood leaning against the wall at the end of the lobby wearing a ball cap pulled down over his eyes and his hands pushed into his pants pockets. I would know that grin anywhere.

I walked past the group as they boarded the large elevator. "Where you headed, Reynolds?" Kyle called out as I passed.

"I'm taking the stairs. I think my room is at the other end of the hall anyway," I announced as the elevator door shut. I was thankful that he hadn't jumped out to follow me. Kyle seemed like a loose cannon.

Alec held the stairwell door open for me, and I slipped past him. As soon as the door shut, he took my bags.

"The hotel is going to give me your receipt as soon as I check out," I said, smiling up at those green eyes that gleamed with a quiet fire.

"So I heard," he answered as he pushed a lock of my hair away from my cheek.

"As did everyone in the hotel," I groaned.

Alec pulled me closer to him with his free hand. "I don't mind if everyone knows I'm taking care of you."

As much as I loved hearing Alec say that, something nipped at me. At some point, I needed to take care of myself. I reached up and touched his stubble with the back of my hand.

"We should go in case someone comes looking for me," I said as I started up the steps.

The second hotel room door next to the stairwell was mine, with Stephen and Alec's room next door. When I was sure no one was around, I slid the key card, and we both entered and closed the door. The suite was huge with a king-size bed, a living area to watch the flat-screen television, and a kitchenette with a refrigerator, stove, microwave, and coffeemaker.

A dozen roses sat in the middle of the coffee table in a crystal vase. "Where did these come from?" I picked up the card sticking out from the bouquet. It read: **For Ainsley, the most beautiful woman in the world. Alec**

I glanced at Alec, who'd set my bags on the sofa, slipping his hands in the front pockets of his pants again. He whistled as he looked about the room, not meeting my gaze. I leaned in and gave him a quick kiss on the lips. "Thank you for the flowers, Alec."

He smiled as he watched me move around the room, checking out the rest of the suite. The bathroom had a walk-in shower with glass doors and little travel-size products that smelled like coconut. I walked back out to see Alec leaning against the wall that separated the kitchen space from the bedroom.

"Do you like it?"

"I love it. I don't know what I expected, but not this. What's your room like?"

"Pretty much the same. Except we have double queens." We stared at each other, and I felt a burning begin to form below my chest. Only the dresser separated us.

"Someone needs to interrupt us," he said.

"Why?"

"I'm thinking about picking up where we left off at your house last week when I kissed you."

A knock on the adjoining door interrupted the memory. It was for the best. Just the thought of it had left me breathless.

Alec walked over to the door and opened it to see Stephen Reeves standing there. The preacher who had worked with Dad in the past stepped in wearing a tee shirt and distressed jeans. He had trimmed his beard, and he flexed his arms as he walked in, his tattoo sleeve moving as his muscles rippled. "Taking you a while to get settled," his West Virginia twangy accent was directed at me, but I saw the look he gave Alec.

"Just admiring the view," Alec answered, unbothered by Stephen's comment.

I did go to the window to survey the view of an enormous in-ground pool and low-hanging trees covered in moss. To be a large hotel, it did seem almost country club-like. "It's charming here," I remarked.

"Good, you're settled," Maren's twang carried through both rooms. She must have somehow let herself into Stephen and Alec's room. I turned to see Kyle coming in through the adjoining door behind her. He took a look around my room and gave a low whistle.

"Maren, you need to talk to the board about skimping on the hotel rooms for the school trips. Ours aren't nearly as nice."

Maren ignored Kyle's statement as she addressed me. "You need to join the others for dinner. In the morning, you're gonna ride down with the group to the site, then in the afternoon, you and Kyle are to meet Stephen and Alec at Ashbury."

"What about you?"

"I'll go down later when I can."

"During the day? I thought we would be investigating at night?"

"We will," Kyle interjected as he stood reading the card on my flowers. He dropped it onto the coffee table with a disgusted look on his face. "The demons are less busy at this place during the day, so it will be easier for you to keep it together for your first time. We'll go back at night. I've already got it sorted out with the owners."

"Did you bring Dad's box?" I asked Maren, referring to a banker's box full of items Dad used during his expulsions.

"You won't need it," Kyle answered for her. He was getting on my nerves.

Maren seemed to sense my aggravation. "With Kyle here, he can help you expel them. He knows the passages by heart."

"You can recite the Latin by memory?" I moved closer to Alec. I'd noticed him studying Kyle's movements.

"Can't you, Little Miss Beacon of Light?" he asked in a sarcastic tone as he sat down on the sofa, pushing my bags over and propping his feet on the coffee table.

"Kyle, come on," Stephen said with a frown. "The group will be gathering for dinner soon. You and Maren should make sure you are available in case they need you."

Kyle sighed. "I've already got to make sure my door stays locked, or that one twin is going to find a way in there."

"I'll take care of Waverly," Maren said. "You behave yourself."

The trio moved to the open door but stopped in front of the coffeemaker so Kyle could complain that his room didn't have a kitchenette setup and Maren could remind him that no one was preventing him from paying for his own room elsewhere in the hotel.

"When you go to make your coffee, check the fridge first," Alec said as he touched the back of my hand. Somehow the gesture seemed more intimate than a hug.

"Did you get me those flavored creamers I love?"

"Chocolate caramel something and a Sweet Cream one, I think."

"Thank you, and thanks for the upgrade in beds," I said to Alec as I motioned toward the bed. The king-size looked huge compared to my twin back home.

"I thought you might approve since you seemed to have liked the size of mine," Alec answered.

When Maren, Stephen, and Kyle turned at Alec's comment, he smiled and winked at me. "Come on, people. Get your minds out of the gutter," he added as he moved past them and into his room.

No one but us laughed.

~ ~ ~

The next morning, I'd had all I could take of being bossed around by Kyle Drekr. We'd spent two hours hauling shingles for new construction to the roofers. Everything I did seemed to irritate the television host as he worked. He made encouraging comments to the other students and snapped at me over little things.

Finally, Maren stepped between us when she saw me place my hands on my hips. He'd acted like it was the end of the world when I'd dropped a bag of nails.

"Really? How hard is it to hold a bag?" he growled at me, his face showing his disgust for my apparent clumsiness. Or perhaps my existence.

"What is your problem with me?" I seethed back.

"Come on now, you two," Maren said quietly. "No need to bring attention to yourselves. Kyle, behave yourself. Did you already reserve a rental car?"

Kyle clenched his jaw as he took his eyes off me to address Maren. "I have a rental company dropping off a car here in about an hour. Then, I guess, Reynolds and I will have to slip away to Ashbury."

"Yes," Maren nodded. "You need to go at lunchtime when the others take a break. Ainsley, you can meet Kyle on the next street over. I'll have to come up with different excuses for each day if anyone asks. I'll just say that you felt dizzy. Low blood sugar or something."

"I don't know," I said to her. "I don't think I can ride in the same car with him and his attitude. There definitely isn't enough room for his ego."

Kyle started to say something to me, but Maren placed her well-manicured hand on his chest and batted her eyes up at him. "Kyle, can I speak to you over there?"

I watched as the two of them walked to the corner of the property, out of earshot. Maren placed one hand on her hip, the other pointing a finger at Kyle's chest, and lit into the tall man as he stood there, holding his peace and nodding. Then, he said something to her that caused her to look up at him with surprise. She glanced over in my direction, but when she saw me watching them, she took Kyle by the arm and led him away from sight.

What had Kyle said to Maren that made her appear surprised? Maren had worked with my father on a few cases, and she had helped me in Charlotte, but she wasn't a Seer. Did this have something to do with whatever role Kyle played within the organization?

~ ~ ~

Reluctantly, I slipped away from the group as they took their break and walked to the next street over. As I waited for Kyle to appear in the rental car, I played with a small palm tree planted near the sidewalk. The smooth leaf was a contrast to the prickly trunk. I thought about how much Ben would love one this size. Could I plant one of these in our front yard? Would it live?

A white Nissan Sentra pulled up next to me, and I peered in to see Kyle motioning for me to get a move on. Even his gestures aggravated me.

"Do we have time to grab a bite to eat at a drive-thru?" I asked as I clicked my seatbelt into place.

"Yeah, I'm starving too," he answered. "Stephen texted me. He's already at Ashbury. There is a tour in about an hour, so I think we should try to make that so you can see the place in the daytime and hear the history."

"But, we are going back tonight?"

"I've already arranged it with the owners."

Kyle pulled the car into a fast-food drive-thru that served greasy hamburgers, salty fries, and beyond large milkshakes. I had to lean over him to scan the menu but quickly decided on a three-piece chicken tender meal and ice water. That was the healthiest thing on the menu. Kyle frowned and then ordered a combo meal with the thickest beef patties I'd ever seen pictured.

When we pulled up at the window, I handed him my debit card.

"No, I've got it," he said as he pushed my hand away.

"I pay for my own." I tried to hand him the card again.

"Not from what I've seen," he countered as he paid the woman at the window using his own card.

"Excuse me?"

He waited until he'd received his card back before replying. "I know Graham paid for your hotel room."

"So? It was a last-minute addition. I didn't have the money, and Father Mahon and the others acted like it was imperative that I do this. Maybe Alec should send *them* the bill." I rubbed my palms on my jeans. Why did I let Kyle irritate me?

"Well, I don't expect anything in return," Kyle said, raising his brows at me.

"Neither does Alec."

The woman at the window handed out our bags, and Kyle set them on my lap. After we received our drinks, he pulled over into a parking spot to eat. Neither one of us spoke. It appeared we were both deep in thought, but more than likely, it was because we couldn't stand each other.

After I finished my chicken, I took another sip of water and then straightened my lip gloss in the visor mirror. I caught Kyle watching me in the reflection.

"What?" I asked.

"You know, Graham is only two years older than me. I just find your relationship, friendship, whatever it is…disconcerting, to say the least."

I studied his blue eyes through the mirror as he talked. The sunlight made them appear almost clear. Kyle was searching for his words. Maybe he was trying not to offend me.

"When *you* date someone, how much of an age gap is there between the two of you?" I asked as I faced him.

Kyle Drekr grinned. "We're not talking about me."

I cocked my head. "Same principle. You can't judge someone else on something you would do."

Kyle stopped smiling and started the car. "Trust me. You're more like my annoying little sister than anything more."

"That's not what I meant," I said quickly.

"I meant-"

"I know what you're trying to say. But I knew your dad. I worked with him. I talked with him. He would not be happy about this. I think if Gerald were here, he would tell you to stay away from Alec Graham."

I glared at Kyle's profile as he carefully pulled the rental back onto the street for us to join Stephen and Alec at the Ashbury Estate.

CHAPTER SEVEN

The Ashbury Estate had stood empty for the last twenty years, except for ghost tours and such, however the home was well-maintained, although somewhat dusty. The roof still held its shingles, and the front porch didn't have one missing wooden slat. The structural foundation appeared stable, but the sparse furniture, peeling wallpaper, and heavy curtains made the house eerie. A look the new owners were clearly going for.

Stephen and Alec were standing at the entrance of the house when Kyle and I arrived. Alec smiled at me and winked as he handed me our tickets for the tour. Kyle, however, was not grateful for Alec purchasing his ticket for him.

"Kyle, just take the ticket," I said as I pushed the paper into his chest.

As he took the ticket from me, his face marked by a great scowl, a tall man appeared with dark hair and eyes and the most beautiful olive complexion I'd ever seen on a man. I was at once jealous. My skin was still threatening to break out from smelling Kyle's greasy burger from earlier.

"Hey, Kyle! It's good to see you again." The man shook Kyle's hand as he glanced at the rest of us.

"It's good to be back here," Kyle threw on his facade of a smile. How could no one tell when he was faking it? "These are my investigators for tonight, Ainsley Reynolds and Alec Graham. Stephen Reeves is here somewhere."

The man nodded to us, but since Kyle neglected to finish his introduction, Alec jumped into the conversation. "Are you the new owner?"

"No, I'm just the tour guide. The owners are Palmer and Helen Meadors."

"Is that right?" Alec asked, surprise written on his face. I made a mental note to ask him about it later.

"Yes, nice people. They bought it when Miss Ivers passed. My name is Ravi. I do both the daylight and occasional nightly tours. Are you guys ready to be scared tonight?"

"I've been looking forward to it for a week now." I smiled at Ravi. "We wanted to see it in the daytime first."

"Of course. In the past, our tours were quite large, but with the two deaths recently and the missing local girls, we've opted to limit the group size."

"Missing girls?" I asked.

"Yes. Unfortunately, we have had three of our own Mire Marsh girls disappear over the last three weeks. Combined with the deaths, well, it is better off that we keep the group size limits in place."

"Kyle told us the deaths were paranormal investigators. What happened to them?" Alec asked.

"I was here both times. The first guy - his name was Robert - went off by himself. I had no idea he'd decided to investigate under the house. Who does that? With all these rooms to look into? He somehow wedged himself between two beams and became stuck. He suffocated to death."

"Oh, wow." I made another mental note to stay with the group and not leave the house.

Ravi continued, "The other one was on a different night. She was an amateur. She'd told me this was her first time investigating a place. Like Robert, she separated from the group, but our cameras picked up her whereabouts in the house. She told the camera she could hear crying and followed it to a small closet in the downstairs study. The video shows her standing in front of the closet for a few minutes with the door open. Then she took her belt off and buckled it tight around her neck before going into the closet and shutting the door. We found her hanging there a while later, but it was too late. As for the three missing girls, I noticed two of them on past tours."

I blinked. It certainly sounded like the Muladach, the demons that influenced people to commit heinous acts of violence or take their own lives. According to Father Mahon, the Ashbury housed around a dozen.

"We'll keep a close eye on everyone tonight," Alec assured Ravi.

"Good to hear. It's hard trying to keep track of people in the dark. Have a look around. We also have a gift shop located on the enclosed back porch if you want to shop after the tour."

Stephen came through the hallway then, and Kyle took the time to introduce him to Ravi as Alec guided me down the hall a bit to allow other people through the door to purchase tickets.

"You don't look too happy to be here," he said as he reached out and played with a lock of my hair.

"No, I'm happy. Now that you're here," I smiled. "Just working with Kyle on the building site is rough. He treats me like this kid that can't do anything right. It's infuriating."

Alec watched Kyle take a selfie with the couple who had just arrived and must have recognized the television personality.

"I think the department would lengthen my suspension if I shot him for you." He smiled down at me and winked.

I laughed, probably a little too loud at the delicious thought, which made Stephen motion for us to join them. Alec was still on suspension for his involvement with me during his last case. However, with his otherwise perfect record and commendations, the suspension was the only reprimand he would receive.

Ravi cleared his throat. There were now seven people crowding the foyer. "Ladies and gentlemen, if you will please follow me into what was once the formal living room area, we will begin the tour shortly."

"What do you think about this house?" I whispered to Alec.

"I bet it was beautiful once upon a time."

"It looks huge on the outside, but not so much inside."

Alec interlaced his fingers in mine and pulled me closer to him so that he could whisper in my ear. "The rooms have been divided up throughout the years. It's probably about 8,000 square feet, give or take." He pulled away and searched my face. "Do you think this house is large?"

"Of course. You don't?"

Alec smiled but didn't answer as Ravi began his spiel. "Welcome to the Ashbury Estate, where the air you breathe is pure madness. Ladies and gentlemen, we are thrilled that you have decided to join us for the daily tour of Ashbury. I do ask that you stay with the group as we make our way through the house. The Ashbury is a historical gal with plenty of stories. Many of these tales originated in the last one hundred years, thanks to the tuberculosis epidemic of the 1920s and 1930s. As you entered the house, did you notice the mahogany and cypress banister and stairwell? That is an original work that survived the fire in 1916 that consumed a chunk of the home."

We all turned to look through the doorway and into the foyer. In period clothes from the 1940s, a woman smiled back at us from the bottom step as she leaned across the railing. Her black hair was pulled back into a sleek bun, and she wore a small white hat situated perfectly. It looked like a nurse's uniform.

Ravi continued, commanding our attention again. "The owners reconstructed this portion of the house in 1918, and the rooms that were once a large sitting room, expansive library, ballroom, and gentleman's study were made into smaller rooms. Because of this change, the townspeople asked the Ashbury family if the downstairs could be used as a temporary tuberculosis clinic in 1938 when the disease swept through the poorest section of town. No one wanted the poor in the large and clean hospital."

Ravi displayed a look of disgust, as I'm sure we all did.

The woman wearing her white belted dress and short heels came into the room and stood near Ravi. I liked that they had period costumes for the tour. Hopefully, they would break out the other periods. From what I'd read, the Ashbury Estate had a rich and extensive history.

The group began to move into the next room, but Kyle grabbed my forearm. "Wait," he said as I turned to look up at him.

Alec and I stayed back with Kyle and Stephen until only the woman, and we remained. The woman smiled at me. "I'm sorry," I said. 'We'll be along in a moment."

"What did you say?" Alec asked.

The woman barely raised an eyebrow acknowledging she'd heard me before turning her attention to Kyle.

"It's all right. I'll see you again tonight." He smiled at her as if she was the most beautiful woman in the state.

Her smile grew wider. Nodding, she walked out of the room.

"What are you talking about?" Stephen asked.

Kyle looked from the doorway the woman had just walked through to join the others to me. "Nothing. Nevermind, we need to go back into the foyer. Ainsley needs to look at something."

We followed him out into the foyer until we stood in front of the wall directly under the stairs.

"This was the original staircase from the mid-1800s. It's witnessed more than its fair share of tragedies, especially with the TB clinic located on this floor for a few years," Kyle said and knocked on a wooden stair. "Stephen, do you think you could make sure the group doesn't come back this way for a little bit? Maybe fifteen minutes or so?"

"Sure, what do you have planned?"

"Something is coming through the locked door under the stairs, and if it's what I think it is, Reynolds can push it open."

Stephen didn't ask any more questions and instead nodded and left back through the house to find the others.

Alec moved closer to me. "Ainsley can push what open?"

"I think this is a portal," Kyle answered as he waved his hand over the peeling paper on the wooden door. Someone had attached wallpaper to the door to make it unseen to visitors, but I could see the outline.

"Why do you think that? Why is this door covered?" I asked.

"The ghosts seem to gravitate around the staircase. The last time I investigated this place, most of the sightings originated from here. Ravi said the door has never been open as far as he knows. Not even the owners go in there."

"Someone has recently. There are broken seams around the door. But do you seriously believe this is a doorway to another realm?" Alec asked. "We haven't so much as heard a creak in this house that a person didn't do since we arrived."

Kyle frowned. "If you're skeptical, you don't have to stay here. You don't serve a purpose anyway."

Alec worked his jaw. "I leave, and Ainsley leaves."

"She's not here with you."

I held up my hand. "Enough, both of you, please. Let's just get this over with."

"Are you sure you want to do this?" Alec asked as he leaned his head closer to mine, ignoring Kyle while the professional ghost hunter walked to the front door as if he needed to prepare himself.

"I think so. I don't mind trying new things." I met Alec's gaze and felt the tingle of electricity shoot through me that only occurred when he was around. He must have thought it too because he gave me a grin that showed he secretly wished we were alone right now.

As I tried my hardest to send Alec a very desirable telepathic message - if only I had that gift instead of the other - a low crying sound started. We both turned around expecting to see a child standing in the hall, perhaps separated from a parent, although I hadn't noticed any children in our small group.

Kyle turned from the front door and made eye contact with me. "Do you hear her?"

I swallowed as dread began to work its way up into my throat. "Yes. Who is it?"

He shook his head. "It's coming from the door under the stairs."

I turned back to the peeling paper below the stairs. With a final whimper, the crying died away.

Alec touched the door before turning to look at me. "Is there a child on the other side of this door? What in the-"

Kyle interrupted him before he could finish. "Not a live one. We need to hurry."

CHAPTER EIGHT

"You don't have to stay here, Ainsley. If it's too much, we can leave," Alec said as he stood in front of me with his back to Kyle.

I shook my head. It wasn't too much - I simply didn't understand what was happening here. Was this an actual haunting? Could there be such a thing? Or, was this a case of the Muladach as Maren and Stephen believed?

Kyle walked past Alec and stood so close behind me that I could feel his breath on my neck. He was staring at the hidden door as well. Alec frowned at Kyle's proximity. I felt like I was in some weird sandwich between the two men, and for a second, I wondered what Waverly would have to say about this.

"Reynolds, give me your hand," Kyle said as he held his left palm up. Without a word, I laid my left hand in his. He turned my hand over, palm side up, and interlaced his fingers into mine so that his grip was firm. "Can you feel the vibration?"

Not only could I feel the familiar warmth I'd felt before while in Charlotte a few weeks ago, but I could feel a deep sensation utterly new to me. It was a vibration from inside of me at my very core. I touched my stomach. The waves of energy passed through me instead of remaining outside of me as they had in the past. The tingling moved up my legs through my abdomen and finally through my chest and arms.

I peered over my left shoulder. Kyle's breathing was coming rapidly now as he stared at me. He could feel the vibration through his body too. Slowly, he guided our hands to the papered door in front of us; my hand still intertwined with his. He stopped the movement with my palm only inches from the door. The heat emanating through that door was so hot I expected to see the old paper begin to bubble and curl away.

I swallowed. "Kyle?"

He continued staring, utterly focused on the peeling wallpaper. He licked his lips, pressed his right hand on my hip, and then addressed Alec. "Whatever happens, don't leave her side."

With that, Kyle shoved my palm against the wall.

The room shifted as I fell through a black hole. I felt my body rise and twist in the air. However, Kyle's hand was still strangely interlocked with mine, and he seemed to have strengthened his grip, refusing to let me go as we both screamed.

Suddenly, the room righted itself, and I was standing in the front hall once again. Except this wasn't the front entrance to the Ashbury Estate with peeling wallpaper and dusty wood floors. This was Ashbury in its heyday. Everything was new and gleaming, and I could smell the oil on the furniture, door frames, and paneled walls. The light above me shone through what was probably a handcrafted painted glass chandelier. I felt Kyle's hand tighten over mine into a fist.

"This isn't real, Reynolds. Not anymore," he whispered as he looked about the hall. We stood across from the wooden staircase at the ornate front door.

"Where's Alec? Where are the others?"

In the distance, I barely made out Alec's voice. He sounded muffled and far away in the house someplace, calling my name.

"He's still here, but in the other realm. He can hear us talking because our bodies are still there."

"I don't understand," I said as I tried to shake Kyle's hand free of mine, but he wouldn't release me.

"Will you stop?" he asked in his aggravated voice I'd become quite accustomed to over the past few days. "We are here in this realm as spirits. Our bodies are still back in our reality, our realm. This is an easier way to see."

"What if someone comes along and sees us just standing there? *Are* we just standing there?" I could imagine the strange sight of Kyle holding his hand over mine against the wall as we stared at it. How would Alec play it off if someone came by? As aggravated with Kyle as Alec was, he'd probably just tell them to move on - at gunpoint.

Kyle rolled his eyes. "I don't know. That's not important. Just don't let go of my hand."

"Why?"

"Shh. Listen," Kyle pointed up the stairs as we heard a man's voice carry downstairs. "Come on. The spirits can't see us. They're like a recording that the house is replaying."

"Are they ghosts?"

"No, not ghosts. Your spirit is what lives inside you – it moves to Heaven when you die. Ghosts are spirits that are trapped between realms; not completely spirit, not completely flesh. Remember the story in the Bible when the disciples thought Jesus was a ghost when He walked across the water?"

"No, I don't know the Bible very well."

"Oh. Well, we'll go over that later. But, I think if there were no such things as ghosts then Jesus would have said, "Nah, Peter, there's no such thing." But He didn't. There are numerous times in the Bible when ghosts are mentioned including King Saul summoning the spirit of Samuel. Plus, God warns us not to seek mediums and familiar spirits. He warns us because they exist."

"But you seek them all the time."

Kyle frowned as he led me up the stairs by my hand that he refused to let go. It was awkward, and he had to shift his fingers in my hand. What would happen if I pulled away? Would we be stuck here forever? If we were like spirits in this realm, why could I hear the stairs creaking under our weight? We stopped at the landing and listened again. This time an older woman's voice rose above the man's burly one. Kyle pulled me again up the next set of stairs, and I jerked his hand back once. I couldn't stand being stuck with Kyle Drekr in a spirit dimension listening for ghosts with the occasional echo from Alec's voice in another realm. I'd heard Alec very faintly ask if I was okay.

"I'm okay," I answered.

Kyle stopped on the stairs and glared back at me. "Shh! We don't want them to hear."

"You said they couldn't see us. So they can hear us, but not see us?" I asked.

Kyle threw his head back as if he was stuck in an alternate reality with an idiot. He came down the step and edged me backward into the wall. For a spirit, I could smell the onions from his burger at lunch on his breath. He leaned down to my ear, never once letting go of my hand.

"The spirit recordings can't see or hear you. However, the demons *can* hear you." He pulled his face away from my neck to give me a pointed look before resuming his climb up the steps with me following mutely behind.

The demons were here in this realm. They could see us, which meant they could probably interact with us. Could they physically hurt us here?

We stopped in front of a door that stood open and silently entered the large suite. It was a sitting room suite, but I could see that it connected to a large bedroom. In a moss green dress, an older woman sat casually on a chaise, her long silver hair wrapped neatly into a low bun. She wore a look of hatred that I'd never seen before on a human being.

An older man stood above her with neat white hair and a gray suit with a tight black tie. His expression matched hers. These two individuals did not like each other.

"You insult my intelligence, Dr. Graham," the woman said with a flick of her wrist as if in dismissal of the tall man standing before her. Her accent was a deep Southern, more profound than the accents of the people I'd met so far on this trip.

"Mrs. Ashbury, that is not my intention at all. It's just that the tuberculosis is sweepin' through the poverty-laden part of town, and we don't have time to construct a separate buildin' for patients. Your house is the perfect size for a clinic." The words were in a hateful tone, but Dr. Graham's stance revealed a desperate man.

Mrs. Ashbury stood and walked to the fireplace. Even at the door, I could feel the heat filling the room. "This isn't the Civil War. My family doesn't have to bend to appease anyone. We will not house poor sick people and risk infectin' our family."

Kyle pulled me into a far corner behind the door and placed a finger over his lips to remind me to stay silent.

MELISSA PLANTZ

Dr. Graham - was he a relation to *my* Alec Graham?- grew angry and even more desperate. "Your family could easily live on these upper floors and allow the patients and medical staff the downstairs. You have multiple exits with the servants' stairs and all. Please, Mrs. Ashbury, our small town needs a place to house the sick ones."

"I said no."

"Do you realize that some of these patients are mere children? The youngest we have is an innocent ten-year-old girl."

"None of us are truly innocent, Eugene." The woman practically spit the words from her mouth.

As Dr. Graham turned to leave, resigned to her answer, I watched as one of the Muladach, a silver demon, sauntered into the room. I pressed my body as flat against the wall as I could. I could see the demon's organs and muscles under its stretched skin. As it breathed, its heart pumped blood through the arteries. How could something supernatural appear so real? If I possessed the courage, I could reach out and touch its silvery skin. This one was large, the size of a gorilla, but with a gargoyle's body minus the wings. Its sharp teeth jutted out at strange angles; nevertheless, it was impressive and horrifying.

The man stopped as if he might try again to convince Mrs. Asbury that the town needed her home for a clinic.

Instead, the Muladach stood on its hind legs and whispered into the man's ear. As it landed back onto its sharp claws, Dr. Graham hesitated, then turned and advanced towards the obstinate Mrs. Ashbury until he stood almost nose to nose with the woman. She took a step backward to peer into the man's eyes.

"I beg your pardon, Dr. Graham. I think you should leave before I have someone escort you out."

"And who would that someone be, Mrs. Ashbury? Your husband is dead, and your son is at work. You've only one housemaid left, and she's somewhere downstairs."

Mrs. Ashbury's glare faltered. She tried to move past Dr. Graham, but he grabbed her by her hair, and as she let out a surprised scream, the man brought up a poker from the fireplace. I turned my head into Kyle's chest as I heard the woman's scream become shrill and then garbled.

However, the fear of the bloody sight swiftly left when I heard a growl. The demon had spotted us in the far corner of the room. Kyle moved in front of me as he tightened his grip on my hand again. "*Revertetur nobis,*" Kyle said with a growl that rivaled the demon's as the thing moved closer to us. "Return us! Take us back!"

The floor flew out from under me, and the sensation of falling again filled me with dread. I felt my feet land on solid ground, and I opened my eyes to find myself standing in the dusty front entrance with Kyle still holding my palm against the wall.

Alec cupped my cheeks in his hands as he searched my face. "Ainsley! Can you hear me? Ainsley!" I realized he was yelling at me.

I blinked several times as I brought his face into focus. "Yes, I'm fine. I'm okay," I managed to say.

Alec dropped his hands and pulled me away from Kyle, who stood dazed.

"Drekr, what the Hell was that?" Alec barked.

Kyle shifted his gaze from the wall to Alec's angry face. "Hell is right. What was your great-grandfather's name?"

"What?"

"What was your great-grandfather's name? I think that would be right. Maybe two greats."

"I don't know. Why?'

Kyle frowned. "The man we saw in this house was Dr. Eugene Graham. Does his name sound familiar?"

Alec shook his head. "I don't know. I know that my great-grandfathers were in the medical field and invested in other industries, but that's all I know. Why?"

I looked from Kyle to Alec. "Because Dr. Eugene Graham murdered Mrs. Ashbury in the sitting room so he could open the TB clinic here," I answered. "The demon, a Muladach, made him do it."

"What is going on?" Alec asked with confusion etched across his face.

I pulled on the front of his jacket. "Come on, let's get out of here. I'll explain it back at the hotel."

~ ~ ~

I managed to slip back onto the construction site without too many questions. Izzy asked me if I was feeling better, and I told her that sometimes I got dizzy. Everyone seemed to believe Maren's story. Unbelievably, Kyle was quiet the rest of the day. He seemed to be lost in thought, probably over the events at Ashbury.

I took the bus back to the hotel with the others and then showered and redressed in my room. I felt gross from not only the construction site and sawdust but the dustiness from Ashbury. After I'd dressed in a pair of black skinny jeans and an olive green tee with a black cardigan, I slipped on a pair of peach socks with little avocados on them. I knew they were silly, but I needed something lighthearted right now.

A knock on the adjoining door stopped me from pulling on my Converse. I opened the door to see Alec, fresh from the shower and dressed for our investigation tonight at the Ashbury Estate.

"Hey, are you ready for this tonight? After what happened today?" he asked as he shut the metal door between the rooms.

I grabbed a bottle of water from the refrigerator and took a drink before I answered. "I think so, but what I saw was as real as you and me. Those people were arguing… and when the man pierced that fireplace poker through the woman, I heard it rip through her body." I clutched my belly. The thought of it made my stomach turn.

Alec sat down on the sofa and rested his elbows on his knees. "I'm still trying to put together what you saw. You think you saw Mrs. Ashbury and a Dr. Graham in the upstairs sitting room, quarreling over using the estate as a temporary tuberculosis clinic for the poor, right?"

I nodded.

"Then a demon entered the room and influenced the doctor to take the woman's life?"

"Yes."

"I take it Kyle has checked up on me, and that's why he thinks I'm a relation to this doctor."

"I'm not sure, but could you be? You said you grew up less than ten minutes away."

Alec rubbed his hand through the stubble on his chin. Part of me wanted to sit on that sofa and make both of us forget about Ashbury and-

"I think I'm going to pay my grandfather a visit while we are here," Alec said, interrupting my way-too-juicy thoughts.

"Your grandfather is still alive?" I moved to sit beside him on the sofa.

"He still lives in the family home."

"I can't wait to meet him," I said, smiling. I would finally get to meet some connection to Alec's past.

"Ainsley, my grandfather is not a good man. I don't think it would be the best idea for you to go."

"Oh. But you said you would drive me by your childhood home," I reminded him.

"I didn't mean I would take you inside."

"You said whatever I want."

Alec sighed as he finally met my stare. He reached up and pushed a lock of my hair back over my shoulder. I watched as he swallowed. "My parents never married, even after I was born. My father was always on the road for his job, and my mother moved back home to her parents in Alabama when I was in grade school. I lived with my grandfather."

"They just left you with him?" I whispered.

"My grandfather has high ideals about how the world should work, and my parents didn't follow those rules. My dad refused to follow in his father's footsteps as he had done with his father. I don't think Grandfather gave them a choice."

"Do you ever see your father?"

"He died when I was in high school."

"Like mine,' I whispered. "And your mother?" I asked quietly. My heart was secretly breaking for Alec.

"I haven't seen her since my graduation from Basic when I was eighteen," he wrapped my hair around his finger absentmindedly. "My grandfather Edward was a surgeon. He also owns part of a steel manufacturing company with his best friend. He's on the Board of Directors for several companies, including a pharmaceutical manufacturer. His father Richard and Richard's father were also doctors. The Dr. Graham you think you saw was probably Richard's father. Now that I think about it, his name may have been Eugene."

He searched my eyes. "Are you sure you saw what you think you saw? I mean, are you sure Kyle Drekr isn't deluding you somehow?"

I shook my head. "No. He's not an illusionist or a hypnotist. He's just a grade-A jerk."

He dropped his hand from my hair as he rubbed his hand over his chin again. "The crazy thing is that I could hear you two."

"Kyle said you could hear what we were saying to each other."

"Not just that. That was weird enough. It was like I could hear the two of you moving within the house. The stairs creaked, and there was shuffling on the landing. And we all three heard that crying. For a second, I thought it might be a human child locked behind that hidden door, but my gut told me I was wrong."

I frowned. Somehow the two realms converged. Was it always like that? Or, had Kyle focused our energy on opening a portal of sorts?

"Wait," Alec said as he reached down and pulled my calf onto his lap. He grabbed my avocado sock-clad foot. "What is this? Are these avocados?"

I laughed as I tried to pull away, but Alec held my ankle firmly. The grin that spread across his face told me that I was in trouble.

"Don't you dare."

"What?" Alec feigned innocence.

"I know what you are thinking," I said as I tried to pull my foot away again.

Alec narrowed his eyes at me as his lips formed into a playful smile. "You have no idea what I am thinking."

Before I could make some flirtatious remark, Alec began tickling my foot to the point that I fell off the couch and landed on the floor, forcing him to stand to dodge my other flailing leg. He pulled me away from the coffee table to keep us from hitting it.

"Okay, okay, I give up," I said with tears running down my face from laughing so hard. My cheeks hurt.

Alec stood above me, holding my socked foot high in the air. My bum floated above the floor by at least six inches. Since only my head, shoulders, and upper back touched the carpet, the only way I could get away from him was if I kicked him with my free leg. Sensing my new ninja skill, Alec grabbed that leg too.

"I said I give up," I sputtered out.

Alec was now laughing so hard he could barely stand and support my weight; however, when a knock came on the adjoining door, he dropped my legs like hot potatoes. I landed with a thud.

"Oh, sorry. I didn't mean to let go like that," he apologized as he helped me stand.

I quickly ran to the dresser mirror and used my fingers to fix the makeup around my eyes as Alec opened the door. I came around the wall in time to see Kyle walk in. "Everything all right?" he asked me. "It sounded like someone fell."

I straightened my shirt and cardigan. "It was me. I'm a klutz sometimes."

"Hm," Kyle answered.

"Are we ready to go?" Alec stood adjusting his shirt cuffs that had managed to work their way free. He rolled them back up his forearms and then straightened the bottom of his shirt over the holster on his hip. He was taking his gun on this adventure.

Kyle's eyes flitted over Alec's gun before landing back on me. "As soon as Reynolds gets her shoes on and does something with her hair."

I looked in the mirror again. I'd only checked my eye makeup. My messy ponytail was indeed messier than usual from rolling around on the floor. I quickly pulled the holder out and redid it without commenting on Kyle's observations.

"Let me run to the bathroom before we leave." When both men looked at me, I added. "I don't want to have to pee at Ashbury and use their bathroom in the dark." I rushed into the bathroom and shut the door.

The hotel suite was lovely, but it was still possible to hear conversations from the bathroom. I realized this midstream.

"So, what exactly are you doing with Reynolds?" I heard Kyle ask.

"What do you mean?" Alec answered.

"What's your game? Coming on this trip, hanging around her, paying for her fancy room?"

"I'm not doing anything. As for Ainsley's room, she deserves something nice."

"Deserves it for doing what?"

"Drekr, I don't know what ideas you've got in your head about Ainsley, but you need to drop them."

Quietly, I leaned on the bathroom door, trying to hear more of the conversation. It sounded like both men were moving about the room. Were they circling each other like sumo wrestlers or what?

"I'm not interested in her like that. And neither should you be," Kyle remarked.

"What did you say?"

"She's got her whole life ahead of her. Don't mark her as your property."

"Don't mark her as my property? Are you listening to yourself? She's a woman, not a new toy."

"Exactly."

The room grew quiet. Hurriedly, I flushed the toilet and washed my hands. When I emerged from the bathroom, Alec was sitting on the sofa again while Kyle was looking through the coffee pods.

"Are we ready to go?" I asked a bit nervously, the tension in the room increasing by the second.

"As soon as you put on your blasted shoes," Kyle growled as he turned to go back into the room next door.

CHAPTER NINE

Maren and I stood in the foyer at Ashbury while we waited for Alec, Kyle, Stephen, and Ravi to finish bringing in the equipment. Due to the volume of sightings, the owners kept cameras and audio equipment on site. Not to mention some of Kyle's equipment that Stephen had brought in his truck.

It took at least an hour to set the cameras up throughout the house. Kyle insisted that we place one in the upstairs sitting room and at the bottom of the main staircase. Ravi set another camera up in front of the closet where the last paranormal investigator died. Stephen and Alec installed smaller cameras with suction cups in the hallways and a few rooms downstairs.

"How are you hanging in there?" Maren asked me.

I shrugged. "It's beautiful down here, but I miss Molly. Mrs. Hiroto text me that she's doing a lot better.

She's awake, but her vocal cords are weak, and they're testing her to make sure she doesn't aspirate when she eats or drinks."

Maren nodded. I knew she still felt guilty over Molly being in Charlotte - and coming so close to death. The Psych teacher ran her manicured hand through her wavy red hair. "I'm glad. As soon as we get back, I'm going to visit her."

"How are *you* feeling?"

Maren touched her side where a bullet had managed to miss her major organs. "I'm still a bit sore, but better. I can do more on the job site now. Of course, I'm still taking pain meds in the evenings."

"Well, take it easy. You have enough help on-site with the other students and the staff present. You could sit all day, and no one would say anything to you."

"But what kind of example is that?" she asked.

"Example of what?" Stephen asked as he walked into the room carrying a large tripod.

"Ainsley thinks I should sit on the building site and let everyone else do the work," Maren answered.

Stephen laughed. "Ainsley's not from West Virginia. You don't work, you don't eat."

The two laughed at their, what I guessed, was an inside joke. They'd both grown up near each other in Charleston, which was quite evident by their accent. Although I seemed to be spending all my time with adults now, Maren and Stephen were really cool. I'd been bitter toward Maren when I found out she was secretly friends with my father. But nothing ever happened between them because my father loved my mother more than life itself.

Stephen had worked with Dad on numerous cases throughout the years. I adored his disarming laid-back nature and respected the way he could get to the root of a problem without sounding preachy. I still thought Maren and Stephen would make a cute couple, both in their forties. However, it seemed like they were just close friends.

"Apparently, Reynolds doesn't believe in working," Kyle's growl pierced my thoughts.

"Kyle," Maren said with a tone of warning in her voice.

"Is this going to be a problem tonight, Kyle?" I asked as I watched the broad-muscled man carry in more equipment.

He stopped in front of me, towering down with his glare. "Unlike the other people in this room, you can see and hear things. You need to get your game face on."

"What does that even mean?"

"It means I need you in the foyer by the stairs." He shoved a flashlight and a small recorder at me. After a moment, he grabbed a helmet that looked like it belonged to a coal miner. "Oh, and put this on."

Alec and Ravi came in carrying more equipment. "I'll run these upstairs," Alec said.

I slid on the too-big helmet. "If I have this, why do I need the flashlight?"

Alec stopped beside me and grinned. He set the bulky cases down and adjusted the strap under my chin, pulling the helmet to a tighter fit. I felt the hairs on the back of my neck raise as his warm fingers brushed against my skin. "Better?"

"Yes, thank you," I whispered.

He winked before picking up the cases and resuming his quest to the upper floor.

"If you're done looking like a lost puppy, you need to monitor the hallway, please," Kyle commanded. "The chandelier is on a dimmer, so turn it down but leave enough light for us to have some while we finish setting up."

I rolled my eyes but did as Kyle told me. The house lights were still on, so it didn't have that creepy effect it would have later in the pitch dark. I lowered the dimmer until it gave off a candelabra effect. A camera was set up directly across the stairs, so I slid by it to look out the front door's window.

With the porch light on, I could faintly see the trees on the front lawn. They looked like they each had eight arms with sagging moss hanging off them. They were pretty in the daylight. But not now. Not so close to the darkness.

A stair creaked behind me, and I turned, expecting to see Alec. Instead, the woman dressed as a nurse slowly descended. She stopped on a middle step and stared at me with a look of surprise on her face.

"Hi, I'm Ainsley. I didn't know you were joining us tonight."

The woman tilted her head at me as if she wasn't sure what I'd just said. But her confused expression broke out into a smile when Kyle entered the foyer. He looked from the woman to me.

"What are you doing?"

"Turning the light down like you so graciously requested."

The woman sat down on the step with her fingers wrapping around the banister spindles as she watched Kyle lean against the wooden railing.

Kyle sighed and smiled at the pretty woman with her dark hair pulled back and tucked under her hat. "This is Matilda, also known as Nurse Mattie."

"Hi," I said to her again. The woman looked up at me again as if she was confused before turning back to Kyle.

"Reynolds," Kyle said slowly as he looked at me. "What do you see?"

"What do you mean?"

"On the stairs, what do you see?"

Was this a test? I glanced from Kyle to Mattie. "Mattie is sitting on the stairs, dressed in her nurse's uniform."

"That's what I thought. You can see them too." He motioned me closer.

I came forward as Kyle turned and placed his hands near Mattie's and brought his face closer to the spindles that Mattie still held. Their faces were only inches apart. "Beautiful Mattie was a nurse here during the epidemic. They say everyone loved her. She took care of the children that were brought in with TB. Unfortunately, Mattie contracted it and died just fourteen days later."

I stood beside Kyle and studied this woman that was as real as me. "Is this a joke?"

Mattie stopped smiling at Kyle and turned a stone-cold gaze on me. She understood that. However, Kyle didn't turn away from her. Instead, I watched as he slowly covered her fingers with his own on the spindle.

"The demons within this house tricked Mattie into staying here. Give me your hand," he said as he reached for me.

My first instinct was to run past this crazy couple and find Alec, but instead I found myself sliding my hand into Kyle's. He'd already shown me something otherworldly once today. What would happen now? What was the saying about curiosity and the cat?

The woman watched Kyle bring my hand to hers on the spindle. I gasped and tried to pull away when my hand touched something fleshly and cold, but Kyle held my hand firmly against Mattie's as the woman looked back and forth between the two of us.

"When you die and go to God, your body transforms into something new, something imperishable, something glorious," Kyle whispered. "When you die like Mattie, the body and spirit can't quite transform. She's just here. She is a ghost."

The sound of footsteps descending the stairs made Kyle and I look up to see Alec coming around the landing, but he stopped short when he saw us.

"Everything all right, Ainsley?"

"Yeah…" I trailed off as I realized Mattie was no longer sitting on the steps. I could no longer feel her dead flesh under my fingers. She was gone.

"Then what's going on?" Alec asked as he came down each stair slowly. He was glaring intently at Kyle, who still had his hand on mine.

"I needed Reynolds to feel something," Kyle answered with a smirk.

I pulled my hand away from Kyle's when Alec stopped on the staircase. "It was the nurse from earlier."

"What nurse?"

"He didn't see her. No one can see her but us," Kyle said.

"Did we catch her on camera?" I asked, suddenly feeling the need to justify why I was holding hands with Kyle in front of Alec.

"Maybe. We'll find out when we go over the footage."

"The cameras are ready to go upstairs," Alec said as he walked past us into the living room. I quickly followed him to the large dining room where Stephen and Maren were finishing setting up the equipment.

"Are you mad?" I asked, but he didn't answer as he lifted out the bag of batteries for the recorders. He started replacing the old batteries in each recorder and device with new batteries. I pulled on Alec's jacket sleeve to get him to slow down. He was like a man on a mission.

Finally, I guess sensing my awkwardness over Kyle, he sighed and smiled down at me.

"No, of course not. It's fine, Ainsley. Kyle is here to teach you the things your father knew. Come on, let's finish this. We're almost done."

"I want to stay with you tonight," I said and then bit my lip when Alec stared at me wide-eyed. Stephen and Maren stopped talking, and I was keenly aware that every ear was open to our conversation.

"I *mean* during the investigation. I don't want to go in any of the rooms by myself."

A playful smile appeared on Alec's face as he tugged at my ponytail. "I wouldn't have it any other way."

~   ~   ~

Two hours later, Alec and I sat quietly in the upstairs sitting room, waiting for something to happen. But nothing did. We'd done everything Kyle had told us, asking questions, listening for sounds, and watching for lights on one of the machines. Unfortunately, there was no one interested in us. I didn't even feel the demonic energy I should have from what everyone said about Ashbury.

"Do you want to go downstairs or investigate another bedroom up here?" Alec asked softly from beside me. We were both stretched out against the wall with our legs crossed at the ankles. We'd placed the recorder and light device on the floor in the middle of the room.

"Where are the others?"

"Kyle and Ravi took the downstairs. Stephen and Maren are on the third floor."

"I like sitting here in the dark with you," I answered and reached for Alec's hand.

"The camera and audio equipment are recording everything," Alec whispered again.

I sighed. "I can't wait until my birthday. I hate the way people stop and stare at us like we're doing something wrong."

"Just a few more weeks, okay? But I have a feeling people are still going to give us a hard time."

I sighed again as I snuggled closer to his arm. Just as Alec intertwined his fingers in mine, a cold blast of air blew through the room. The device lit up at once creating a buzzing noise.

"Is someone here?" I asked.

The lights lit up in red and green, throwing images onto the wall. I crawled to the middle of the room to check on the device. Maybe it was shorting out. However, there was a small noise that sounded like electrical sparks coming from the fireplace, not the box.

"What's wrong?" Alec asked when I moved to the fireplace.

"There's a sound like electricity coming from here. Do you hear it?"

"No. The only thing I can hear is the buzzing from the box."

I ran my hand over the mantle as I struggled to focus on the low crackling sound. The box seemed to be getting louder. "Can you turn it off?"

Alec went back to get the box as I continued feeling the edges of the fireplace. The fireplace where Mrs. Ashbury had breathed her last hateful breath before Dr. Graham killed her.

With that last thought, my fingers touched cold brick to the left of the fireplace. The cold air was coming from behind the old red brick. What was there? The bricks were larger than the ones used today for modern buildings. I started tugging at the loose mortar. It crumbled easier than I expected.

"What are you doing?" Alec asked after he'd managed to turn off the box and see me destroying private property.

"There's something back here."

He placed his hand over mine. "That doesn't mean you tear down a wall to get to it."

"It's one brick, Alec. If I can remove one, then maybe I can see what is behind this wall."

"Okay, here, then let's use my knife." Alec pulled his pocketknife out and bent down to work the brick loose. "Shine your light here."

When he'd finally removed the brick, he took the flashlight and peered inside before looking up at me from his stooped position. "If I tell you there is nothing there, can we quit?"

"What do you see?" The buzzing sound was growing. There had to be something there.

"I can see steps leading down a narrow stairwell."

"The servants' stairs. Dr. Graham told Mrs. Ashbury that her family could use the servants' stairs to keep away from the TB patients. Can we get in there?"

"Not without removing several of these bricks. I don't think the owners would be too happy about that."

"Please? We can repair them tomorrow."

"It's destruction of property, Ainsley."

"But we will put them back first thing in the morning. We'll use the same bricks with fresh concrete or something."

Alec studied the wall, frowning. "If we remove these ten, I think we can slide through," he said, outlining the bricks with his knife.

I dropped to my knees again beside him and used the barrel from the flashlight to work the crumbling mortar loose as Alec worked with his knife. It took us about an hour to carefully pull away the ten bricks, leaving an opening just barely large enough for each of us to squeeze through. The sound of electrical wires crossing became louder as I followed Alec into the hole.

"You seriously don't hear that noise?" I asked.

"It's dead quiet in here." He shone his light ahead of us, then reached back for my hand.

"Hey, before we head down to who-knows-where, I just want to say that I'm glad you came. Having you here makes me feel like I'm braver than I really am."

Alec touched my cheek. "The Ainsley I know is already pretty brave. She doesn't need me or anyone else to give her strength. I will back you up though."

"Thank you for saying that. I'd kiss you, but I think our helmets would get in the way." I glanced up at the small bright light on Alec's head.

Alec gave me a half-grin before he turned away, tightening his grip on my hand. "Do you think I would let helmets stop me? Come on, let's see where this goes."

With our backs to the wall, we slowly descended the old wooden stairs. The passageway was extremely narrow, and the ceiling was lower than I would have expected, giving off a claustrophobic vibe. The buzzing sound grew until it felt like it might be coming from within me with every step.

We finally came to a door, and Alec tried the knob.

"It's locked," he whispered.

"Knock on it. Maybe Kyle or Ravi are nearby. This is the first floor, right?"

When Alec pounded on the door, the buzzing suddenly stopped.

"Shh," I said. "The buzzing stopped."

"Why am I shushing?"

"I'm trying to listen."

"For what?"

"I don't know," I admitted.

Alec pounded on the door again. This time the knob began to turn back and forth as if someone was trying to open the door from the other side.

"Hey, Kyle? Ravi? It's us," Alec yelled through the door, but neither man answered.

The knob continued to turn back and forth faster and faster.

"Who's there?" Alec asked in his sternest cop voice. But instead of a voice, someone or something began pounding on the door in response.

Alec drew his gun. "Turn around and go back. Now."

"I'm not leaving you here."

"I'm right behind you. The door is opening."

I turned, and as quickly as I could, with only the flashlight beams and our helmet lights to guide the way, rushed up the stairs and to the hole in the wall. I had barely squeezed through when Alec came through the gap quickly. So quickly that he pushed me over onto the floor, landing on my back, to get away from whatever it was. He quickly rolled off me.

We both laid on the floor in front of the hole we'd created in the wall near the fireplace watching as we heard footsteps coming up the wooden steps. Alec and I both scooted on our backs across the floor, and it took me a moment before I realized Alec was pointing his gun at the wall.

When a small hand reached around a brick, I screamed.

CHAPTER TEN

I screamed the loudest I'd probably screamed in my whole life and scrambled to stand. Alec was on his feet quickly, reaching over and swinging the camera to point to the hole in the wall. The little hand remained on the brick as if unsure what to do now that it had our attention.

I slowly became aware of the vibrational energy forming around me. The energy was different than the buzzing from earlier. This vibration meant that there were Muladach somewhere close. Were they on the old stairs? Would one, or more than one, come bounding out of the hole any second?

Alec grabbed my upper arm and dragged me toward the door, but I hesitated with my hand on his chest. I needed to know. We hadn't come this far not to see what was attached to that hand...if anything.

"Who's there?" I asked.

Another hand appeared on the opposite side of the hole, and I heard Alec let out a breath when a figure began to emerge from between the bricks.

"What the-"

"Can you see her?" I interrupted him.

"Hm-mm," Alec answered. He tightened the painful grip he had on my upper arm.

A girl with stringy black hair wearing a hospital gown stood at the entrance to the hole. Her eyes reminded me of the Muladach's eyes – reflective and gleaming from our flashlight beams. Her skin color reminded me of the cold of Mattie's flesh when I'd touched her hand earlier tonight. No life in her.

"Who are you?" I ventured.

The girl turned her head a bit as if sizing us up, and Alec's grip intensified to the point that I knew I would have bruises on my arm by morning. I pushed his hand away as I took a step forward.

"No, Ainsley," he whispered. I could hear the fear in his voice.

But I wasn't sure where my fear was at the moment. It seemed overcome by curiosity. "Were you sick here? Did you have tuberculosis?" I asked the girl.

Her lips turned upward into a strange grin.

Demonic. The word hit me suddenly, and I knew it was true. I rushed back to the door and swung it open. Kyle could handle this one.

"Don't go. Don't leave me." Her little voice sounded desperate. If I had planned to turn around, Alec didn't give me a chance. He pushed me out into the hall and slammed the door behind us.

"We need to find Kyle," he said as we raced down the dark stairs, our beams of light swinging wildly over the dark paneling. Ravi had turned off all the power to Ashbury for tonight's investigation.

When we hit the first floor, we both started yelling for Kyle. In less than a minute, we ran into Kyle and Ravi coming through a small parlor room.

"What's wrong?" Kyle asked.

"There's a girl in the upstairs sitting room," I answered, a bit out of breath.

"A girl?" Ravi ran his hand through his hair.

"I felt cold air and heard a buzzing sound coming from beside the fireplace, so we pulled a few of the bricks away. We found a staircase, but something followed us back into the room."

"I could see it," Alec said.

Kyle nodded as he considered what we were saying. "If you could see it, then it's strong. Probably not a ghost."

"I think it's demonic," I added.

We followed Kyle back through the house to the upstairs sitting room, but the girl was nowhere to be seen. The bricks still lay stacked on the floor near the hole. I noticed Ravi frowning at the mess.

"We'll repair this in the morning. I promise," I said to him.

"I hope so. The owners won't like this," he said.

"Hopefully, the camera or audio picked it up," Kyle said as he checked on the camera and its tripod focused on the brick wall. He shined his flashlight back over to the hole. "We need to see where the staircase goes. Alec, you come with me. Unless the ghosts are getting to you?"

I didn't have to look at Alec to tell Kyle's remark aggravated him. "After you," he said with more bravery than I could muster at the moment.

Kyle peeked inside the hole before turning around to face us. "Ravi, do you know where this leads?"

"No, I didn't know there was anything here."

"We did," I said to Kyle. "Do you remember when we crossed over, and we were in this room with Mrs. Ashbury and the doctor? Weren't there two white doors, one on either side of the fireplace?"

Kyle slowly nodded, remembering the scene that had played out in front of us earlier. "They must have removed the door to the servants' stairs and bricked it up for some reason. The other door leads to a bedroom."

He shined his light into the stairwell. "What if the door at the end doesn't lead to the first floor? What if it's another portal?" he asked into the darkness.

"Then you'd better go first," Alec answered him.

Kyle looked back at us and grinned. "Ravi, will you keep watch downstairs to see where we come out? Reynolds, do you want to stay here or wait downstairs?"

"I'll go downstairs with Ravi. Shouldn't we turn on the lights?"

"We'll leave them off for a little while longer. I want to see this girl. Did she feel like Mattie?"

"I didn't get close enough to touch her."

"No, I meant did her presence feel like Mattie's?"

"No, it was demonic. I know it."

"Then it's probably a demon masquerading as a child that died here. What easier way to get paranormal investigators to follow than to appear as a little child?"

"Isn't that what we're doing now?" Alec asked. "Following the demon that appears as a child to wherever it wants us to go?"

"Scared?"

"Cautious," Alec answered.

I watched as Kyle and Alec slid between the bricks and into the dark stairwell again. Ravi and I quickly made our way to the first floor to listen for them.

"When we were on the stairs, we banged on the door. You didn't hear us?" I asked Ravi.

"No, it's been quiet down here the entire time. Well, except for Kyle occasionally talking out loud."

"I wonder how Stephen and Maren are doing?"

"We'll check on them as soon as we find this door. I'm wondering if the owners bricked this door up too."

I hadn't thought about that. The ghost girl/demon could've made it appear that the door was opening from somewhere else in the house, but it might not be accessible. Maybe it was another portal like the wall under the stairs.

I ran my hand over the wall in the dining room. This was the room under the upstairs sitting room. "Where are you guys?" I whispered.

I heard a small thumping sound. It was subtle, like the bass of someone's car stereo playing a couple of blocks away. I continued to run my hand over the wall until I suddenly felt the wall pulsate. I jumped back.

"What's wrong?" Ravi asked when I yelped.

"The wall moved here." Hesitantly, I placed my hand back on the cool wall. "Where are you guys?" I asked again, and in response, the wall pulsated gently under my palm and then under my fingers. It was moving toward the soft thumping sound.

I followed the movement out of the dining room and into the kitchen. I almost lost the small bubbles forming under the wall through the doorway, but they resumed on the other side until I came to where the refrigerator must have set at one time. Ravi and I exchanged glances before I placed my ear against the painted drywall.

"We're here," I heard Kyle's faraway voice.

"They're behind this wall," I told Ravi.

"Are you sure?"

"Yes, I can hear Kyle. I think he's talking to me."

Ravi felt the wall. "I don't hear anything. Wouldn't they bang on the door?"

"I think they are. Somehow I think the house is absorbing the sound."

"If we do this, then we have to fix it tomorrow."

I nodded. Ravi left the kitchen and came back a minute later with an ax.

"Wait, how do you know that you're not going to hit one of them?" I practically screeched.

"Can we tell them to move?"

I placed my hands on the wall just as Kyle had shown me earlier. "Alec? Kyle?" I raised my voice. "We're going to break through the wall. Stand back!"

Ravi swung the ax, and immediately drywall dust blew into the air. I coughed but tried to stay focused. If I saw either man, I needed to stop Ravi from swinging and killing someone. It only took a few more hits to the wall to bring it down. There was no insulation. This must have been the doorway to the servants' stairs, but where was the door I had seen? Why was this end of the stairwell drywall and not brick?

Sure enough, Alec and Kyle were standing on the stairs, shielding their faces from the drywall dust.

They both emerged, dusting themselves off in the kitchen.

"But where's the door?" I asked as I examined Ravi's hole.

"It's gone," Alec answered. "It was a dead-end at the bottom of the stairs."

Kyle coughed, still trying to clear his throat. "I guess the demons wanted you to open the portal, so they used a door."

"But we didn't open it. It was locked. That thing opened it," I said.

"I don't know, Reynolds. At least we know where it ends."

Ravi shook his head. "We're going to have a lot to clean up in the morning."

~   ~   ~

It had taken time to find Stephen and Maren since no one's radio was working. All of the new batteries had died. Once we did, Ravi turned on the lights, and we quickly broke everything down. Maren couldn't believe that they hadn't heard anything from the third floor with the commotion of me screaming when I saw the girl to Ravi hacking through the kitchen wall.

I was exhausted by the time we reached the hotel, but I knew I needed to shower before I could get in bed. Maren said she would try to sleep for a few hours before meeting with the students for breakfast. It was going to be a long day.

As I toweled off, I caught sight of my upper arm again. Alec had been so afraid of the girl/demon that he had squeezed my arm with such force, it left a handprint. I could see his fingertips as bright blue and purple bruises that circled my bicep. I didn't want to mention the bruises to him because I knew he would feel horrible. I climbed into bed to see a text on my phone from Alec. It read to call him if I wasn't too tired. He answered on the first ring.

"Hey," he whispered. "Are you okay after tonight?"

"I think so. What about you?"

"That was…strange. I've never seen a ghost before or whatever that was. I didn't expect to see anything tonight."

"Where's Stephen?"

"He's asleep. The reason I wanted to talk was to ask you about how you knew where we were inside the wall. Precisely where we were on the stairs."

"Oh. I was in the dining room thinking about you and Kyle, and I began to hear a thumping sound. When I placed my hand on the wall, the thumping turned into a pulse, and it led me to you."

"Hmm. When we were on the stairs and realized it was a dead-end – the door was gone –

Kyle touched the wall as if he was feeling around for something. He kept saying, 'Reynolds, we're here. We're in here.' I thought it was Drekr being Drekr, but now I realize that maybe he was somehow telling you where to find us."

I rolled onto my back across the bed. I'd heard Kyle through the wall when Ravi could not. Why were we so connected to each other? Was it because I was a Seer and Kyle had worked with Dad as his Protector?

"Did you fall asleep?" Alec's soothing voice came over my phone.

"No, I'm just thinking."

"I think it's time we both went to sleep. We've got a long day tomorrow."

"I know. Good night, Alec."

"Sweet dreams, Baby."

~ ~ ~

Alec, Kyle, Ravi, and I spent the entire next morning repairing the damage from our previous night's investigation. Maren told the other students working on the site that Kyle was researching a location for a future show and that she'd sent me to look into another construction site in case we finished earlier than expected. I doubted that anyone believed her story about me, but no one said anything at breakfast.

Kyle arranged for us to do another investigation later at dusk, although I wasn't sure I was up to it. With the brick wall repaired in the upstairs sitting room, we had just finished sanding the kitchen wall after replacing the drywall when we heard a voice coming through the downstairs. Thankfully, the Ashbury was closed to visitors.

"Hello? Is someone here? Ravi?" a man's voice bellowed through the first floor.

Kyle stood and went to the kitchen doorway. "We're in here. In the kitchen."

A tall white-haired man, easily in his seventies, fit and dressed in a tailored suit, appeared in the doorway.

"I'm Palmer Meadors," the man said as he glanced about the kitchen.

Kyle reached for the man's hand. "Hi, I'm Kyle Drekr. We spoke on the phone."

"Yes, of course," the man said as he glanced at me, and then his eyes lit up with recognition when they settled over Alec, who was leaning against the counter. "Alec Graham! Is that you?"

The man bounded towards Alec and enveloped him in a bear hug. Alec grabbed the man just as hard.

Kyle and I exchanged looks, and I bit my lower lip to keep from laughing out loud. The expression on Kyle's face was one of utter surprise.

"Yes, sir," Alec answered the big man as he pulled away. "It's good to see you, Mr. Meadors. How is your wife?"

The man patted Alec on the back. "She's good, I tell you. Fit as a fiddle as usual. She'll outlive me by forty years, I'm sure of it!" The man literally guffawed at his own joke. "Have you seen my son Harold? He's been getting involved with Ashbury more."

Alec smiled and reached for my hand, pulling me to stand in front of him as if offering me to the man. "No, sir, not yet. Mr. Meadors, I'd like to introduce you to Ainsley Reynolds. She's here with a group working on a housing project up the road, but she volunteered her time to help us do some small repairs here at Ashbury."

Mr. Meadors' gaze quickly swept over my dusty jeans and hoodie before he took my hand in his. "It's a pleasure to meet you, Miss."

"Mr. Meadors is my grandfather's best friend and partner in a few successful business ventures."

"Including Ashbury," Mr. Meadors said.

"Grandfather invested in the Ashbury Estate?" Alec asked, surprised.

"Why, yes. You know everything that man touches turns to gold. At least, in the last thirty or so years."

I nodded. Of course, that was where I had heard the name Meadors. Ravi had mentioned the owners yesterday. No wonder Alec had sounded shocked at the revelation. But to find out his grandfather was financially involved was probably more of a shock. We would need to discuss it later.

"Mr. Meadors, if you wouldn't mind not mentioning anything to my grandfather about me being in town, I would appreciate it. I plan to visit him soon, but I need to get some work done before I head to the house."

"Of course, Alec. I won't say anything, even to Helen. Now, what repairs needed doing around here? Where's Ravi?"

Kyle moved into the conversation at the mention of Ravi, as the tour guide had left to pick up lunch for the four of us. Kyle explained that we'd bumped into the kitchen wall with our equipment and had to repair it this morning.

"Not a problem at all," Mr. Meadors said as he looked at Alec. "Alec, my boy, you could've called me, and I would've sent workers in here to take care of it. No reason for you to do it."

"I wanted to," Alec said. "It's been a while since I've worked with my hands."

"That's right. You're a big shot detective now."

Alec gave a little laugh as he looked down at the floor. If I didn't know any better, I would have believed Alec was embarrassed by Mr. Meadors' praise.

"Well, it's easy to be a big shot in a small town," Kyle quipped.

Mr. Meadors turned his attention to Kyle, sizing the equally big man up with a cold stare. "So, Mr. Drekr, tell me how your investigation is going." It wasn't a question but more of a command.

Kyle half-smiled at Mr. Meadors, clearly understanding that the older gentleman was a fan of Alec's. "I think it's going rather well. No problems to report, but rather some paranormal activity last night."

"How many people are investigating Ashbury this time?"

"Well, there's me, Ainsley, Ravi, my friends Maren and Stephen. Oh, and Alec."

Mr. Meadors frowned as he turned towards Alec. "Why are *you* ghost hunting with Drekr's crew?"

Alec clenched his jaw as he pulled me closer to him. "No particular reason. Ainsley wanted to check it out, so I joined her."

Mr. Meadors slowly nodded as he studied my face as if waiting for me to oust Alec in a lie. Instead, I smiled. "Building a house is hard work even with lots of other students to help. Ghost hunting at Ashbury seems like a great way to blow off steam."

The man smiled before patting Alec on the shoulder. "Back in my day, we drank and hung out at make-out spots to blow off steam. I guess things have changed." He turned to leave. "Tell Ravi I said to call me when he gets back."

The rest of the day went by relatively quickly after lunch. We painted the kitchen wall and had everything back to normal a few hours before our next investigation. I rode to the hotel with the silent duo of Alec and Kyle. The two men didn't like each other, and the tension in the rental car was smothering, to say the least.

By dusk, once again, we stood in the empty Ashbury house, waiting to start the new investigation that either would lead us to the cluster of demons hiding in the other realm or across more spirits of those trapped within its walls. Honestly, I was leaning towards the Muladach for this one. Seeing Nurse Mattie in her tragic condition was too much to contemplate.

"Stay with me, okay?" Alec asked as he readjusted my loose-fitting helmet.

"It's probably best if she's with me," Kyle said. "I may need her abilities again to open a portal."

Alec frowned, but before he could disagree, I placed my hand on his. "It's okay. I'll be fine."

Maren sighed loudly. "If you two are done playing Tug-of-War over our Seer, we can get this over with."

Stephen and Maren took the downstairs, Ravi and Alec chose the second floor, and Kyle and I worked our way up to the third floor. The floor consisted of a vast hall with wooden doors on both sides that I guessed had once led to bedrooms.

"At some point, we need to take that smaller door there and go to the attic floor," Kyle said in a low voice.

"What's in the attic?"

"Smaller bedrooms for the servants. The stairwell on the other side of the door connects all the floors."

"But it's not the same hidden staircase we found last night?"

"Nope. This house holds many exits. Some literal, some invisible."

"Just like Dr. Graham said in yesterday's vision. Mrs. Ashbury and her family could've used any of the stairwells to stay away from the TB patients downstairs."

Kyle nodded. "Yeah, except it wasn't a vision, but more of a recording. Houses record highly emotional scenes. What we saw was a replay of sorts. However, the demons could see and hear us. Especially you."

"Why me?" I asked, turning my flashlight suddenly on Kyle, who'd stopped in front of a bedroom door. He put a hand up to shield his eyes from my light. The frown under his helmet was quite visible.

"You're the Seer, the Beacon." He turned away from me and placed his hand on the door.

"What is it?" I asked.

"Not sure. Wait."

We stood motionless for a few minutes. I moved closer to Kyle so I could see his face. His eyes were closed, but he seemed focused, intently listening for something. Whatever it was, was outside of my scope of hearing.

"Touch the door," Kyle whispered.

I hesitated. Would it be like the portal that opened downstairs yesterday in the foyer? Would I find myself alone on the other side of this realm?

"Touch the door," Kyle repeated. This time he stood staring at me.

"Shouldn't you hold my hand, so I don't get lost somewhere?"

The side of Kyle's mouth turned up into a half-smile. "I just did that to irritate you."

Highly descriptive words filled my mind, but I pushed them aside and instead focused on the door. Arguing with Kyle wouldn't help the situation.

I raised my arm until the palm of my hand hovered a couple of inches from the door.

"Focus on the sound," Kyle whispered.

"There is no sound," I whispered back.

"There is. Just below the surface."

I squeezed my eyes tightly shut and focused. After a minute or two, I peeked out at Kyle. He stood in the same place as if waiting for me to do something.

"There is no sound. It's silent."

Kyle's typically impatient tone of voice dissolved. "It's beneath the surface of the silence. Try again." He gently pushed my hand until it touched the wood.

I closed my eyes and focused on the door in front of me. At first, it was silent, and then, slowly, came a sound. It was what I would imagine people sound like when they are drowning, mouth full of water, and the lungs fighting hard to breathe, to gain one last intake of fresh air.

"Underwater screaming," I murmured.

"Not underwater."

I opened my eyes and studied Kyle's face as he moved closer, listening to the sound as well. He stopped only inches from my face. "Reynolds, that is screaming in the other realm."

The palm of my hand began to feel clammy as I listened to the sound. Who was doing the screaming? The demons? The trapped spirits?

"I don't want to be here anymore," I said as I withdrew my hand and rubbed my sweaty palm across my jeans. "We've only seen the one Muladach."

"There are more here," Kyle explained as he touched the door. "Even if only one or two come over at a time, they are just outside the portal door. I can feel them. Can't you?" He turned his head to face me again as he waited for my answer.

"No, I can't. This doesn't feel like the demons I came across in Locklyn. The one we saw yesterday was definitely a Muladach, but I don't think we are dealing with the same creatures aside from that one. Couldn't it be something else?"

"Like what?"

I was surprised to see the look of curiosity on Kyle's face. Was he interested in my opinion?

"I don't know anything about the demons other than what I found out a few weeks ago. But could the demons have a hierarchy? Like lower-level demons are assigned for certain tasks while the more powerful demons work on a larger scale?"

Kyle didn't answer. He seemed deep in thought.

I pushed on. "We've all heard stories about guardian angels, but those angels are not the same as the archangels."

"The archangels are warriors."

"Right. What if people are assigned demons to derail them? While massive tragedies are orchestrated by... 'arch-demons?'"

Kyle smiled. "I don't think they would be called arch-demons."

"Well, you know what I mean. Maybe what we are dealing with here isn't a demon cluster of lower-level Muladach, but something else?"

"Something more sinister than our run-of-the-mill demons?" Kyle asked. "Angels have a hierarchy, and demons *are* fallen angels." He blinked. "You might be onto something, Reynolds. Let's get this investigation over with, and then we can spend time researching the archives."

"What archives?" I asked as I followed Kyle through the dark hallway.

"Our organization keeps records from past investigations and expulsions. I bet if we dig deep enough, we'll find something from a Seer or a Protector about demon hierarchy. Of course, you not being able to decipher the energy could be because there are both demons and ghosts here. You're so new to this, and it's a lot to take in. I know. Come on, let's check the attic next."

~   ~   ~

I stood in the doorway between the formal living room and the foyer, shining my flashlight around, trying to locate a live person. Where was everyone? How had I managed to separate myself from Kyle and the others? The one thing I was supposed to *not* do under any circumstance. The last thing I remembered was walking with Kyle on the third floor. We'd stopped at the narrow door leading to the attic and the servant staircase - the one that connected all the floors. I'd grasped the doorknob and turned it, only to suddenly find myself staring into the dark emptiness of the first-floor foyer.

I was already creeped out from learning that the woman I thought was an actress in a 1940s nurse's uniform was a nurse from the early 1940s who contracted tuberculosis and died. I didn't want to run into any more ghosts or demons pretending to be ghosts, like the little girl. The thought of her straggly hair made me want to cry; knowing she was a demon made me want to run.

"Alec? Kyle?" I asked into the empty entrance. I eyeballed the camera on the tripod watching me from the front door. It had a clear view of the stairwell and the foyer.

When no one answered me, I tried harder to listen for them. Surely, I could hear someone somewhere in this place. There were six of us for crying out loud. "Where are you guys?" I whispered, hoping a thumping sound would alert me to their whereabouts like it had last night with Alec and Kyle.

Suddenly a bright light appeared on the staircase as if someone had dropped a flashlight from the second floor. I moved to the side of the camera to make sure I didn't block its view. I expected Nurse Mattie to materialize, but instead, the figure was of a man sitting halfway up the stairs with his head down, arms outstretched palms down, his elbows resting on his knees.

I stopped breathing. I tried the radio Alec handed me at the beginning of the night, but it made a crackling sound again and died. The energy of this house was draining the batteries again. I pressed myself up against the front door behind the camera. Even in the dark, I could see the man. Unlike Mattie, his body emitted a blue glow around him like an aura that lit up the hallway.

"Ainsley, what are you doing here?' he asked in a raspy voice, sounding tired. And familiar. The husky voice, although low, sounded as if it were right in my ear.

Tears stung my eyes. This was either a horrible trick by the Muladach...or it was him. I didn't answer, afraid that he would look up, afraid of what I might see.

I guess, sensing my dread, the figure raised his head to look at me.

I gasped as I tried not to cry. Gerald Reynolds stared back at me with eyes that reflected the beam of my flashlight.

"What are you doing here, Baby Girl? You shouldn't be here."

"Dad?"

He raised himself to a standing position, studying me as I peeked around the camera. His face remained expressionless as he raised his gaze from my face to something above his head. The foyer's ceiling blocked my view.

I didn't have a choice.

I shouted, "Be gone, demon!" in English as I couldn't remember any Latin while staring up at the image of my father. Suddenly, the image of the figure blinked at me, then disappeared.

"Dad?"

I heard creaking right above the foyer from the floor above. Someone from our group had to be up there. I shined my flashlight at the stairs and began climbing when something dropped in front of me.

It was Ravi with something wrapped around his neck. He dangled a few inches from the stairs and shook violently, almost knocking me back down the steps. I screamed, grabbing him around the legs and pushing him up to hopefully help him breathe. The thin man was heavier than I would've expected.

I kept screaming for help until I felt strong arms pulling me away from Ravi and taking over. Someone switched on the formal living room light. As my eyes adjusted to the brightness, Kyle carried Ravi over his shoulder down the stairs.

"We need to get him to the hospital now," Alec said as he pushed the camera out of the way of the front door and reached for me.

We loaded Ravi in Stephen's extension-cab truck, and Kyle sat in the back with him. Alec rode with Stephen while Maren and I followed in Kyle's rental car.

Two hours later, a nurse came out of the emergency room and said Ravi was stable. He was breathing on his own, but it was a wonder he hadn't broken his neck.

We drove back to the house to break down the equipment. I still hadn't told anyone about seeing what I was pretty sure was a demon mimicking Dad's spirit. He'd said I wasn't supposed to be here. I prayed that it hadn't been Dad's ghost. I'd expelled whatever it was to Hell. I wasn't even sure I could free ghosts.

I found Kyle in the entranceway on his knees packing up the camera.

"I don't know how I got down here by myself. It's like I stepped through the doorway into the stairwell and found myself here," I said, standing behind Kyle.

"I know. You stepped through, and then you were gone. It's like the house transported you down here. Probably some type of portal." He sighed, sounding weary.

"Kyle, I saw something tonight."

Kyle looked over his shoulder at me as he continued packing. "You mean the nurse? Or the girl?"

"I think I saw Dad. Or a demon pretending to be Dad."

Instead of turning to face me, Kyle rested his hands on his knees and lowered his head.

"Did you hear me? I saw something, and it spoke to me."

"Where?"

"On the staircase, only moments before Ravi…" I trailed off.

Kyle still didn't bother to face me. "If you did, the camera will have picked up something. I'll look at it back at the hotel."

"Whatever it was, I expelled it back to…wherever. I was able to banish it quickly with just a command. I'm getting stronger. But it said that I'm not supposed to be here. It sounded sad like Dad might if he were here. Do you know why he would say that?"

Kyle slammed the case shut and stood. He placed his hands on his hips before answering me. "Your dad wouldn't have wanted you to be a Seer. He wouldn't have wanted *this* for you."

I repeated the words to myself. "Is that why he never told me about the gift? He didn't want me following in his footsteps?" I leaned heavily against the wooden railing. "*Am* I disappointing him?" I tried to keep the tears out of my voice, but it only revealed the shakiness I felt.

Kyle sighed. He slowly moved to the stairs until he stood in front of me. As if Kyle wasn't sure if he was doing the right thing, he hesitantly placed both hands on my shoulders. "You could never disappoint him," he said slowly. "We can take a look at the video later. Demons love to mimic, but if Gerald told you something personal, then maybe it was him."

I tried to remember. "Dad said my name and that I wasn't supposed to be here. But then he called me Baby Girl. It was his name for me."

Kyle lightly squeezed my shoulders. "Yeah. Your dad used to call me Kyle-the-Kid. I was sixteen when I met him, and I had a huge chip on my shoulder."

I smiled up at him. "You? That's hard to believe."

Kyle smiled back. "Believe it or not, I was an even bigger hind-end than I am now."

"What's going on?" Alec stood in the main living room entranceway, staring at Kyle's hands on my shoulders. The blond man dropped his arms and went back to his camera. "Nothing. Reynolds thinks she saw something on the stairs before Ravi hanged himself."

Alec looked from Kyle to me. "Is that true?"

I nodded, but before I could answer, Kyle grabbed up the case and tripod and shouldered Alec in the wide doorway.

"Sorry, man. The load's heavy," Kyle said as he went on to the next room.

Alec took a deep breath and let it out slowly, a look of warning clearly in his eyes.

"Hey," I said, trying to pull his attention away from Kyle's asinine behavior. "Let it go. He's got issues. I think I saw Dad sitting here on these stairs tonight. But, it could have been a demon. It probably was a demon. I was able to banish it."

"Like the child?" Alec leaned on the railing as he studied the staircase.

"Yes. His eyes gleamed like hers, but he called me Baby Girl. That's something my dad only called me when we were alone. I think it was his way of reminding me I was always going to be Daddy's Little Girl." I could feel the heat forming behind my eyes.

Alec must have heard the small crack in my voice because he reached out and cupped the side of my face in his hand, bringing me closer to him.

"Are you okay?" he whispered, his thumb running across my jaw.

I nodded. "It probably wasn't him. But it looked and sounded like him. The way I remember."

Alec wrapped his arms around me into a hug, and I fought the urge to cry.

"Maybe the video picked it up, and we can analyze it later," Alec suggested.

"That's what Kyle said too," I said as I pulled away to catch a grimace cross Alec's face. "You two don't like each other much, do you?"

"I don't have a problem with Drekr. He's the one who has an objection to us seeing each other. Honestly, I don't think he's the only one. Stephen had a few things to say on the way down here."

"Like what?"

"It's not important. Come on, let's make sure everything is back where it belongs so that we can go to the hotel."

CHAPTER ELEVEN

The king-size bed felt luxurious for the second night in a row, and I silently sent good thoughts to Alec for paying for the fantastic room. It didn't take long for me to fall into a deep sleep as I was exhausted from the long day and even longer night at Ashbury.

However, I dreamt that I was back at Ashbury, standing in the gift shop I'd only casually glanced through while we were at the house. The room was an addition to the back of the house with screened-in windows, properly enclosed in glass during the cooler months. The small covered porch was filled to the brim with miniatures of the estate, mugs, keychains, postcards, and other tourist treasures. I touched a coffee mug with an image of the Ashbury printed on the front.

"Still drinking coffee? Didn't anyone ever tell you it would stunt your growth?"

I looked up to see Dad leaning against the cash register counter. Since this was a dream, I strangely wasn't shocked to see him at all.

"My dad used to tell me that a lot. But I'm five-foot-six now, so I think I proved him wrong."

Dad smiled. "You've turned into a beautiful young woman, Ains."

"I saw you tonight."

Dad shook his head. "No. Not me, Baby Girl. I'm in heaven, not haunting around at an old house, overrun with demons. But I felt your sadness and your confusion. That's why I decided I needed to visit you."

"Can I touch you?" I asked, vaguely aware that I was softly crying.

Dad opened his arms, and I ran to him. I hugged him tightly. His body felt solid, and I smiled when his beard rubbed against my cheek. It felt good to be in my father's arms again. I looked up at him, at his thick dark hair and eyes; a man taken in the prime of his life.

"Ainsley, there is something I need to share with you, and there's not much time. You'll be waking soon."

I took a step backward, but I didn't let go of his arms. "I inherited the gift of discerning spirits. I'm the Seer."

He didn't answer for a moment. He only half-smiled the way he did when he had to tell me something hurtful. Like when I was eleven, and our cat died.

"Listen to me. The demons mimic, as you now know. There are three rules, and you are breaking them all, making it that much harder to fight them, and putting yourself in danger."

"What rules? Why didn't you tell me any of this?"

"I thought I had more time. I knew you had the gift, and I tried to get things together to share with you. If I'd known…" he shook his head. "At home, inside the fireplace, you will find a loose brick with a key. Take the key to the bank. You'll find what I left you there."

"Okay. Dad, I have to ask…are you disappointed in me?"

Gerald Reynolds grabbed the sides of my face with his hands. "No. There is nothing you could do that would ever disappoint me. I let you down by not telling you the truth, teaching you about God, or revealing to you about the resurrection power of Jesus. But if this is your purpose, then it doesn't matter what I did or didn't do. What will happen will happen. Surround yourself with people who can help you. The demons don't want Kyle and you in the same place, but Kyle keeps breaking all the rules for approval. There are consequences to breaking the rules.

He needs a reminder. You need to remind him. He'll listen to you."

I laughed. "Clearly, you haven't seen us together."

Dad smiled. "I know both of you. It will be fine." He dropped his hands and took a step away from me, which only made me clutch his arms tighter.

"Ainsley, it's time you woke up now. I want to visit your mother in her dream while there is still time. I need to tell her something." He pulled my hands from his shirt and kissed the tips of my fingers. "I love you, Baby Girl. Stay strong."

I opened my eyes to find myself clutching the large bed pillow. I pulled it closer to me as I glanced at the alarm clock on the nightstand and wiped the tears from my face. Was that a real visitation from Dad or just a dream? Maybe when I returned to Locklyn, I would check the fireplace in the family room for a loose brick. Just in case.

~ ~ ~

Early the next morning, I knocked on Maren's hotel room door to ask her if she could tell everyone I wasn't feeling well so I could travel with Alec to his grandfather's home. At first, she balked at the idea.

"Ainsley, you know I adore Alec, but if someone sees you with him and it gets back to the Board, I could lose my job."

"No one will know, I promise. This is the only chance I will get to meet Alec's family. He and his grandfather are estranged."

Maren finally sighed as she pulled up her long red hair into a sleek ponytail to head out to the construction site after breakfast. "All right, but no funny business. Don't make me regret my decision."

I crossed my heart and smiled. "You won't regret it. Thanks!"

I slid out of her room and around the corner to mine. Once inside, I knocked on the metal door separating my room from Stephen and Alec's. Stephen opened the door.

"Good morning, Ainsley, are you headed to break-fast?" Stephen asked as he let me into their room. He sat down on the sofa to put on his shoes.

"No, not yet. I'm going to see Alec's grandfather with him."

Stephen frowned. "Is that such a good idea? Have you talked to Maren about it?" he asked as he stood to adjust his belt.

I concealed my growing agitation with the well-meaning adults in my life with a smile. Nevermind, the fact that I would turn eighteen very shortly. "Maren said that was fine."

Alec emerged from the bathroom, already dressed. Except what he wore wasn't his usual jeans and a tee-shirt from his off-duty attire. Today, he wore a pair of dress pants and a tailor-made button-down shirt with a tie. Unlike his standard untucked shirts, this one was tucked in, complete with his belt and a tie clip. I cringed. I was totally underdressed in my jeans and hoodie.

"Maybe I should change," I said.

Alec's eyes flitted over my outfit. "No, you look great. Plus, if you insist on going, you're not getting out of the truck. You can go your whole life without meeting Edward Graham."

"Everything all right?" Stephen asked Alec.

"Yes, just family drama. I'm sure you know what I mean."

Stephen nodded thoughtfully. "Well, if you need me to go, I will."

Alec shook his head. "It's fine. I just don't want Ainsley to get her feelings hurt."

"Why would I get my feelings hurt?" I asked.

"I told you that my grandfather isn't the nicest man in the world," he said as he adjusted his watch and took in my outfit again. "He has certain expectations."

I bit my tongue from stating the obvious; I didn't meet those expectations, and not because of my clothes. I was a senior in high school, and Alec was eight years older than me.

Sensing the tension growing between us, Stephen tossed his truck keys to Alec. "Well, you two, be careful. If you need me for anything, just give me a call." He turned to me but didn't speak until I looked him straight in the eye. "Ainsley, do you have my number?"

I nodded. Maren had given me Stephen's phone number before we left Locklyn.

"Good. Call me if you need anything. Kyle's supposed to go over last night's video footage after they work on the site today. If you're not back by then, I'll have Maren text you."

I nodded again as I watched the tall preacher walk out of his room to join the others for breakfast downstairs. Then I turned my attention back to Alec, who was holstering his gun.

"Why are you taking your gun?"

"I don't want to leave it in the safe," he snapped without looking at me.

I took a deep breath and let it out slowly before I approached him and placed my hands on his forearms. Alec stopped moving as I guided his hands onto my hips. He still refused to meet my eyes.

"I may not be what your grandfather would want for his grandson, but there is nothing that he, or anyone else, can say or do that will make me not want to be with you."

Alec's eyes finally met mine, but the usual fire wasn't there. Instead, those deep green eyes housed a look of inevitable defeat. He touched my cheek with the back of his hand and then planted a light kiss on my lips. He gave me his half-smile. "Come on, let's get this over with."

~   ~   ~

Alec drove Stephen's truck down the two-lane highway in the direction of the Ashbury Estate with one hand on the steering wheel and the other resting against his temple, a posture I'd seen before when he was deep in thought. Typically, Alec badgered me about making sure I'd eaten, but his mind was a million miles away, and I was thankful I'd grabbed a couple of cereal bars and a banana from the kitchenette before we left.

Alec slowed the truck and turned onto what appeared to be a narrow paved road. The asphalt stretched ahead of us, deeply surrounded by lush green trees and vines. No one had told this part of South Carolina that it was late October.

"I bet this road stays cool in the summer with all the foliage," I remarked.

"It's a reprieve from the sun, that's for sure." He let out a sigh.

"You know, we don't have to do this," I said quietly to his handsome profile with the lines of worry etched across his forehead. "Maybe we could find out something through the town's archives?"

Alec shook his head. "No. The archives will only have surface information. If one of my great-grandfathers murdered a woman, he was never charged. If the woman died from a stab wound, why didn't someone put it together that it was murder?"

I stewed on that suggestion. I hadn't looked at the woman after Dr. Graham impaled her with the poker. My attention had been on the demon coming towards Kyle and me. The scene had to have been horrific.

Alec made another slight turn, and the trees opened up into a clear view of the only house at the end of this road. Not road, driveway. *This long paved road was someone's driveway.* I sucked in my breath. I was pretty sure I'd seen a picture of this place on the front cover of a southern home magazine.

"You grew up here?" I marveled at the four-story white home with its wide columns and iron balconies. Well-maintained flower gardens bloomed along both sides of the steps that led to the front door.

Alec didn't answer as he pulled the truck through the circular drive to the point that I thought he might have changed his mind about seeing his grandfather, but then he parked. Through the rearview mirror, he peered at the house as if summoning the courage to get out of the truck.

"Alec?"

"Look, I need you to stay in the truck, okay? At least until I've got a handle on my grandfather." He was asking me, but his eyes betrayed his suggestion for a command.

"Sure, I'll stay," I said, then smiled. "Unless you need me. The house is huge. No wonder you weren't impressed with Ashbury. How big is this place?"

"Over 13,000 square feet. I told you I grew up right down the road from Ashbury, so no, big houses don't impress me at all." He grazed my cheek with his thumb.

"But it's not the least bit cozy either. Now, please stay in the truck until I come back, okay?"

"I'll stay here."

Alec squeezed my knee and then took a deep breath before opening the truck door. I watched through the back glass as he slowly walked around the circular driveway with his head down and hands in his pockets. He mounted the steps, but before he could knock or ring a doorbell, the wooden door swung open, and an older lady greeted him.

I couldn't hear their exchange, but the woman covered her mouth like she might cry when she saw him and then grabbed Alec and pulled him into a tight hug. Was this his grandmother? I'd never asked Alec about her. I watched as the woman pushed him into the house and shut the door.

I sat in the silence of the truck and studied the mansion. That's really what it was. A glorious estate probably passed down from generation to generation in the Graham family. Was this what Alec meant when he said I didn't know anything about his finances?

Then again, this was his grandfather's family home, and I'd seen enough movies and read enough books to know that sometimes people put on "airs" so others didn't think they were broke. Even if his grandfather did have money, it didn't mean that Alec did.

My eyes scanned the gardens until I noticed a young boy sitting on a large rock near the trees. He watched me with amusement on his face until I waved, then his smile disappeared. It was as if he'd been quite content to observe me from his perch as long as I didn't see him. He continued watching me as I fished the extra cereal bar out of my handbag. Maybe I could make friends with the boy over food.

I waved the bar, and crooking my finger, I motioned for him to come over to the truck. The boy, clad in shorts and a tee and a metal knee brace on his right leg, slowly stood on the rock and pointed up at the house.

I watched a curtain in a first-floor room move. Was someone watching me through the window? I glanced back at the boy who stood staring at me with a sad look on his face.

A sudden rap on the passenger-side window caused me to yelp. I turned to see the woman who had greeted Alec smiling at me through the glass. She had short white hair and appeared slim and active. The only indication that she might be older was the smallest of fine lines between her brows.

"Hello, I'm Tilda," she said in a drawn-out Southern accent after I'd lowered the window. "Alec said you are waitin' for him."

"Yes, I'm Ainsley."

"Won't you come inside? Alec's speakin' with Edward, and it might be a while," she said as she drew out the last word entirely too long.

I looked back towards the boy, but he was gone. He'd probably made his way into the house.

"Alec told me - I mean asked me - to stay in the truck," I stammered out.

"Well, that's just foolish," Tilda said as she waved her hand. "Alec's been gone so long that he's forgotten his manners. Come with me. I'll get you some tea. Or, would you prefer coffee?" Tilda opened the truck door, leaving me no room to argue.

I grabbed my bag and followed her. Part of me was excited at getting a chance to see the inside of the house. The other part of me was worried I would disappoint Alec by not staying in the truck. The marigolds and other flowers' overwhelming scent along the steps forced me to cover my mouth to keep from coughing.

"Oh, you're not allergic to flowers, are you?" Tilda asked when she saw me stifle a sneeze.

"Not normally. I guess there are just so many."

She waved her hand. "Yes, I have a landscaper come with pallets of assorted flowers. It cheers the place up, don't you think? Ed thinks it's a waste of money, but he's also very proud of how I keep the house up." She opened the wide oak door to reveal a foyer that was really like a giant room.

The foyer greeted me in bright, rich hues of green, orange, and brown with dark paneled walls. It was as wide as my living room at home and featured a circular marble table under a massive chandelier. I trailed Tilda into a room on the right with expensive-looking antique furniture.

"Please, take a seat, sweetie. What can I get you?"

"I don't want to be any trouble."

"You're certainly no trouble. I'm excited to see Alec come home. Now, what would you like? Maybe iced tea?"

I nodded and said thank you as Tilda left. There wasn't a television anywhere in the room, however a grand piano set in one corner and a series of bookcases lined the opposite wall. This had to be a parlor or sitting room. Since Tilda had left the door open, I moved to peer around the thick wooden doorframe. There was another set of sliding wooden doors directly across the hall.

Further down the hall was an entranceway into another room. At the end of the foyer was a sun porch with long windows that almost ran floor to ceiling. Maybe I could get Alec to give me a tour.

Suddenly, I heard raised voices coming from the room next to the sitting room. I was pretty sure I'd just found Alec and his grandfather. It sounded like a physical fight was about to occur.

As if on cue, a sighing Tilda walked into the foyer from another doorway. She smiled apologetically at me as she set a tray with four iced tea glasses on the marble table. She went to the next room over and slid open a pair of wooden doors.

"How dare you accuse your ancestor of such a heinous crime, boy!" The man's booming voice caused me to brace myself against the doorframe of the sitting room. No one had ever yelled at me with such extreme authority, and I couldn't imagine being raised by the likes of someone like that.

"I'm not accusing anyone of anything. I'm asking you if you've ever heard of such a story, maybe while you were growing up in this house? Any stories about your grandfather and Ashbury?" Alec's voice remained calm but rigid.

"Gentlemen," Tilda said in her sweet southern twang. "It's been so long since we've had any guests that I think we've forgotten our manners. Let's keep our voices down, shall we?"

"What guests?" the older man's voice growled. "The boy grew up here."

"Not him," Tilda said as she leaned backward and pointed at me, still glued to the doorframe. "Her."

An older man, probably in his seventies, charged out of the room. He stopped when he saw me, and at that moment, I wished to God I had the power of invisibility. I was so thankful that I'd taken the time to do my hair and makeup before we left the hotel. Maybe the man wouldn't judge me so harshly based on my jeans and hoodie.

Edward Graham stood at least six foot three with a full head of hair, and although it was peppered now due to age, he still appeared distinguished. It was like looking at an older version of Alec. Right down to the suit.

The man looked back at his grandson, who had finally emerged from the other room. Alec shoved his hands in his pockets, his lips in a tight straight line; he was not happy that I was in the house.

"I apologize if we seem rude, Miss. And you are?" he asked with a patient, albeit forced, smile.

I cleared my throat. "My name is Ainsley, Ainsley Reynolds," I answered. I shifted my gaze from the older man walking towards me to Alec and back again.

"Miss Reynolds, I must say that Ainsley is a beautiful name. I'm not sure I've ever met a young woman with such a unique name in my life." He reached for my hand, and I gave it to him as I swallowed the lump of fear in my throat.

"Well, I didn't think it proper for her to wait out in the truck with so many missin' girls. It's just not safe. Here now, I've poured us all some tea. Let's go in and sit a spell and talk," Tilda said as she carried the tray past Edward Graham and me. "Come, Alec. Come join us with your friend."

"What do you mean missing girls, Tilda?" Alec asked.

Alec's grandfather let go of my hand, and I followed Tilda back into the sitting room and quietly resumed my seat on the little sofa. Alec sat down rigidly beside me. I had a feeling he would not so much as brush against my leg with his grandfather present.

"Tilda came out to the truck and coerced me into coming inside for tea," I said quietly to Alec.

He half grinned as he took a glass from the sweet woman. "I doubt she had a tough time coercing you."

"What did you mean about missing girls?" Alec tried asking Tilda again, a little louder this time.

Tilda waved her hand. "Oh, about three or four of em over the last three weeks or so. Disappeared from right here in town. Around Ainsley's age, between sixteen and twenty. Even small towns have their problems. But, I heard the police have a lead." She looked at me. "You just stay with Alec, and you'll be fine."

I took a sip of the strong tea with its half-pound of sugar in the glass. When Tilda had said sweet, she'd meant syrupy sweet. Between the caffeine and the sugar, I expected to see sounds very soon.

Alec's grandfather whipped a chair around to face the sofa and sat down. He moved like he was eternally young, and, frankly, it was a bit intimidating.

"Please feel free to call me Edward," he said to me.

"Thank you, Edward," I forced my voice to sound normal.

"So?" Tilda started as she sat down on the little sofa across from us. "Alec, have you come home?"

Alec smiled. "No, ma'am. I still live in Locklyn. I'm just down this way for an investigation," he answered, and for the first time, I could hear his Southern roots.

"What kind of investigation would include Ashbury?" Edward asked.

"It's a cold case. Someone brought up information that the lady of the house was murdered in the late 1930s before the estate became a TB clinic."

"How horrible," Tilda said. "Tuberculosis was an awful thing back then before they had a vaccine. So many people died."

Edward took a deep breath as he narrowed his eyes at Alec. "But why would you believe it was my grandfather that murdered that woman? You know very well that Eugene Graham was a well-respected physician in these parts, as well as his son - my father, Richard - after him."

Alec licked his lips. "Someone may have been in the house that day and witnessed Eugene stab a fireplace poker through Mrs. Ashbury."

Tilda let out a gasp and covered her mouth.

"If that was true, then why didn't they report it to the authorities?" Edward asked, raising his eyebrows.

"Perhaps they were frightened. Or, someone received something as compensation for her death."

"What are you saying, Alec?" Edward asked.

"I'm just trying to put the pieces together, Grandfather."

"Well, obviously, you have a theory."

"Perhaps Dr. Graham was desperate to save the poorer people of the community and took matters into his own hands. I've been told that Mrs. Ashbury was a difficult woman. Some would go as far as to say heartless."

"And he brought you along for this trip?" Edward asked me.

I opened my mouth, but before I could mention I was here for a school project - and possibly my own investigation - Alec reached over and squeezed my hand.

"I brought Ainsley down here to see where I grew up."

Edward tilted his head as if considering this comment. I had a feeling that trying to get things past this older version was just as difficult as dealing with his grandson. "Are you hungry, Ainsley?" he asked.

"Oh no, thank you, sir," I said. "I ate in the truck."

"I ask because you've been grippin' that cereal bar in your hand since I laid eyes on you."

I glanced down and realized that not only had I been holding onto the bar, but I'd also managed to smash the package.

Tilda stood up. "Oh, sweetie, let me throw that out for you. I can bring you somethin' to eat. I have an apple pie that I baked yesterday if you want some."

"No, that's okay," I said as I tossed the smashed bar into my purse. "I was going to give it to the boy outside, but then he must have come in the house."

"What boy?" Tilda asked.

"A blonde boy was sitting on that rock past the flower gardens near the trees," I motioned with my hand in the general direction. "I tried to get him to come to the truck, but I guess he was taught well. Stranger danger and all that," I said, smiling until I felt Alec's grip tighten on my hand again.

"What was the boy wearin'?" Edward asked quietly.

I shrugged. "Um, a tee shirt and shorts, which I thought was a little odd for October, but it is warmer here. He also has a metal brace on his leg. His right leg."

Edwards's face turned red as he shifted his gaze from me to Alec. Alec stood and pulled me up with him.

"We should go," Alec announced as he started leading me through the room toward the doorway.

"Alec Edward Graham, stop where you are," Edward growled, and Alec stopped so suddenly that I bumped into his back. He didn't so much as budge.

The older man walked around until he was nose to nose with Alec. "Is this some kind of a joke?" he demanded. "You think bringin' your most recent mistake here, and makin' fun of my brother is somehow the way to get attention? Is that it?"

"We're not making fun of-" Alec started, but Edward interrupted him.

"How is that not makin' fun of a dead ten-year-old boy?" he roared, and I instinctively took a step backward, but Alec didn't let go of my hand.

"Dead?" I whispered but regretted the word as soon as it left my lips.

Edward Graham turned his glare on me. His dark green eyes scanned me again head to toe as if seeing me for the first time. "Yes, as I'm sure you know. My brother Teddy died when he was ten after being bitten by a tick. The fever from Lyme Disease took him. Just who are you to Alec?"

Then the man scoffed and shook his head as if meaning had dawned on him at last, meeting Alec's now hardened glare. "Are you repeatin' your father's mistakes? Is this girl pregnant?"

"We're leaving," Alec said as he pulled me around Edward and to the foyer and out the front door. I could barely keep up with his stride as we walked quickly to the truck. Thankfully, Edward did not follow us outside.

Alec peeled Stephen's truck from the circular driveway with a sudden jerk that pushed me forward in the seat as I fought to pull on my seat belt. "Alec, stop!"

Instead of stopping, he slowed down, his breathing sounding heavy. I could almost see his nostrils flaring in the sunlight streaming through the windshield. He looked at me. "I told you to stay in the truck," he seethed.

"Tilda insisted that I come inside. It seemed rude to say no."

Once my belt was securely on, he sped forward down the narrow lane.

"Is your grandfather always like that?"

"Pretty much. I had it handled before he saw you."

When I didn't answer for a moment, Alec let out a pent-up sigh. "I'm sorry, Ainsley. I don't mean to take it out on you. He's a difficult man, set in his ways. He was already suspicious of me being there asking about his grandfather, and then he saw you. He thinks I'm repeating what my father did with my mother." He reached over and took my hand. "But, I promise you this. No matter what our future holds, I would never bring you here to live in my grandfather's house while he is still alive. That man will *never* raise *my* son."

I remained quiet. I wasn't sure what to say. Was Alec thinking about our future together, or was this some vow he was making to himself? I didn't want to ask him either.

"I didn't mean to snap at you. Are you mad at me?" he asked, squeezing my hand.

"No. I am angry with your grandfather. I've never heard anyone yell at someone like that in my entire life."

"Really?" he asked and smiled as he kept his eyes on the road. "I can't remember a time when my grandfather didn't raise his voice. For the longest time, I thought that *was* his inside voice."

I half-smiled. The man was demanding, that was for sure. The house was gorgeous and well-maintained. Tilda was a sweetheart. But for all the bonuses, Edward Graham was not fit to raise a child - probably never was.

"So, did he tell you anything about his grandfather that could help us?"

Alec shook his head. "No, not really. He wouldn't even entertain the idea that the man may have been so desperate for the clinic that he killed Mrs. Ashbury."

"So what now?"

"Now I go back to the hotel and try to dig up some news articles on the Ashbury from the time of the TB clinic. Maybe I can find a death certificate for Mrs. Ashbury. Do you want me to drop you off at the building site?"

I shook my head. "The other students cannot see you. That would only make things worse."

"I can call Drekr and have him pick you up from around the corner or something."

I stared at his profile. "You want Kyle Drekr to pick me up?"

He shrugged. "No, I don't, but it's important that you maintain a good reputation. No one will question it if Drekr brings you to the site."

I bit my lower lip as Alec pulled his cell out of his suit jacket pocket and called Kyle.

CHAPTER TWELVE

"**S**hould I even ask?" Kyle groaned after he pulled up next to Stephen's truck at the gas station three blocks from the construction site.

Alec didn't answer him as he got out of the truck and opened the passenger door for me. Kyle rolled his eyes when Alec opened the door to the rental car and waited while I climbed in. Then Alec leaned down to see Kyle.

"We went to see my grandfather about Ashbury, but it was a bust."

"That doesn't surprise me. Why would he want to tarnish your family name around here? I've done the research. The Grahams helped build this town. I bet he was none too pleased to see you with Little Miss High School." Kyle waved his finger back and forth. "As a matter of fact, you may want to keep these side trips to a minimum. All it takes is for someone to see her sneaking off with you."

I shook my head at Kyle. Now was not the time to push Alec. To my astonishment, Alec only narrowed his eyes at the man.

"Alec, maybe I should just go back to the hotel?"

"No. Everything is fine," he answered, his jaw clenching. Then he surprised me by tilting my chin up and giving me a quick kiss on the lips before slamming my door shut.

Kyle stared straight ahead while he waited until Alec pulled Stephen's truck out of the gas station parking lot before putting the car in reverse.

I began pulling my hair up into a ponytail. "I don't know why you say things like that."

Kyle looked at me like I'd grown stupid in the last few hours. "Gee, I don't know, Reynolds. He's going to ruin your reputation and your integrity. What's it going to take? How much longer until you give him what he wants?"

"Which is what exactly?"

Kyle's eyes flitted over my hoodie and jeans, but he didn't bother to answer me. It didn't matter. I knew what he was insinuating, the same thing everyone else was.

We drove to the site in silence. I tried to pretend that I didn't notice that the other students stopped working when I got out of the car. As I walked to Maren to ask her where I should start working, I overheard Waverly.

"Well, that sucks," she said to Ethan. "Looks like Ainsley's moved on to a different guy. I guess no man is safe."

I turned my head and looked her in the eye, but that only caused the blonde Barbie to smirk. "That didn't take you long. Does this mean your cop boyfriend is free now? Or, is this a side thing?"

I sighed. "You're wrong about me."

"Am I? You keep disappearing. Now you show up with Mr. Drekr."

"Ms. Bell sent me on an errand, but I needed a ride back here."

"Just saying, and I thought you were sick, not running errands. Isn't your room away from ours? I mean, you could slip anyone in there for Netflix and chill, and no one would be the wiser."

Ethan cleared his throat. "Ainsley, don't let her get to you. Waverly is just giving you a hard time because she has a crush on Drekr."

Waverly let out a huff. "No, I don't, Ethan."

The two began bickering about Waverly's apparent crush on the television celebrity, and I used the distraction to get to Maren. The red-haired woman wore her usually perfect hair in a perfect ponytail and was balancing herself on a stool as she held part of a doorframe for Jamal to hammer in a row of nails.

"Any good news?" Maren asked.

I whispered in her ear when Jamal took a break from hammering. "No. Edward Graham was no help. Alec is going to try to find something online. You seem to be doing well today."

"So far, thank God."

"Well, where do you want me?"

"Go help Freya. She's on the second floor."

I climbed the stairs to the second floor. It was strange seeing a house without all of its walls complete, like a skeleton with only bits of muscles and tendons and organs here and there.

I found Freya in what would soon be an upstairs bedroom. "Hey, Ms. Bell said to come help you."

Freya tousled her blonde hair in my direction. "Thanks. I'm assigning the drywall pieces to this room. Then, I guess, we will hang the drywall."

"Are we supposed to patch and sand it too?" I asked.

Freya looked up from the drywall she was leaning against the wall, clearly shocked that I knew what I was doing. "I think so. Probably tomorrow." She studied me for a moment. "You're full of surprises."

'Well, don't believe everything you hear about me." I moved one of the drywall pieces over to a blank space with only two by fours and a roll of insulation for an outer wall.

Freya nodded. "Oh, don't worry. I never believe rumors, and I mostly keep to myself what I see." She moved closer to me and gave me a pointed look.

"Like what?"

"Like I saw you and a man getting into Mr. Reeves' truck this morning."

I studied Freya for a second. "Ms. Bell sent me on an errand."

She smiled. "I'm not going to tell anyone. The truth is, I only saw it because I was running late to the dining area for breakfast. He looked familiar. Is he from Locklyn?"

I glanced nervously through the door frames that offered absolutely no real privacy. Maren and Kyle were downstairs somewhere.

"Freya-"

"It's okay. I won't tell anyone. I promise. My father's the mayor of Locklyn. I know how to keep my mouth shut."

What could I tell this girl? How much should I tell her? Wasn't the Mayor like the boss of the police department?

I sighed. "My friend paid for my room because it was so last minute. He came to settle the bill, and then he gave me a lift to run an errand for Ms. Bell." I blinked as I waited for Freya to decide if I was telling the truth or not.

Her eyes searched mine, then widened. "I knew I recognized him. He works on the police force. He's the one everyone says is your boyfriend."

I turned back to the drywall and started pulling on the gloves. "We are not officially dating yet. Not until I turn eighteen."

Freya put her gloved hand on my arm. "I won't say anything about him being here. You can trust me. I know it would get both of you in a lot of trouble. I remember when the Police Chief called my dad about Detective Graham and his teenage witness."

I winced.

Freya removed her hand from my arm and helped me hoist the drywall piece into place. "Well, I will tell you this. He *is* steamy," she said through gritted teeth while we tried to position the heavy board correctly.

"Who's steamy?" Kyle suddenly appeared and steadied the drywall so I could drill the screws in.

"We were both agreeing that you are steamy, Kyle," I purred as I glanced up at him. Freya turned three shades of pink.

For a second, Kyle's face registered shock, and his eyes locked with mine, but he recovered quickly. He cleared his throat. "Thank you for the compliment, ladies. Especially you, Great Sarcastic One."

I continued working with Freya for the rest of the day. Freya filled me in on all of the happenings at the school that I missed in the last month wrapped up in demons and murder. By the time we'd finished hanging the drywall, I had decided that I liked Freya. According to her, she used to have a bubbly personality, but all that changed when something happened to her best friend, Ava.

"I'm only telling you this because I know how people can judge someone when they don't know anything about what that person has gone through," Freya said as she packed up the scattered nails on the floor.

"Yeah. Before my dad died, I was more like Molly. Then I found it easier to hide behind everyone else. When I met Alec, something lit inside of me. It was like someone lit a match, and I'm always blazing with this fire that seems to grow every day. It's not *just* because of him. I've learned more about my dad and more about what he believed in."

Freya stood. "Like what?"

"Well, he was a Christian, but he never talked about it. I'm not sure why, but I know my mother's parents didn't believe in what they considered ridiculous notions. Maybe he didn't want to offend them."

"Are you a Christian?"

"I believe in God. I've seen things. So, I guess I am."

"You've accepted Jesus Christ?"

We were standing at the top of the stairs, and I turned to look at Freya. She'd hoisted her thick blonde hair into a bun with a large pink headband. "Are *you* a Christian?"

"Yeah, I am. I got saved when I was fifteen, baptized when I was sixteen. My best friend and her sister are Christians too."

I studied Freya's eyes for a second. To know someone my age who was a Christian, or rather who admitted it out loud to others, was rare. At least in my life, in my circle.

"You're the first person my age I've met who professes that out loud," I said. "Most people keep it to themselves, saying it's personal. Maybe I need a new circle of friends." A little nervous laugh slipped out of me.

"Or, maybe you need to influence your circle of friends." Freya smiled a wide grin at me. "Come on. It's time to leave, and I am starving."

~ ~ ~

As soon as I reached the hotel, I showered and put on fresh jeans, an eggplant purple lightweight crop sweater, and a pair of socks. I would have thrown on my pajamas; however, we still had to appear downstairs for dinner. I reapplied my makeup and started to braid my slightly wet hair as I sat on the side of the bed.

I was thinking about the events of the day when a soft knock sounded on the adjoining door I'd left unlocked this morning in case Stephen or Alec needed me for some reason.

"Come in!"

Alec appeared in a pair of cargo pants and a black thermal Henley, and his hair pushed up the way I'd seen him do when things got stressful.

"Find out anything?" I asked.

He smiled as he sat down on the bed, scanning me up and down with his eyes. "That I miss you. That I hate leaving you with Drekr even for a minute. That not only do you own socks with avocados, but you also own more socks featuring fruit." He tilted my chin up and kissed me again, but instead of the quick kiss in Kyle's car, Alec kissed me slowly, drawing out the moment until I dropped my comb on the floor.

Alec pulled away only slightly from the kiss and grinned. "You dropped your comb."

"Something must have distracted me from the urgent business of me braiding my hair."

"Something good?"

"I think so."

Alec took a deep breath, the expression in his eyes growing hot, and then he suddenly stood and moved to the wall that separated the bedroom portion from the living room suite.

"What's wrong?"

He shook his head as he pushed his hands into his pockets. "Nothing's wrong. I just have to keep myself in control with you at all times. Hands off. Sometimes it's a bit hard to do."

"Does this have something to do with what Kyle said today?"

"Drekr and Stephen have their opinions." He lowered his head and stared up at me through his lashes. "I do admit it is true that I don't want people to think I have nefarious plans for you."

My lips turned up into a devilish grin. "Well, your stare is pretty nefarious. Are you sure you don't want to make good on those plans?"

I watched as Alec's tongue popped into the side of his cheek like he was considering the proposition. Then he stood a little straighter and crossed his arms as he leaned against the wall.

"You make it very hard to be good. Instead of me sitting on your bed, why don't you come sit on the couch with me, and I'll tell you what I found out?"

Maybe it was because of the rare occurrence of fun I'd had with Freya today – where I'd momentarily forgotten about everything – or because Alec was looking extra handsome, but a boldness grew inside of me. I locked my gaze with Alec's as I stood and tried my best to walk over to him in the most enticing manner. For a moment, Alec watched me with amusement until I reached up and touched the back of his neck and pulled him closer to me.

"Seduction won't work, Ainsley. I'm immune."

"I'm not trying to seduce you, Detective. I just want a kiss," I whispered before I touched my lips to his.

Alec gave a sound that resembled both a groan and a sigh. I breathed him in as he slowly turned, backing me into the wall. I ran my hand across his broad shoulder, feeling the warm muscle through the thermal material and up to his stubbled jaw. My other hand found its way under his shirt and to the cut muscles of his abs.

It was another minute before I realized Alec wasn't touching me. I opened my eyes as Alec trailed a kiss down my neck. His hands were on either side of me, palms flat against the wall.

When he saw me notice, he grinned. "I told you. I don't think I should touch you."

"Even if I want you to?"

"Even if you want me to." He rested his forehead on my collar bone before straightening but never took his hands off the wall. "Ainsley, this is where there is a fine line. Dating is one thing. Lusting is a whole other ballgame. I absolutely cannot cross that line with you. It would be too difficult to stop."

"You could keep your hands on the wall," I suggested with a grin. "Think of it as a challenge."

Alec raised his brows at me, then shook his head. "You drive me crazy. Plus, I am pretty sure that if you were to ask Stephen, lusting is a sin. *This* would definitely be a sin." He pushed himself away from the wall, then grabbed a bottle of water from the refrigerator before moving to the sofa in the suite's living area.

Reluctantly, I followed him to the couch and dropped onto the plush cushion. I didn't have to ask Stephen. I already knew. No wonder people used to marry young; it was better to marry than to burn.

"Okay, Mister-Wait-Until-Ainsley-Is-Thirty, what did you find out?"

Alec smirked at my only slightly joking comment as he pulled his cell from his pocket. "Well, as we know, Grandfather was no help. He shut me down at the mere mention of his grandfather doing something so heinous as murdering Mrs. Ashbury with a fireplace poker."

"Murdering Mrs. Ashbury with a fireplace poker in the upstairs sitting room. Good grief, it's like *Clue*."

"However, I did find a news article from the local paper after she died."

"Her obituary?"

"Better. Read this." He handed over his phone, and I zoomed in on the image of an old article, but before I read it, I asked, "Did you know Freya is a Christian?"

"Freya who?"

"Freya Montgomery, the Mayor of Locklyn's daughter."

"I know the Mayor goes to church."

"Well, Freya is on this trip too. We hit it off today. I think she's pretty cool."

"I don't know the family, but I'm glad you're making new friends. Especially Christian ones." He tapped the phone in my hand to bring my attention back to the article. I ignored it.

"Are you a Christian?" I asked him.

His eyes flitted from the phone in my hand to my face. "I…I'm not sure what I am. Stephen and I have been talking about some stuff."

"Like what?"

"Stuff from my past." He shrugged. "It's hard to reconcile the things I've done with a God who says He forgives everyone who believes in Jesus with everything they've done."

When I didn't comment, he ran his finger lightly over my wrist. "I've served in the military. I've served overseas in a war. I defended our country, and I defend your town. I've killed people, Ainsley." His blunt words were spoken with only the softest of tones; harsh words barely breathed.

"What did Stephen say about that?"

I watched his chest rise as he took a deep breath and slowly let it out. "That I only kill when necessary to save people." His eyes darted back to me. "I don't want to talk about this with you right now." He tapped the phone in my hand again.

This time I zoomed in on the image of an old newspaper and tried to silence the million questions flying through my head. But it wasn't the headline *Mire Marsh Loses Town Matriarch* that caught my attention. It was the smaller headline that read *Missing Local Girls, Total Now Four, Police Zero.*

I scanned the article above about how Mrs. Ashbury and her late husband, and the prestigious Graham family, founded Mire Marsh and brought innovation to the small community. The town would miss her dearly as she had succumbed to tuberculosis only days before the clinic opened in her home. I let out a snort. "Tuberculosis. No one questioned why she had a gaping hole in her chest?"

"My guess is that Eugene Graham performed the autopsy."

"Your family founded the town?"

"Yeah," he answered quietly.

When he didn't explain, I continued, "Did you see this article about the four missing girls at that time? They were local girls."

Alec took the phone away and zoomed in, reading the article. "All four were from Mire Marsh, ages ranging from 16 to 20."

"Just like the girls Tilda mentioned. Do you think they are connected? I mean, you're from around here, right? Please tell me this isn't a common occurrence in this town."

"Of course not," he said, a frown forming between his brows as he stared at the thumbnail-size portraits in the write-up. "But if demons were roaming around the estate then, maybe they were influencing someone to take the girls. Look at this one." He scooted closer to me on the couch, and the sudden warmth of his leg against mine made my mouth go dry. "This girl's last name was Tarsey. I'm pretty sure that was Tilda's maiden name. This girl may have been a relation to her. I'll call Tilda in the morning."

I smiled at him. "Look at us solving crimes together. We should have our own reality series."

Alec grinned. "Oh, yeah," he said, tossing his phone onto the armchair and leaning over me on the couch. "And what will we call it?" His breath felt hot against my face.

"I don't know," I whispered. "The Senior and the Detective?"

His gaze dropped from my eyes to my lips. "You're terrible at titles."

"The Senior and the Drop-Dead Gorgeous Detective?"

"Try again."

"The Seer and the Skeptic?"

Alec grinned again, then leaned down for a kiss.

There was a knock on the door from the hotel corridor, breaking the spell. Alec sat back on the couch as far away from me as possible.

I sighed as I got up to answer. I opened the door to see Kyle leaning over the doorway. "Of course," I mumbled.

"Hey, you got a sec? I knocked on Stephen's door, but he's not there. Is he in here?" He peered down the hall, looking out for a random student, not where they should be.

I held the door open and saw the grimace cross Kyle's face when he saw Alec leaning against the couch. "I take it Stephen is not here. What are you doing in here without proper adult supervision?"

Alec narrowed his eyes. "Guess I should ask you the same thing."

"I found some stuff on the video footage. Some of it is actual spirit manifestations, ghosts, like Mattie," he said, turning to me. "I saw the entity on the stairs who mimicked your father."

"Really? Was it clear?"

"Yes. Reynolds, it wasn't your father. It moved… wrong." Kyle picked up the phone on the armchair and tossed it to Alec before sitting down.

Alec leaned forward. "What do you mean it moved wrong?"

"Ghosts move differently. They're caught between the realms, part spirit, part flesh. This thing moved like a projector image."

"Jerky," I said.

"Exactly."

"That's the way the girl moved too. Did you see her?"

Kyle's eyes darted from me to Alec. "I heard and saw everything from that room."

"Meaning what?" Alec asked.

Something passed between the two men that I couldn't quite decipher. It was like a silent testosterone competition.

"So, you saw the way she moved when she emerged from the brick wall?" I asked.

"I saw her. She was a demon."

"Can a demon mimicking a ghost kill us?" Alec asked.

"Well, you heard how the two paranormal investigators died. I don't think they can physically kill you, but they can trick your mind. Delusions, hallucinations, what you think are your thoughts. If they go another step further, then they can influence a human to do things."

"So far, that hasn't happened, right?" I sat down beside Alec, and without thinking, I grabbed Alec's bottle of water from between his legs, unscrewed the cap, and took a drink.

When Kyle noticed, Alec quietly removed his bottle from my hands.

"What?" Surely, I hadn't broken some rule now.

Kyle rubbed his right eyebrow as if he was summoning a great deal of patience from the other realm.

"There you guys are," Stephen announced as he came through the adjoining door with Maren close behind. "I stopped by Kyle's room." He turned to Maren. "That Waverly girl is hanging out in front of his room again."

Maren groaned. "I should have packed a leash for her. Sorry, Kyle. I'll see if I can get her under control."

Kyle leaned back in the armchair, eyeing Alec. "Don't worry, Maren. You won't catch me dead alone in a hotel room with a high school girl."

Alec's jaw clenched, but he remained silent. Instead, he motioned for Maren to take his seat on the couch, but she refused.

Stephen went to the fridge and retrieved a bottle of water, offering one to Maren before settling on the arm of the couch. "Okay, I talked to some people at Malus Navis over the archives. There are hierarchies of demons, but I don't know if that is what we are dealing with here."

"Why?" Kyle tapped his thumb on the armchair.

"The higher level demons possess people, not just influence them. The ones at the very top are more concerned with global issues…"

"Not Ashbury and its few deaths," Kyle finished for him.

"Right. That isn't to say a ghost can't possess an unbeliever. They can do that for a short amount of time if they are strong enough."

Kyle shook his head. "I've seen Mattie clearly from Day One, and she has never tried to possess a visitor. The energy in Ashbury isn't like the other sites. It's as if we are dealing with several different things."

Maren moved away from the wall. "What do you mean?"

"Reynolds said the energy at Ashbury is different from the energy she felt with the demons in Charlotte and Locklyn. We saw one in its original form in the portal, but one mimicked the girl and Gerald on the videos. I don't believe they are the same type of demon."

"Can you banish them the same way?" Maren asked.

"She can expel them regardless of the type, I guess."

"You're not sure, are you?" I asked Kyle.

He shrugged. "Every case is different. No one is an expert in this sort of thing."

"Gerry was," Maren said softly.

The five of us were quiet for a few minutes. I chewed on my bottom lip. Maren was right. It seemed like my father was the man who swooped in to save the day, whether he was in Afghanistan, Israel, or North Carolina. How could I live up to that without him here?

"Well, what Gerald wouldn't want is for us sittin' around remembering him instead of out expelling these creatures back to Hell," Stephen said, standing up to stretch. "I say we eat and then get a good night's sleep and regroup after breakfast."

"Agreed," Maren chimed in and headed for the adjoining door with Stephen. "I'm exhausted after today."

I observed Kyle frown as he studied Alec, who hadn't made a move off the couch yet. Alec was texting someone on his phone.

"You coming, Kyle?" Maren asked from the door.

"I'll walk down with Reynolds."

She shrugged. "Suit yourself. See you in a bit."

With that, Alec looked up at Kyle. "Is there a problem?"

Kyle leaned his body forward. "You can't be seen with her downstairs. It will cause too many questions, too many rumors."

"You know what?" I asked, finding my voice. "I think I'm just going to order a pizza and have it delivered to my room. Why don't the two of you go down for dinner?"

"Are you sure?" Alec asked, surprised, probably by the tone of my voice.

"More than sure. I've had a long day too. I'm just going to throw on my pajamas, eat a slice of pizza, and go to bed."

Kyle stood. "Not a bad idea. I think I'll order room service and call it a night." But he stood there, clearly not leaving until Alec did.

Alec gave a half-grin at Kyle's ridiculous behavior and then, standing, gave me a quick kiss on the cheek. "Is there anything I can get you from the dining room?"

"No, I'm good. Thank you."

After the two men left, I blew out the breath I didn't realize I'd been holding in. This was stupid. What gave Kyle the right to act as my guardian? Even Stephen and Maren trusted us enough to leave us alone in the room. The more I thought about the injustice of it all, the angrier I grew. Alec was not going to cross a line with me. He'd already vowed against it, and there was no changing his mind, so Kyle acting as if Alec was going to toss me down on the floor and make all my fantasies come true was unfounded.

Fuming, I grabbed my key card, slid it into my back pocket, and stormed out of my room wearing my black socks with their images of tiny grapes.

CHAPTER THIRTEEN

I rapped on Kyle's hotel room door and hoped he would open it quickly before someone saw me. Thankfully, he did.

"What's wrong?" he asked as he looked up and down the hall.

"Nothing, I need to talk to you," I answered.

"You can't come in, Reynolds. Unlike your boyfriend, I care about my reputation," he said with a know-it-all smirk.

"You were just in my room."

"With other people present."

"I want to know what your problem with Alec is," I said, raising my voice. "If you don't let me in, I'll just keep getting louder."

Kyle groaned and pulled me inside by my sweater. "If you get me into trouble…" he growled.

As Kyle shut the door, I looked around his room. It was smaller than mine with a queen-size bed, a dresser with a flat-screen television, and a desk. He didn't have a mini-fridge or a microwave. I did notice the small coffeemaker on the desk. No wonder he griped about my room.

"So," I continued as I turned to face Kyle, who'd sat down on the edge of the bed. "I don't care if you are belligerent to me, but there is no reason for you to be that way toward Alec. He's here to help."

"I'm not belligerent to your Alec."

"What do you call it then?"

"Hostile?" he answered as he blinked up innocently at me.

"Why? Why are you so hostile toward him?"

Kyle stood and walked past me toward the large window with his hands behind his head. He sighed loudly before turning to face me. "Alec is not who you think he is."

I frowned, but Kyle held up his hand.

"He's just a guy who happened to be in the right place at the right time. He's not your Protector."

"Father Mahon said he is my Protector. He called us the Seer and the Protector." I remembered the conversation with the white-haired priest vividly as he asked me to continue my father's work within the organization, Malus Navis.

"Father Mahon is wrong," Kyle said quietly.

"What makes you say this? Where are you getting your information?"

Kyle rubbed the back of his neck as he searched for the words. "He doesn't possess any supernatural abilities. A Protector has a little of both of the Seer and Protector gifts. He can't protect you from the demons."

"You can't make that judgment. You just met Alec." I took a step back, getting angrier by the second. "You know what I think?"

Kyle narrowed his eyes at me before crossing the room and sitting down at the head of his bed. He swung his legs over and stretched out, crossing his arms over his chest as if settling down to watch a movie. "Go ahead. I'm sure you'll fill me in on how chivalric Detective Graham behaves and what a pig I am," he said sarcastically.

I took a deep breath as I stood at the end of his bed with my hands on my hips. "I think you're jealous."

Kyle raised his eyebrows but remained silent.

"I think you wanted to be a full-fledged Seer, but you don't have the entire gift. You can do some things like you did back at Ashbury, but you aren't THE Seer. I think you feel insecure about your position within the organization, so you're taking it out on Alec. I mean, why should he play the role you clearly can't?"

Kyle was staring at me, but his face didn't register the emotion I was sure my words would bring forth. I wanted to cut him down to size.

Kyle's face was expressionless. "Well," he finally said. "Then I guess your father was wrong."

I blinked. "What?"

Kyle got up off the bed and came to stand in front of me. He leveled his gaze to meet mine, standing less than a foot away. "On my last investigation, it was Gerald's spirit that came through. He shouldn't have been there, which means he sought me out."

"A visitation?" I leaned away from Kyle, searching his face for the hint of a lie. He had to be lying. Why would Dad visit Kyle?

Sensing my doubt, Kyle continued as he walked over to the little coffeemaker and began making a pot of coffee. "We were investigating an abandoned asylum of all places. I was sitting in the middle of a room on the floor, asking my usual questions with the recorder, making sure to stop at the right places to make things easier during editing." His eyes darted over to me at this confession.

"I asked if I was alone, and a voice audibly said, 'No, Kyle, I'm here with you.' It was Gerald's voice; that rough and gaspy sound like he drank whiskey or something. The way he always sounded like Indiana Jones. I'd know it anywhere."

I swallowed. I remembered Dad's voice very well. I'd just heard it in an extremely vivid dream.

"Where is it?"

"Where's what?" Kyle asked, looking confused.

"Did your equipment capture the voice? Or did you edit that in later?"

Kyle studied me for a moment. "It's on my computer, and, no, there hasn't been any tampering with it."

"So show me," I demanded.

Kyle moved his laptop closer to him on the desk and opened it. It powered on right away. As he typed in his password and found the audio, I took a small styrofoam cup from his dresser and poured myself a cup of coffee, leaving just enough in the tiny carafe for Kyle a cup. By the time I'd added the little pod of creamer, the screen was ready. But it wasn't just audio. The recording was a video of Kyle in the room at the sanitarium.

Kyle stood and motioned for me to sit in his desk chair while he got himself the last of the coffee. He hit the play button.

"Testing. I'm in Room 16 and sitting on the floor to see if I can pick up the restless voices of the undead as they reach out to me to share their secrets," video-Kyle said solemnly into the camera.

"Nice touch," I said.

"Would you just watch?"

I turned my attention back to the video. "To the ghosts in this place, now is the time for you to speak. Let me hear you. Show the world that you exist, so we don't forget you."

The room remained quiet. This prodding from Kyle continued for several minutes with no sounds coming from the sanitarium. "Is anyone here that would like to speak, or am I alone?" video-Kyle asked.

"No, Kyle. I'm here with you."

I pushed away from the computer and knocked into Kyle standing behind me, dumping his hot coffee onto his shirt. He howled as he pulled at the fabric against his skin.

"Was that him? Or a demon?" I asked breathlessly.

Kyle pulled his shirt off, exposing broad muscles and quickening-reddening skin from the coffee. "I told you. Keep listening," he growled as he went to the closet in search of another shirt.

I wheeled the chair back to the desk and had to reverse the video in case I'd missed something.

"No, Kyle. I'm here with you," Dad's disembodied voice said again. It couldn't have been any clearer if he'd had a microphone.

Shock registered on video-Kyle's face. "Gerald?" he asked in a whisper.

"Hey, Kyle-the-Kid," the voice answered. "I only have a moment. I need your help in that realm."

"What can I do?" video-Kyle asked, now up on his knees. I'd never seen the real Kyle this vulnerable.

"My daughter is a Seer. She needs your protection. Keep her away from Ja-." The rest was garbled.

"Keep her away from what?"

When the voice didn't answer, Kyle repeated the question. "Keep her away from what, Gerald?"

Several minutes passed, and I waited with bated breath. Finally, video-Kyle looked directly into the camera. "This is for my video techs: This segment is not to be altered in any way or deleted. Nor is it to be shared. This was a personal message from Gerald Reynolds to me." The video stopped.

I looked at Kyle, who stood at the closet door with a clean shirt in his hands. He was staring at the computer screen but slowly moved his gaze to me. "I don't know what Gerald wanted me to keep you away from but as I said Alec Graham is not your Protector."

I stood. I desperately needed air. "I need to go," I said as I pushed past the shirtless Kyle to the room door. He didn't try to stop me as I swung the heavy door open and stepped right into Alec's chest.

Alec caught me as I jumped back, startled that he was standing at Kyle's door. Apparently, he had started to knock when I opened the door. Alec's eyes scanned past me, and I turned to see Kyle pulling his shirt on over his head. Alec's eyes landed on me again.

"I came to talk to Kyle about Ashbur-," I said, but the look in Alec's eyes made the last word freeze to the roof of my mouth. It was as if I'd knocked the air out of him.

Kyle pulled the door open a little wider. "Is there something you need from me too?" he asked Alec in a tone that I could've sworn sounded like a challenge.

I glanced down at Alec's hand as it clenched into a fist. "Alec, why don't we go back to my room and talk about this?" I whispered.

When he turned his glare on me, I felt it all the way to my soul. "I don't think so," he answered as his jaw clenched. He turned away but had only taken two steps when Kyle spoke.

"Look, man, it's not what you think. I'm no competition when it comes to the girl. I'm not interested in high school girls. I'm not you."

Alec spun around and pushed past me and into Kyle's chest, knocking the much larger man back into the room. The door slammed behind them before I had a chance to run in. I tried the metal doorknob, but the heavy door was programmed to lock automatically. I could hear things crashing from behind the door.

"What on Earth?" I heard Maren's voice as she came out of her room, clearly alarmed. If Maren could hear the commotion, it wouldn't be long until the other students came out of their rooms or off the elevator from the dining room.

"It's Kyle and Alec," I whispered to her.

"Get to your room. Now!" she seethed. She was seconds away from screaming at me.

I ran around the corner to my room, swiped my card, and dove inside. Before the door shut, I could still hear the sound of crashing and Maren's voice rising as she ordered the men to open the door.

I leaned against the closed door, tears streaming down my face. I'd inadvertently hurt Alec when all I had wanted to do was clear the air between the two men.

~ ~ ~

"What on Earth happened, Ainsley?" Maren towered above me as I sat on the couch in my suite. The Psychology teacher was furious and perplexed; her red hair seemed even redder somehow.

"I don't know," I sniffed. "I went to Kyle's room to tell him to ease off Alec, and then he showed me a video of my father's voice communicating with him on location somewhere."

Maren placed her hands on her hips. I glanced over at the armchair where Stephen sat, but he only watched me quietly.

"Why did a fight break out?" Maren demanded.

I sighed. "I knocked hot coffee on Kyle, then I opened the door while Kyle was putting on a clean shirt, and Alec saw him. I guess he thought the worst."

"Well, you guessed right. It took forever to get both men calmed down once the manager opened the door. I'm surprised the man didn't kick us all out. He threatened to, that's for sure." She paced back and forth between the coffee table and the kitchenette.

Stephen raised a finger off the armchair to make a point. "Except that Alec explained he would pay for all the damages. He told the manager that he was Alec Graham, Edward Graham's grandson." Stephen studied me carefully before adding, "When the manager heard the name, *he* apologized to Alec for the interruption and *left* the room."

I wasn't sure what to say. I hadn't told Stephen or Maren the details about our meeting with Alec's grandfather, but clearly, the man's name held power in the town.

Stephen leaned forward where he could meet my gaze easily. "Kyle and Alec are great guys, Ainsley, but they're both grown men; real men who don't play games. You can't go in and out of their lives without problems." He reached over and took my hand. "I know you care about

Alec, and I think on some level, he cares deeply for you. But sometimes the best thing you can do for someone is to disconnect yourself from them. At least for a while."

"What are you saying?"

"I talked with Alec after the fight. He's going to stay elsewhere for the remainder of this investigation at Ashbury. He's going to distance himself from you."

I pulled my hand away. "What? That's not fair, Stephen. I didn't do anything wrong. Ask Kyle. He'll tell you."

Maren sat down on the edge of the coffee table facing me, the knees of her skinny jeans barely grazing mine. "Honey, we've all talked about your relationship since Alec agreed to come on this trip with you. Now, we learn that his grandfather's name *alone* strikes fear in the residents of this town. This Edward Graham is not a man to be trifled with, and there is a good chance that Detective Graham is the same way."

"Alec is nothing like him. Who told you that about his grandfather?"

"Alec told us after he'd had time to calm down," Stephen answered. "He and Kyle are both bruised up." Stephen smiled then. "Good news, both of 'em are tough enough to come out of it walking away - and with all their teeth."

"So," Maren began as she reached for my clenched fist, "You will still follow through on the investigation at Ashbury, you will work with Kyle to expel the cluster of demons, and you will only associate with Alec when it is necessary while on the remainder of this trip."

When I narrowed my eyes at her, she added, "Alec made those rules, not me. He said he's done, Ainsley."

"What's does that even mean?"

Stephen sighed. "It means that after we get back to Locklyn, he will move on with his life, and you'll go on with yours."

~ ~ ~

A soft knock on wood made me sit up in bed. Was that on my door or another room's door? The soft knock repeated, confirming that someone was indeed in the hallway in front of my room.

I pushed myself off the bed, not caring to look in the mirror at my appearance. Did it matter if I looked like crap at this point? Alec had nothing more to say to me as he'd made abundantly clear to Stephen and Maren. I wasn't proud of it, but I needed some time to come to terms with that before I could pull myself together again.

I peeped through the hole in the door to see Tilda standing there. I slowly opened the heavy door, not hiding my surprise.

"Well, hello dear," the woman said as she looked over my shoulder into my suite. "Is Alec here?"

"No, he's not. This isn't his room. It's the next one over," I said, pointing to his room door. "But I don't think he's in at the moment. Actually, I think he is moving to a different hotel." *Because I may have destroyed any hope of there being an us.* I swallowed and hoped Tilda couldn't read my mind.

"That's alright, Ainsley. I actually would like to speak with you." She waited patiently for my answer.

"Of course." I opened the door a little wider for her to enter. Tilda was dressed in wool dress pants tailored for her elegant figure with an emerald green blouse and a black pea coat. She unbuttoned her coat and draped it casually over the chair.

"Can I get you something to drink? I have bottles of water, or I could make you a hot cup of tea or coffee?"

Tilda patted the cushion beside her on the sofa. "No, dear, I'm fine. Please come sit so we can talk."

I did as I was told and lowered myself as gracefully as I could on the sofa beside the woman. I quickly wiped my face with my sweater's sleeve and hoped I didn't have smeared eye makeup everywhere.

"Ainsley, is it true what Edward thinks? That you're gonna have Alec's baby, and that is why he brought you home with him?"

I almost laughed at the irony. "No, Tilda. That is *not* true. Alec and I aren't even an official couple," I sighed before I added, "we might never be at this point."

Tilda studied my face. "He's a good boy. He just has a lot of his father and grandfather in him. Let's his anger get the best of him."

"May I ask how you are related to Alec?"

"We're not. I was childhood friends with Ed and his brother, Teddy. We did everything together. After Teddy passed, Ed became self-absorbed, and we grew apart for a while. I married someone, and then Ed married Ethel. My husband died in Vietnam, and I didn't have any children. When Ethel passed away, she left behind little William. I knew Edward wasn't the type to spend time with the boy to raise him. So, I came by as much as I could to help."

Tilda ran her thin hand through her white bob. "Later, William brought home a beautiful brunette with a child in her belly, and I found myself jumpin' at the chance to be a mother. I had no idea that Edward would drive the couple away and apart, but he has that way about him."

"Yet, you stay?" I asked, frowning.

"Ed's not hateful to me. He's the sweetest and gentlest man I know. He only behaves that way when it comes to Alec. Well, and his businesses."

"How did you know where we were staying? Did Alec tell you?"

"No, Edward has his sources," she waved her hand dismissively. This was a gesture I needed to add to my life.

"May I ask you another question? A question about Alec?"

"Of course, sweetie," Tilda smiled the most grandmotherly smile I'd ever seen.

"Do you know what happened in Wilmington? The reason why Alec decided to move to Locklyn?"

"He hasn't told you?"

I shook my head. "I need to know."

"Well, in that case, I will take a cup of strong coffee." She smiled again.

I hurriedly made Tilda a cup of the hotel coffee, and I could've used a mug myself, but decided I didn't want to take the precious time to make it. It seemed Tilda wasn't going to spill until she had her cup, and I was seated beside her again.

"Alec was always a heartbreaker. Girls fell for him just about everywhere he would go, but it was in the Corps that he fell in love with a woman."

"The Marine Corps?"

"Yes. Her name was Annika. Pretty woman with dark hair and eyes, very exotic lookin', and they were together for probably about four years, give or take. Annika got out of the Marines two years before Alec's contract was up, but they moved in together."

Tilda sighed as she took a sip of her coffee. "Alec was comin' back from his second tour when he ran into a good buddy of his that lived on the same base as he and Annika. His friend told him that Annika was cheatin' on him with an officer that both men knew. So, Alec arrived back on base without tellin' anyone and went straight home."

My eyes had to be the size of saucers as I waited for Tilda to take another sip of her coffee.

"Sure enough, he found his girlfriend with another man in his own bed."

"Oh, no!" I remembered the look Alec had given me when he'd seen me hurrying out of Kyle's room like I'd knocked the air out of him. "What happened?"

"Alec broke the man's jaw. The officer knew he was in the wrong, you know from sleepin' with Annika and all, so he didn't press charges. Alec did have to pay $25,000 for the man's surgery and things."

"Oh. I bet Edward was angry. That is a huge amount of money to pay for losing your temper."

"Well, the Graham family has temper and money. Alec is a trust-fund baby that refuses to spend anything. That's one thing his grandfather has taught him is how to invest and remain wealthy. He'd rather work as a policeman and live on his income than cash in. But, he paid the man's medical bills and moved on."

"What about Annika?"

"Oh, Honey, it was over the minute he saw her with that other man. Alec Graham will never play second fiddle to anyone."

I swallowed the growing lump in my throat. I couldn't get Alec to listen to me. He didn't play second to any man in my life. But as of right now, he thought I was just another Annika.

Tilda patted my hand. "Sweetie, why don't you walk me down to the lobby? I need to get back to Ed and whip up somethin' for supper."

Reluctantly, I grabbed the suite keycard and checked my face in the mirror above the dresser. I wasn't in the mood to see anyone outside of my room, but it seemed rude to say no to Tilda. I slid on my shoes as Tilda elegantly draped her coat around her shoulders. I had a feeling she could make a tarp look classy.

We didn't say much on the ride down in the elevator. My mind swirled around me. How could I get Alec to listen to me? As the doors opened to the Ground Floor, the building swayed. Or rather, the veil separating the real Ground Floor from the supernatural realm swayed. I grabbed the elevator opening to keep the doors from closing again while I gained my bearings. I always felt like I might tip forward and pass out on the floor when this happened.

Why was this happening now?

Tilda wrapped her small hand around my elbow. "Oh my, Ainsley! Are you all right?" Then she eyed me suspiciously. "Are you *sure* you're not pregnant?"

Good grief.

I stepped out of the elevator, and the room expanded and collapsed with a sudden thrust that if I hadn't pressed my weight against the marble wall, I would have fallen from the sheer force. I tried to focus. Where was it coming from?

"Ainsley, answer me, Sweetie. Could you be pregnant?" Tilda's voice sounded distant.

As I muttered a 'no' in response, I scanned the lobby. Waverly, Ethan, and Freya stood near a vending machine, gawking at me. Of course, my classmates would overhear such an insistent question. But what alarmed me wasn't the smirk on Waverly's face or the shock on Freya's. It was a Muladach moving menacingly behind Freya. What was it doing?

The creature stood on its hind legs, sniffed at Freya's hair, and then gave a hollow-sounding bark. Freya's hair moved slightly, and she turned to look behind her, but obviously, she couldn't see the demon.

I started towards her when two more Muladach came from the right and flanked the three humans, watching Freya. I froze. Why were they so interested in her? Why not someone evil like Waverly? The demon closest raised its head to stare at me, its eyes reflecting the light from the chandelier above my head.

I opened my mouth to banish them when they suddenly took off through the open front door of the hotel as two bellhops wheeled in a luggage cart.

"Sweetie?" Tilda asked again.

I turned away from my classmates. "I'm okay, Tilda. Really. I just get a little dizzy sometimes." I heard Waverly snicker at my answer.

Tilda studied my face, unconvinced, but then someone caught her eye over my shoulder. She moved quickly to my side and raised her hand in a wave. "Harold Meadors! Don't you pretend you don't see me!"

A man with a full head of white hair stopped mid-step and turned. I didn't think Tilda noticed the grimace on his face. My guess was the man was in his fifties. "Tilda, of course not." He joined us under the chandelier that was beginning to sway suspiciously above my head. I glanced over my shoulder, but Waverly, Ethan, and Freya had left the lobby. I was sure that Waverly would probably inform the rest of the students of Tilda's question/accusation by bedtime.

"Harold, I want to introduce you to a friend of the Grahams. This is Ainsley."

Tilda sweetly laid my braid over the front of my shoulder, presenting me as a gift. It reminded me of how

Alec had introduced me to another Mr. Meadors at Ashbury. I probably looked like crap at this point.

"Ainsley, this is Harold Meadors. His parents, as well as Edward, own the Ashbury Estate."

Meadors. Of course, why hadn't I put that together? I shook the man's hand. "Mr. Meadors, yes. I met your father."

The man smiled as he looked me up and down, making me feel uneasy. It wasn't a glance like most men or one of observation like Edward Graham's look. This was flat-out leering. "Well, in that case, call me Harold. I don't want you to mistake me for my father."

A chill crept up my spine. I glanced up at the chandelier that swung with a little more energy. The Muladach might be gone, but there was some type of energy charge moving the thing.

Harold noticed me eyeing the lamp. "I'm not sure what is going on with that." He looked back at me, wide-eyed. "Perhaps this hotel is as haunted as the Ashbury. So, you must be a friend of Alec's."

I nodded, although it felt like a big, fat lie.

Harold frowned. "I thought Alec was older, like mid-twenties." He glanced at Tilda, who placed her arm around my shoulders protectively.

"Oh, Harold! You can barely keep track of your own age, let alone the age of someone else's boy. Anyway, what are you doing here?"

Harold's eyes widened as he stammered, "I-I was waitin' on a friend."

Tilda's clear blue eyes narrowed. "What kind of friend? Not a young female one, I hope?"

"Maybe I should go back to my room," I interrupted. I didn't want to be in the middle of, well, I wasn't sure what I was in the middle of between creepy Harold and elegant, yet nosy Tilda.

Tilda squeezed my shoulders. "All right, Sweetie. But if you need me, you know where I am." Then she gave me the biggest and warmest hug I'd ever had from someone who wasn't related to me.

By the time the elevator door closed and I was on my way back to my room, the tears were falling hard and fast. And silent.

CHAPTER FOURTEEN

I joined the other students in the hotel's dining room for breakfast the next morning at Maren's insistence. I settled into a chair beside Freya, who didn't try to hide her look of shock.

"Are you okay, Ainsley? You look like you haven't slept much."

"I'm fine," I answered as I took a sip of my coffee. I was wearing my distressed black jeans, a black tank, and a chunky black cardigan with absolutely no makeup. I was tired of crying off all my eyeliner. I'd pulled my hair up into one of my mother's pineapple buns and left it.

"You know what I heard?" Ethan whispered across the table. "That Kyle Drekr got into a fight with some guy yesterday evening."

"Didn't you hear the crashing?" Jamal piped in. "I tried to get in to see what was happening once the manager opened the door, but Ms. Bell ordered us back to our rooms."

Freya watched me before she shrugged. "Probably just a crazy fan who got too close. I'm sure it's nothing."

Everyone got quiet when Kyle showed up and joined us at our long table, sporting his new black eye.

"Hey, Mr. Drekr," Waverly ventured. "What happened?"

"Wave!" Everly elbowed her twin.

Kyle threw the girls a somewhat flirtatious smile. "I disagreed with someone. Don't worry. You should see the other guy, ladies."

The girls giggled as they went back to eating. Kyle shifted his eyes over to me, the fake smile still attached. I dropped my glare to my breakfast plate. Who was I even mad at? I was the one who had gone to Kyle's room. I was the one who put myself in this position, not Kyle.

However, I still wanted to punch that look off his face.

"You know what I heard last night in the lobby?" Waverly asked the table.

"Waverly, don't!" Freya practically yelled from the chair beside me.

"What?" Waverly asked, innocence dotting her perfectly contoured face. "I'm sure you heard it too, Freya." Her eyes rolled over to me. "Such a juicy rumor."

Kyle's eyes darted between Waverly and me. "Waverly," he started in a smooth like hot butter voice that made the girl turn and look at him. "I don't think the breakfast table is any place for rumors. Especially about other classmates."

Waverly considered his words and then sighed. "You're right, Mr. Drekr." She eyed me again. "I guess we can wait nine months and talk about it then."

The entire table erupted into a fit of whispers and low laughter. Kyle leaned back in his chair and threw his napkin on the plate in front of him.

"That's enough," Maren said in an authoritative tone. Everyone got quiet.

"Ainsley? Are you sure you're okay?" Freya asked in a low voice.

I nodded, forcing myself to swallow a bite of bacon.

"Well, if you're interested, a group of us plans to ask Ms. Bell if we can tour a haunted house tomorrow before we head back home."

"What haunted house?"

"The Ashbury Estate," Jamal answered for Freya. "It's supposed to be scary."

My mouth went dry. I glanced at the head of our table where Maren and Kyle sat whispering, but neither of them overheard.

"What makes you think she'll let us go?" I asked.

Ethan leaned in closer to our little group at this end of the table. "Kyle has been there, so we are thinking of having him talk her into it."

Waverly raised a neat brow at me as she toyed with her thumbnail on her bottom teeth like a viper sharpening its fang. "Unless you have Mr. Drekr too busy tomorrow night."

"Shut up, Waverly," Everly sniped. "Give it a rest, will you? Ainsley, if we say Ashbury would be a great experience for us, then Mr. Drekr will relent. He seems pretty cool."

So Jamal, Ethan, Waverly, Everly, and Freya wanted to tour the haunted Ashbury of all places. I bit my lower lip.

"You're not scared of ghosts, are you, Ainsley?" Jamal asked laughter clearly in his voice.

"No," I answered softly. "I'm not scared of ghosts."

It's the other things you can't see that scare me. "When are you planning on going?"

"Tomorrow evening," Freya said.

"What if Ms. Bell isn't convinced?" I asked, wondering when Maren, Stephen, Kyle, and I were supposed to go back again to try to banish the small horde of demons haunting the place.

Ethan lowered his already quiet voice, "Honestly, have you noticed that every evening, we are pretty much on our own? Ms. Bell says to stay in our rooms after dinner, but she never checks on us. I made a trip to the vending machine at 1am the other night and never heard a peep from anyone."

So, they were planning on sneaking out to the Ashbury Estate for an evening tour if Maren didn't permit them to go.

Crap.

I wouldn't have cared except for the two paranormal investigator deaths, Ravi's alleged suicide attempt, and that I'd already seen three Muladach circling Freya like she was a box of Girl Scout Samoa cookies in the Spring.

"If you end up going, I'll go," I heard myself reluctantly saying and wondered if the students would consider me a snitch if I told Maren about the group's plans. Of course, and snitching would do nothing to raise my popularity within the senior class. Not that it mattered to me, but I preferred not to be hated by the student body. But without Kyle serving as my Protector inside Ashbury, how would I keep a group of students safe from the demons? Especially when the Muladach seemed to trick me too?

My phone beeped with a text message. *Please be Alec.*

It was Mom: **Molly is awake and coherent! She's asking about you [a row of smiley faces].**

"Thank God," I whispered before raising my voice. "Ms. Bell? My friend Molly is awake and coherent. Would it be all right if I drive up to see her today? I'll return tomorrow."

Maren slowly nodded her head. "I'm glad to hear about Molly. Let's talk about you leaving after breakfast." She smiled at me, but the smile didn't reach her eyes. Was she not going to allow me to leave? What was worse, I couldn't ask Alec to take me home either.

I text Mom back, and after a moment's hesitation, I made myself send Alec a message.

Me: **Molly is awake and coherent. I'm going to try to return to Locklyn today to see her.**

I waited. Nothing. I was so excited about seeing Molly but also hurt about the situation with Alec. He wasn't even going to return my text.

"I'm glad Molly is better. How long before she can leave the hospital?" Freya asked, taking a bite of her omelet.

"I don't know. Hopefully, I can see her parents today."

I glanced over at Kyle, who was silently eating his breakfast with his head down. Maybe Alec had knocked some humbleness into him.

"So, did you see that old man in the lobby last night?" Freya asked before taking a drink of her orange juice.

"The white-haired man?"

"Yeah. He gave me the creeps."

"How?" Harold Meadors had given me the creeps too, but I couldn't put my finger on why.

"I don't know. It seemed like everywhere I turned downstairs, there he was, watching me."

I made a face. "That is creepy. I met him last night. The woman who came to visit me knew him. He is an odd one."

"Wonder if he is staying here?" she asked with a small frown between her brows.

"I don't think so, Freya. He said he was waiting on a friend."

Freya gave me a small smile, but she still looked unconvinced by the time we'd finished breakfast.

After the students loaded onto the bus to go to the worksite, Maren pulled me aside. "Kyle is going to drive you to Locklyn. You must return by tomorrow evening."

I groaned. "Kyle? Come on, Maren. Do you *want* me to murder him?"

"Kyle's not at fault for this, Ainsley. Alec threw the first punch. If you want to go see Molly today, then you have to go with Kyle."

I knew there was no use arguing with her. I didn't have a car here I could drive. "What about Stephen?" I volunteered, remembering his truck.

Maren put her hands on my shoulders. "Stephen is not going to drive you. Either you go with Kyle now, or you wait until we head home at the end of the week."

"I can't wait that long. I promised Mol I would come to her when she woke."

Maren dropped her arms. "Then it's settled. Kyle?" She raised her voice when she yelled for Kyle, who stood casually leaning against the bus, apparently observing our conversation.

"I need you to drive Ainsley to Locklyn, please."

"Her detective not available?" he asked, a bored expression on his face.

Maren shoved her manicured nail into the chest of Kyle's hoodie. "Don't start with me, Kyle. I'm still aggravated at all three of you. You're taking Ainsley. It'll give you two time to talk." She pushed past Kyle towards the bus.

"Talk about what?" Kyle called after her, but the Psych teacher boarded the bus without looking back.

~ ~ ~

"I'm not happy about this either," I said to Kyle about an hour into our drive after I turned down the radio. Neither one of us had spoken until now. I'd spent the time putting on my makeup to hide the drama of the last few days and simmering about being forced to ride to North Carolina with Kyle.

"It's just another three and a half hours, or so," he said, sounding resigned.

I took a deep breath and then exhaled slowly. "I can't believe I'm going to say this to you of all people, but...I'm sorry."

"For what?"

"I should never have come to your room. I should have talked to you about Alec when other people were around."

Kyle sighed. "If you hadn't come to my room, then I couldn't have shown you the footage from the asylum. It's not your fault. Your boyfriend assumed something when he saw you. Of course, now that I think about it, it didn't help when you spilled coffee on me, and I took my shirt off. I hope you realize Alec Graham is a jealous guy."

"He thinks I repeated a mistake from his past." I looked down at my lap. "Stephen and Maren said that Alec told them that he is done with me after we finish at Ashbury. He's not even staying at the hotel anymore."

Kyle was quiet for a few minutes. "I'm sorry," he finally managed to say.

"I somehow doubt that."

He looked at me as he drove. "No, really I am. I'm sorry you got hurt."

I motioned towards his face. "I'm sorry you got hurt too."

"Oh, this?" Kyle said, smiling as he pointed towards his eye. "I give as much as I get. Graham is sporting a few cuts and bruises too." He paused. "What did Waverly mean about nine months?"

I let out an exasperated sigh. "Nothing. Alec's grandmother - or she is kind of like a grandmother to him - stopped by to see me last night. When I got off the elevator, I felt the demons nearby, and everything vibrated away from me, so I got dizzy. She asked if I could be pregnant. Waverly, Ethan, and Freya overheard her."

Kyle shook his head with disappointment on his face. "That would explain Graham's overly-territorial behavior. Not to be nosy…"

"No! Would everyone stop asking me these questions?! I've never slept with Alec! I've never slept with anyone! I'm not pregnant." By the time I finished yelling in the small rental car, Kyle was utterly silent.

I turned the radio back up for a while to absorb some of the awkwardness. Kyle didn't argue with me about the station. I figured his mind was about as far away as mine. He might have been a little scared of me too.

A couple of hours later, Kyle hesitantly lowered the radio's volume. "Where exactly are we going?"

"We are going to meet my mother at my house and then ride to the hospital. You're more than welcome to stay at the house while we're gone."

"Hmm. Give me a chance to rummage through your drawers, looking for your diary." He smirked as he said it.

"Haha. Joke is on you. I don't keep a diary."

"Everyone keeps a diary."

"I don't. But you know what? There is something you can look for while I'm gone. If you want to, that is."

"Sounds intriguing."

"The other night, I had a dream about my father. I think it was a visitation. He said to look inside the family room fireplace for a loose brick. He said there I would find a key to a safety deposit box at the bank. Well, I'm assuming it's for a box."

"What's in the safety deposit box?"

"A collection of things he had for me. In my dream, he said that he had planned to tell me everything. He thought he had more time." I swallowed hard. I could feel hot tears building behind my eyes, and there was *no way* I would cry in front of Kyle.

"I hope we find it. I'd like to see what Gerald put in there for you."

"Me too. He also said that I needed to remind you of something."

Kyle let out a breath. "What?"

"Of course, this could've just been a dream. I don't know," I said quickly. I was suddenly worried that what I was about to say would upset Kyle. And for a second, it seemed like we were getting along.

"Reynolds, remind me of what?" he asked with a little more force to his voice.

"He said to remind you that you know the three rules, and you're breaking every one of them."

Kyle looked at me with wide-eyed alarm, his blue eyes almost transparent in the sunlight. He turned his head quickly towards the road again.

"Kyle, are you all right?" I asked. His hands gripped the steering wheel so tightly that his knuckles were turning white.

"You had a visitation from Gerald. An actual one. There is no way you could know about the three rules. I never told you about them. I doubt Maren or Stephen know them all," he spoke so softly, I strained to hear him.

"Tell me what they are. Then tell me what the consequences are for breaking them."

"Not now, I will soon. I need to think about what you told me. Tell me about the demons at the hotel last night."

~ ~ ~

I plastered a huge smile on my face as I opened the door to my house with Kyle carrying our overnight bags.

"Mom?"

"Up here, Honey!" Mom's voice greeted me.

We ascended the stairs to the living room where Mom was coming through, wiping her hands on a dishtowel. Since she'd been out visiting Molly, she was wearing a pair of dressy dark-wash jeans and a purple blouse. Her pineapple bun was down, so her blonde hair spilled below her shoulders. "That didn't take you too long. Was the drive uneventful?" she asked me, but her eyes landed on Kyle.

"It was fine. Mom, this is Kyle Drekr, the host of *Paranormal Houses*."

"Of course," Mom said. "I am very familiar with your show, Mr. Drekr." She shook Kyle's hand. "What happened to your eye?"

Kyle smiled what I could've sworn was a genuine smile as he rubbed lightly over his black eye. "Just a raving fan. Thank you, Mrs. Reynolds, but please call me Kyle."

"Well, I'm Stella. So how did they get you to drive Ainsley back to Locklyn?" She motioned for Kyle to take a seat on the couch.

Kyle shed his hoodie to reveal a tight tee-shirt and then handed the hoodie to me. Neither noticed my eye-rolling as I hung both his hoodie and my cardigan up behind the front door.

"I volunteer with the organization Serenity that is building the house in South Carolina, near Parris Island. I needed to make a trip up this way, so I said I could bring her home. We need to head back down tomorrow, though."

"Of course. Where are you staying?"

"I thought I would get a room over at the Locklyn Lodge."

Mom threw her hands in the air. "No, no! You can stay here with us. If you don't mind the couch."

"Are you sure? I don't want to impose on the two of you." He glanced over at me with a smirk.

"Never stopped you before," I mumbled, but neither heard me.

"No imposition. My son will be home in a bit. He's nine. He watches your show too."

The two of them went into an in-depth conversation about Mom's books and Kyle's show. I slipped away to the kitchen. Mrs. Hiroto said we could visit Molly around 5pm. I still had two hours before leaving and decided to eat a container of yogurt and a protein bar. I sat down on a stool against the kitchen counter as Mom and Kyle continued to talk.

"Oh, Honey! Before I forget, Alec called for you."

I poked my head around the wall so I could see Mom. "What? Alec called? The landline? When?"

She laughed. "A little bit ago. Is everything all right between you two? He sounded...off." She turned to Kyle before I could respond. "Alec is the man Ainsley has been sort-of seeing. He's a bit older, so they are waiting to date until she's eighteen."

Kyle looked over at me. "Really?"

"He's a homicide detective," Mom added.

"What a noble profession."

"Kyle," I said, my voice full of warning, then turned to my mother. "Alec and I got into a...tiff...over the phone. I didn't expect him to call here. He didn't call or text my cell phone."

"Oh, I see. Well, I told him about Molly and that we planned to see her this evening. Maybe he will come."

"Why would he want to see your friend Molly?" Kyle asked, leaning forward on the couch.

"Oh, Ainsley didn't tell you? The serial killer, The Artist, attacked Ainsley, Molly, Alec, and a teacher a few weeks ago. He almost killed Molly and Alec."

"How did you get away?" he asked. Kyle knew the story. *What was he up to?*

I shook my head at him. "I confronted the killer and distracted him long enough for Alec to shoot him." That was putting it mildly.

"Hmm," he said as if deep in thought. "I guess that would make you feel grateful to Alec. I mean that he was there and could save you and your friend."

I narrowed my eyes. So we were back to this, were we? That I was only attracted to Alec because I felt grateful for his presence - and his presents. And that Alec was taking advantage of my appreciative nature.

"I'm going to try to call him. I'll be back." I walked straight down the hall to my room and shut the door behind me, leaning against the full-length mirror. I pulled up Alec's name on my phone and pushed the icon.

It rang three times before he answered. "Ainsley? I can't talk right now. I'm in a meeting." His voice did sound strange – strained.

"Oh, okay. Mom told me you called. I'll let you go. I just wanted to know if you are going to the hosp-"

"Graham!" I heard a man's voice boom over the phone, and then the call was promptly disconnected. Alec had hung up on me. My guess was that he was at the station, and that pleasant man was the Police Chief. Wait, he was in Locklyn?

I sat down on my bed. He hadn't moved to a different hotel. He'd left South Carolina altogether and came home. He'd left me there with the others to figure out Ashbury on my own.

I must have sat there for some time because eventually, Mom knocked on my door and announced it was time to see Molly. Kyle stood in the living room under the portrait of my parents watching me as I started to follow Mom to the garage.

"Reynolds?"

"What, Kyle?"

"Can I talk to you for a minute?"

Mom was already heading for the car, so I went to Kyle. I looked up at him and saw that he was studying my face.

"Are you okay? Did you talk to Graham?"

"Yes, and no. He's in Locklyn."

"He's here?" Kyle seemed as shocked as I was.

I nodded. "Yeah, I guess Alec is done with me. He came home. He must have rented a car."

Kyle frowned. "Well, I wanted to ask where is the family room? Do you still want me to look for the loose brick?"

I'd forgotten about the possible loose brick and the key. "Oh, yes! Come on, and I'll show you."

I grabbed my cardigan from the hook by the door, and Kyle followed me downstairs. I pointed to the fireplace. "Text me if you find anything."

I started to pull my cardigan on when Kyle grabbed my forearm. "Reynolds! What is that?"

I looked down to see what was wrong. He was staring at the ring of bruises around my exposed upper arm. When

I looked back up at him, his face was full of shock and…anger.

"Are those handprints? Did Graham do this to you?"

"No. I mean, yes, but-"

"No! But nothing!'" Kyle placed his hands on my shoulders and bent low enough so he could see me on my eye level. "Ainsley Reynolds, I want you to tell me the truth. No one will be mad at you, I promise. I won't be mad at you. You can trust me. Has Alec Graham hurt you in any way? Maybe wanted you to do something you didn't want to do?" He quickly looked me up and down as if he were searching for bruises under my clothes. "Maybe something you weren't ready for?"

I pushed Kyle away from me. "No, Kyle! I've told you, Alec is not like that at all. This was an accident. It happened at Ashbury in the sitting room on the first night of our investigation."

"What did he do?" Kyle asked, clearly not believing my defense for Alec.

I sighed. "It was when the demonic girl showed up. Alec grabbed my arm to pull me out of the room, but I hesitated. I tried to talk to the ghost first. I think Alec was just scared, that's all. He doesn't even know that he squeezed my arm hard enough to leave bruises."

Kyle seemed to consider this plausible explanation.

"I would appreciate it if you didn't mention the bruises to anyone, especially my mother."

Kyle turned his head towards the fireplace and ran his hands through his hair. Finally, he turned back to face me. "Fine. I won't say anything. I do think you should stay away from Graham before you seriously get hurt."

"Alec wouldn't hurt me."

Kyle stared at the bruises on my arm again. "I don't think he would mean to hurt you, but that doesn't mean that he won't hurt you."

CHAPTER FIFTEEN

Mom and I hugged Mr. and Mrs. Hiroto as we entered Molly's room, every surface draped with even more flowers than when I had left. Mom went out into the hall, asking the Hirotos questions.

"Mol!" I ran to her bed, and after some moving of several wires, I was able to hug my best friend.

"You look so pretty," Molly said softly after she leaned against the pillow again, her black hair sprawled out around her.

"Me? You were a literal Sleeping Beauty."

"If only," she said with a soft laugh. "I don't think anyone kissed me to wake me up."

"Are you sure?" came a man's voice, and I turned to see Alec standing in the doorway with a colorful bouquet.

He had a small butterfly bandage across the bridge of his nose and a bruise on his cheekbone.

"Hi," Molly and I said at the same time. Molly slowly punched me in the arm. "Jinx."

"Ainsley messaged me that you were ready for visitors. I just wanted to drop these off. How are you feeling?"

"Better, thank you. And I know I'm late, but thank you both for getting me help. The doctor said that if it had been another two hours, I wouldn't have made it. Alec, I know you got hurt. How are you? Is that cut on your face from that night?"

"No, this is from something else. I'm scarred, but I'll live." He smiled at Molly, totally oblivious to me sitting on the bed.

"Me, too," she said with a slight smile on her face. Molly ran her hand over her ribs where she'd received stitches, then reached for me. "And I guess you are better? Mom said you were in South Carolina."

I took a deep breath. "Yes, I have to head back tomorrow. I wanted to see you."

"Reynolds, hey, there you are!" Kyle appeared out of nowhere in Molly's room. "I've been looking for you everywhere on this floor."

"Kyle Drekr? The TV host of that ghost show?" Molly asked the same time that Alec narrowed his eyes and finally growled at me, "What's he doing here?"

"Calm down, Detective. I don't think you can throw a punch in a hospital," Kyle leveled his gaze at Alec.

"I bet I can," Alec answered, his eyes on Kyle.

"What's going on?" Molly's face clearly showed her confusion.

I quickly introduced Molly to Kyle. Kyle moved closer to her bed and away from the glaring detective. "Molly, your friends are very concerned about you. I'm glad to see you are up and about." Kyle smiled at her, but I couldn't read this one. It didn't seem fake.

"Well, I'm not exactly about, but I'm awake, and that's all that matters."

Alec shifted, placing the flowers on the closest table. "Molly, I need to get back to the station. I'm glad you are doing better. If you need anything, don't hesitate to call."

"Molly, I'll be right back," I said and quickly followed Alec into the hall with Kyle on my heels after he motioned for Molly to give him a second.

Alec walked past Nikki Hiroto and patted her arm. She gave him a little wave, but he didn't seem to notice. He was intent on catching the elevator.

"Reynolds, let him go," Kyle groaned behind me in a stage whisper. "Don't chase the guy." I threw him a dirty look.

"Alec, please wait," I said when he stopped at the elevator, slamming his closed fist on the button. "Did you leave South Carolina because of me?" I whispered as Mom and the Hirotos stopped talking and were curiously watching us. Kyle halted about halfway between the trio of parents and Alec.

"I left South Carolina this morning because you said Molly was awake. Then I had a meeting with the police chief."

"Are you going back down?"

"Why is Drekr here?"

"He drove me back."

His jaw clenched as he stood studying my face. The elevator dinged, and he glanced briefly up at the Hirotos and Mom, gave them a nod, and then boarded the elevator.

"Alec," I pleaded. "Will you talk to me, please?"

"Good-bye, Ainsley." The doors started to shut, but I pushed them open again. Alec glared at the ceiling before finally letting his eyes rest on my face.

"Look," I said, removing one hand from the elevator door to point at him and hurriedly pushing my foot and shoulder against the door to keep it from closing. Alec raised an eyebrow as he leaned against the back wall of the elevator, arms crossed.

"Look," I repeated when I was sure the door couldn't shut with me standing there. "I'm not Annika."

"What did you say?"

"I know about Annika. I'm not her. Everything I told you was true."

"That's not what it looked like." He moved closer to the elevator door and leaned in so that he was almost nose to nose with me. "It appears that you are unhappy with our 'hands off' dating. I don't know what you are doing with Drekr or why he acts like nothing is going on-"

"Because there is nothing," I hissed at him. "Why do people assume the worst?"

"Reynolds, come on," Kyle said quietly from behind me.

Alec's glare moved from my face to the figure of Kyle. "You need to stay out of Locklyn."

I felt Kyle move closer behind me. He lowered his voice to match Alec's deadly whisper. "Or what? I don't bruise as easily as Reynolds."

Alec frowned. "What are you talking about?"

"Kyle, don't," I started.

But Kyle moved his head until it was right above my shoulder, so only the three of us at the elevator could hear. "When you grabbed her at Ashbury, you bruised her arm bad enough that it left a ring of blue marks, impressions. I suggest *you* stay away from *her* while in Locklyn."

Alec's face registered shock. He took a step backward and looked at me. "Is that true?" he asked, horrified.

I sighed. "Yes, but I know it was an accident. We were trying to get away from that girl."

He nodded, then looked down at the elevator floor. "Ainsley, let go of the elevator doors." He raised his head, and I could see the tears behind his eyes. "Just...I need you to let go."

Without another word, I retreated quietly from the opening of the elevator and watched as the doors shut.

~   ~   ~

I stood motionless for a moment, trying to decipher if I had just let Alec go for good. Then I realized the muscled man with the blonde highlights was waiting for me to notice something.

"Why *are* you here?" I demanded.

With a smile of triumph on his face, he held up a small key. "I found it."

As angry as I was with Kyle for having shown up unannounced, I was thrilled to see the key. "It wasn't a dream," I whispered.

"No, it wasn't." He slid the key into his pants pocket. "So, are we headed to this bank?"

I nodded as I walked back into Molly's room. Kyle followed me and took a seat in the chair closest to the door. Molly was sitting up a little more in the bed with a tray of food.

"What is going on with you?" she asked with a mouth full of banana.

I sat down at the foot of her bed. In case Mom came into the room, I whispered, "Do you remember the organization that worked with Maren and my father? They have asked me to help expel a cluster of demons in South Carolina at an old plantation house. Kyle works with the organization too. Mom thinks I'm there on a Senior community service project."

Molly's eyes grew wide. "Were you able to stop the ones at Queens University? The ones influencing…" she trailed off as her eyes glazed over.

I squeezed Molly's blanketed foot. "Yes, I expelled two of them. This house in South Carolina has several more. That's why I have to return. But I promise you that just as soon as we defeat them, I'll be back here." I popped one of her grapes into my mouth. "Eating your scrumptious dinners."

Molly smiled, then she leaned forward and glanced at Kyle. I peered over my shoulder to see Kyle scrolling through his phone. "So, what's up with that? Your detective seems mighty jealous," she whispered even lower than I had.

I sat up straighter. "Nothing. Absolutely nothing. Alec and I just had a falling out about something. A misunderstanding."

"Hmm. So is Kyle single?"

"I don't kno-"

"Why, yes, Molly. Kyle is very single," he answered from his chair.

I glared at him over my shoulder. "It's rude to eavesdrop."

"It's rude to pretend I'm not in the room and not politically correct to presume I'm deaf."

~ ~ ~

Molly thought Kyle and me bickering was funny. I told her that she had lost all sense of what humor was in her coma. After throwing a grape at me, she told me to get on with my demon-busting and hurry home.

The next morning before we were to leave, Kyle and I drove to the local bank. "Molly is cute," he said nonchalantly to the silence.

"No."

"No, what? You don't think your best friend is cute?"

"Oh, she's beautiful. *You* don't get to think she is cute. She is *not* dating you."

"I wouldn't date her right now anyway. She's too young. And what do you mean? She has no say in who she dates?"

I parked the car under the bank's marquee sign, turned off the engine, and then spun around to look Kyle in the eye. "She just woke up from a coma. She's not thinking straight, so I'm thinking for her. You're too much..." I scrambled to find the right words.

Kyle narrowed his eyes. "Too much what, Reynolds? Angry? Self-absorbed? Sarcastic? That's only my good side. Don't forget popular, handsome, intelligent, and wealthy."

"You are too much of all of those things, Kyle. You're the center of attention. Everyone, who isn't me, likes you. They are drawn to you. Molly is the same way. You two would compete with each other." I sighed. My comments about both of them were harsh. But with their personalities, I could see Molly getting her heart crushed.

"You're self-righteous and judgemental," he said, getting out of the car and slamming the door.

"No, I'm not!" I slammed the driver's side door just as hard and internally winced. It was a rental car, after all.

Kyle turned on me and shoved his finger towards my chest when I walked around to his side. "And naive."

I gasped. "I am not naive."

"And childish," he added as he stormed off towards the front doors of the bank.

"I am none of those things, Kyle," I loudly whispered as he opened the inner door to the bank, and we stepped into the lobby.

A tall thin man with an equally thin mustache approached us as we must have shown that we had no idea what we were doing. "Can I help you?"

Kyle smiled his fake grin. "Yes, my friend needs to check her safety deposit box." He handed the man the key.

The man looked us both up and down, and I wished I had dressed differently. Since we would be traveling for close to five hours, I'd decided to wear comfortable jeans, sneakers, a tee-shirt, and zippered hoodie with my school's logo on the front.

"What's the last name?" the man asked, motioning us over to a desk.

"Reynolds."

The man checked his records and then asked for my identification. "Looks like everything is in order. The box belongs to Gerald Reynolds. The only beneficiaries are Ainsley Reynolds and Stephen Reeves."

Neither Kyle nor myself uttered a word. Did Stephen know about the key and the box? We followed the man further into the bank and into a smaller room lined with metal doors. "Here it is. Box 1673. I'll leave you to it then."

I stood motionless in front of the door, staring at the box number. Whatever was inside, my father had put it together for *me*. He knew that I was a Seer. He'd made a special trip to visit me in a dream to make sure I found out about this box.

"What do you think Gerald left you?"

"Something to help me be a Seer."

"You're already a Seer. Maybe something to help you understand how to do the job."

I glanced at Kyle. As aggravated as he made me, his remarks tended to be profound. I stuck the key in the lock and turned, then pulled the box from its home in the wall and set it on the table behind me. With a deep breath, I lifted the metal lid.

Kyle and I both leaned over the box staring at the leather-bound book, the only thing in the box. I picked it up, feeling the cover under my fingers. It was a thin book and small, probably four by six inches.

"All right, Dad. What is this? Do I *read* the Muladach to death?"

Kyle took the book from me as he studied the cover. "You're not powerful enough to kill them. You can only banish them for a short time."

"Not helping," I said, grabbing the book back. I moved the gold strap to the side and opened it to see my father's familiar scrawl inside. "It's like a journal, except each entry is addressed to me."

Kyle looked over my shoulder. "He was thinking of things to share with you. It's like a handbook, only out of order and not indexed."

I flipped back to the first page. *Property of Gerald Reynolds. A record for Ainsley Reynolds.* I turned the page. *The Three Rules of a Seer and a Protector.*

"Here are the three rules. The ones you wanted to wait to share with me," I said, then began to read the page out loud.

The Three Rules of a Seer and a Protector

Rule Number One: Never communicate with the dead.

Rule Number Two: Never open yourself up and allow a demon to use you.

Rule Number Three: Never pass through to the other realm unless it is to save a soul.

"Kyle!" I whispered loudly. "I've broken at least two of these! And Dad said you'd broken all three!"

"Shh!" Kyle shut the lid and slid the box back into its place in the wall. He turned the key, locking the box, and then handed it to me. "Come on. We can talk about this in the car."

I followed Kyle out of the bank, only stopping to say a quick 'thank you' to the man who had helped us with the box. Kyle got in the driver's side and held his hand out for the car keys. I slapped his palm instead.

"What are the consequences for breaking the rules, Kyle?"

"We can discuss it once we get on the road." His light blue eyes were wide. Was he afraid?

I took the keys out of my handbag and handed them over before pulling on my seatbelt, Dad's book lying on my lap like a secret treasure.

Once we were steadily on the interstate and Kyle had set the cruise control, he let out a loud breath. "I'm sure Gerald covers it in the book. Ainsley, you have to realize that I make my living using my gift. A fantastically-paid living. Everything I own is because of that gift. I mean, why were we given the gift to converse with the dead and then not allowed to use it?"

"You said Ainsley."

"What?"

"You never call me Ainsley. You're scared."

"What I do, what we do, *is* scary. The first time I helped free someone from a demon, I felt empowered…and special. No one else could do what I could. I could see ghosts. I could hear demons, sometimes see them. I found out my spirit could walk through portals into the other realm with a Seer present. Word got out that I could help ghosts move on, and a cable network approached me about doing a show."

He quieted for a moment. "I talk to the dead, like Mattie. I don't ignore them. During an investigation, I open myself up so they can find me. Sometimes there's a demon present, and I have to pull back."

He took a deep breath and let it out, then reached for the bottle of water in the console and took a drink. "Your father emailed me once, reminding me of the three rules - and the consequences for breaking them. But by then, I was a multimillionaire with a big house in Los Angeles and traveling all over the world on someone else's dime. I don't want to give that up."

"What are the consequences?"

"When we store up treasures for ourselves here on earth where the moths can eat it, and thieves can steal it away, we will lose it."

"That's cryptic."

"Not really. Your heart is where your treasure is."

"So, your treasure is your house and money?"

Kyle looked at me and then spoke quietly, "My treasure is my fame. By breaking the three rules, I put my livelihood in jeopardy."

"Is that all?" I asked, and Kyle stared at me wide-eyed. "I thought maybe you would lose your soul if you broke the rules."

He turned toward the windshield again and swallowed. "I didn't say that I haven't endangered that as well."

"So stop."

He gave a little laugh. "It's not that easy. I don't like living in poverty like I did growing up in Texas. I like helping people, and I like discovering new things about the other realm. I like the thrill of seeing a ghost for the first time or watching something inexplicable happen."

"At the risk of losing everything?"

Kyle was quiet again, clearly deep in thought.

I took my hair down from its bun and then neatly wrapped it back up into a ponytail. "I've already broken two of the rules. Do you think it is too late for me to fix it before something bad happens?"

"The problem is we need to banish the demons from Ashbury. We need the trapped spirits' knowledge of the demons. We may need to cross through the portal again. We won't know for certain until we go deeper. You can't expel the cluster until they all come through."

"I banished that one easy enough."

Kyle threw me a sideways glance as he smiled. "There is only room enough in this investigation for one cocky jerk."

I feigned offense and gently shoved Kyle on the shoulder. Maybe he wasn't so bad after all.

~   ~   ~

We stopped an hour out from the hotel so that I could take a restroom break and we could grab some food. Thankfully, Kyle found one of my favorite chicken places to eat, and I ordered a dozen grilled nuggets, a fruit cup, and an unsweetened tea. We ate quietly in the car.

As I poured two stevia packets into my tea, Kyle leaned against the car seat and rested his head as he studied me, his gaze landing just below my throat, leaving me feeling awkward. "You know, you don't have to wear that."

"What?"

"Your dad's medallion. Gerald wore it because he felt like it offered him some security, like a blanket or a favorite toy. It doesn't offer real protection."

I rubbed the pendant between my fingers, feeling the two riders and horse on one side and the engraved initials on the other. "When we were at Queens, the serial killer told me that the only reason the demons hadn't been able to get to Alec was that I'd given him a blessed object. It was this medallion."

Kyle tilted his head down to peer up at me through his lashes. "Maybe it was because you blessed it when you gave it to him."

"I didn't. I don't know how."

"Reynolds, you have more power than you realize. It's all boxed up in you because you haven't discovered who you are, and no one introduced you to Jesus. There is real resurrection power there, and He gave it to us."

I exhaled loudly. "What are you talking about? Trust me, I'm no Jesus."

Kyle smiled. "Me either. But I strive hard to follow Him. I mess up on the daily. *On the daily.* I break the rules, as I have admitted. Sometimes I'm sarcastic and cynical."

"Sometimes?"

"All right, more than I should. I'll be the first to admit it. But here's the thing that I don't think anyone has told you," Kyle turned in his seat so he could make better eye contact with me. "When Jesus was crucified, He did it to bring every Christian to Him. Three days later, the

Resurrection power brought Him back and defeated death. For every Christian - past, present, and future."

"I know the Easter story. It was the only time we went to church."

"Okay," Kyle pushed his head to one side, trying to stay patient. I suspected that he did have anger issues. "I need you to hear this as a personal story. When Jesus ascended into heaven, He gave a command to go out into all the world doing His work. Then fire came down and landed on each of His followers. This was the Resurrection power. It's still there for those Christians that truly seek Him and are willing to put their lives last."

I studied Kyle's blue eyes under his intense gaze. He believed this.

"So, that's why you do this? Because you think you have some of this power?"

Kyle leaned away from me with aggravation written on his face. "I do this because I have a gift. It's the same reason your father did it. What I'm trying to tell you now is that aside from the gift, you have another power. It's that power that makes you dangerous to the demons. With it, you don't have to worry about saying everything right in Latin or holding a special object. It comes from within you."

I raised an eyebrow.

Kyle sighed loudly and turned back to the steering wheel. "Fine. If you don't believe me, ask God to show you." He started the engine.

"Show me what?"

"Show you who you are," he said as he clicked his seatbelt and guided the car back onto the interstate.

"Okay, I will. But we need to find a way to do these things without breaking the rules anymore. The more I think about it, maybe that is why I lost Alec."

Kyle frowned. "You lost Graham because you weren't supposed to ever be with him. It was a fluke that you two got thrown in together on that murder case. No offense, Reynolds, but you have a crush on the guy."

I narrowed my eyes at Kyle. "It may have started that way, but I don't have a crush now, and Alec never had a crush on me."

"That's evident."

"You don't know what you are talking about."

Kyle sighed. "I think he liked you. Why wouldn't he? You're pretty, smart, capable, curvy as all get out, and not to mention special with your ability to see and hear things that other people cannot. Combine all of those things with the fact that you haven't had a real boyfriend before, and it makes you irresistible." He threw another sideways glance at me again. "Like candy."

"What are you saying? Because I know there is a point somewhere under all that."

"I think Detective Alec Graham likes his candy and doesn't want anyone else to go near it."

"Do you hear yourself? You are comparing me to a Snickers bar."

Kyle laughed. "More like a Whatchamacallit."

"Or a Mounds," I said, laughing.

Kyle laughed harder as his eyes darted to my chest and then back to the road. "That's true." He slammed his hand onto the steering wheel, laughing hysterically. "Or, a gobstopper!"

We both had tears in our eyes from laughing so hard that at first, neither of us heard Kyle's phone ringing. He picked up his mobile, glancing at the unknown number. "I don't recognize it, but that's a South Carolina area code." We calmed ourselves enough for him to swipe the green arrow and place the call on speaker as he balanced the phone on his lap.

"Mr.Drekr? This is Palmer Meadors."

"Yes, Mr. Meadors. How are you?"

"Where are you?" The man's voice boomed through the speaker.

Kyle and I exchanged glances. "I had to drive up to North Carolina yesterday, but I am almost back to the hotel near the Ashbury now."

"As soon as you get back, come straight to Ashbury. There's been an...accident with my son Harold."

"Oh, I'm sorry to hear that, Mr. Meadors," Kyle answered.

"Well, I hate to say it, but I think the ghosts in this house were responsible."

"Why do you say that?"

"Just come straight here," the older man ordered. "And bring Alec Graham with you."

"Well, about that, Mr. Meadors-"

"No excuses, Drekr," the man barked into the phone and then disconnected the call.

Kyle and I looked at each other again. "What do you think happened?"

Kyle shrugged. "I don't know. Call Maren. Tell her I am dropping you off at the hotel and then going to Ashbury."

"Not by yourself, you're not." I pulled my cell phone out to call Maren.

"Aww, are you worried about me, Reynolds?"

"No, I'm worried about Mr. Meadors' son, and whatever he expects you to do, you will probably need my help. Plus, you heard him. He wants Alec there."

"We can't help with the latter."

"Sure, we can. Alec didn't answer the phone when I messaged him about Molly, but he drove from South Carolina to Locklyn." I pulled Alec's name up on my phone.

Kyle watched me from the driver's seat. "He told you to let go. He wasn't just talking about the elevator door, Reynolds," he said, his voice admonishing me for what I was about to do.

I ignored him and instead hit the call button. The phone rang twice and then went straight to voicemail, indicating that Alec had sent the call over to his voicemail when he saw it was me.

I took a deep breath. "Hi, Alec. Look, you don't have to call me back or anything. Palmer Meadors called and said there had been an accident with his son, Harold. He is blaming the ghosts at Ashbury for the accident, but you and I know that it was probably the demons. He asked for you specifically to come to the estate. Kyle and I are on our way there now." I hesitated for a second before disconnecting the call. What good would it do for Alec to show up? He couldn't rid the estate of its demons.

I called Maren next and told her everything from Molly's update to Mr. Meadors' strange call. I told her everything except about the safety deposit box and Dad's book. I wasn't ready to share that with anyone else. She said she would pass the news to Stephen but for Kyle to bring me back to the hotel first before going to Ashbury. When I told Maren about Mr. Meadors' request for Alec, she quieted.

"Well, it's up to Alec whether he wants to come back or not, Ainsley. You just need to focus on why you're here."

"I am," I answered. However, I was secretly praying that Alec would return and sweep me off my feet. Then, I remembered the look on Alec's face as the elevator doors closed at the hospital.

No. Alec Graham was done with me.

~   ~   ~

As we neared the hotel, Kyle tapped Dad's journal I'd laid across my lap.

"Have you read any nuggets yet?"

"A little. He wrote a large entry for me that seems to be advice."

"Read it to me."

I opened the thin leather book to the page after the dreaded three rules that I seemed destined to break. I read the first line silently to myself and choked back tears. This was going to be much harder to read than I thought. I could hear Dad's voice in my head.

When Kyle reached over and patted my knee, I began to read out loud.

My dear sweet Baby Girl, my Ainsley, I know you are probably asking why I would do this for people I don't even know. The answer is it doesn't matter that I didn't know them. They were innocent people victimized by a monster. The moment I knew of their peril, it became my responsibility. That's what duty is; it's fighting for those who cannot fight for themselves. They, in essence, became my people.

I know you're afraid. I know you think that I am always brave, never scared.

You're wrong, Ainsley.

I feel the fear, yet I have pushed through it so many times. I embrace it as a strength, not as a weakness.

If you want to defeat the demons around you, then you need to embrace your weaknesses and allow God's grace to be your strength. You're going to screw up, Baby Girl. That is life because you are human, a fallible thing in a temporary vessel. What counts is what you do with what you have. Never waste your energy, your time, or your thoughts. The demons will try to mess you up - YOU are their assignment.

Don't let them win. Don't give in. They will use everything, and not everything will be bad. Good opportunities can actually be distractions to pull you off your purpose. Your heart might fall in love with someone sent to make your heart grow cold.

Don't let them win.

With God, you have the power of His Son to battle demons, to help people, and to see through the realm. As you learn and grow, you will make this your story. What worked for me might not work for you. Did you know Jesus never performed a miracle the same way twice? Look it up.

Every battle will be different. Why? Because the demons strategize too. You need to keep this feeling of Awakening within you at all times. Stay vigilant, Baby Girl. Stay aware.

There will be times that you must walk away. Sometimes the timing isn't right. Sometimes a person or situation is not your assignment. Let it go for now. If God wants you there later, He will put you there.

I want you to find a Bible that you can read and understand. There are many versions, so find one that doesn't change or leave out the important stuff. Ask my friend, Stephen Reeves. He will help you. I'm not telling you to read the Bible because of the stories. I want you to read it as if God is talking specifically to you - because He is. You will find Him when you seek Him with all your heart. If you are reading this, then I might be gone, but God will never leave you nor forsake you. I am only human, and I only have one life to live, but He is with you always. He will deliver you from all your fears.

You will see and hear the demons. I did. I've seen them while walking you to school, heard them during a company picnic, expelled them in the parking lot of Ben's daycare. You may be called upon to battle one or more.

Before you accept, ALWAYS PRAY. Not every assignment is for you, but you MUST PRAY for guidance once you know about it. I cannot stress this enough. Isaiah 43:2 says, "When you pass through the waters, I will be with you; and when you pass through the rivers, they will not sweep over you. When you walk through the fire, you will not be burned; the flames will not set you ablaze."

That is the kind of backup you need in this fight. Don't be fooled - this is a war.

I know you don't feel like a warrior, Ains. Guess what, Baby Girl?

It doesn't matter how you feel.

Your feelings have nothing to do with your purpose. Get on with it. I know that sounds harsh, but I'm still your dad, and I will always tell it to you straight. You know that.

My biggest mistake was hiding my calling from your mother and you. I worried too much about what my inlaws would think about me "touting off Christian stuff." I can stand up to the supernatural, but not your 5 foot 3 inch Irish hot-tempered grandpa.

Don't hide it. Even if it makes your mother and your grandparents uncomfortable. So what? It is your calling, and you are responsible for it.

The rest of this journal includes some of my favorite Latin passages with the English equivalents. You don't have to use them. They are merely jumping-off points for you. What is important is that you believe what you are saying and tap into the Resurrection power of Jesus Christ and use His authority. I'm also leaving some pages blank for you to write in your own passages and notes.

Remember the three rules.

Keep your heart and mind as pure as you can (trust me, I know exactly how hard this is for us humans).

Don't jump to your own conclusions.

PRAY like you mean it. Don't use fancy words. Talk like you always do. Talk to God like you talk to your mom or me. He knows you better, and He knows your thoughts anyway. Be careful what you say aloud. The demons can hear what you say, but they can't read your mind. They can try to influence your thoughts by whispering to you, but again, they cannot read your mind. Pray in your head and out loud.

Be wary. Be vigilant. Stay aware. Push past the fear.

I love you more than you will ever know. Dad

For a moment, I could no longer see the page with my father's handwriting. The tears spilled over my eyes, down my face, and onto my lap.

"Reynolds." Kyle sounded sad as he took my hand and squeezed, which would have been awkward in any other circumstance. Instead, it was strangely comforting right now.

"I haven't felt this close to Dad since he died. Between the dream the other night and the journal, it feels like he is just on a business trip somewhere. That he will be back soon." I sniffed and wiped what I knew had to be snot on the sleeve of my hoodie.

"In a way, he is on a trip somewhere," Kyle said softly. "You will see him again."

"I want to believe that, Kyle. I do. It just seems…beyond my reach."

Kyle was quiet for a moment. "That's where faith comes in. You believe demons exist because you have seen and heard them. You believe God exists because you have seen Him deliver you and your friends from danger. Have faith that what Jesus said was true about preparing a place for us."

"I don't know what Jesus said. I didn't grow up with any of this." I wiped my eyes again with my sleeve. Why couldn't I stop crying?

Kyle handed me his phone. "Here. Find the app I use for the Bible. We're going to look up a few things, starting with the Book of John, Chapter 14, and ending in the first half of First Peter Chapter 2. Stephen can fill you in on more later." Kyle grinned, then threw me a playful wink. "This is going to be the Kyle-quickie version."

CHAPTER SIXTEEN

The hotel elevator door opened to an orchestra of voices that were definitely out of tune. Waverly and Everly were yelling something to Maren, who was trying to gain control of the situation while the others talked all at once to Stephen.

"Oh, Mr. Drekr! It's horrible! We can't find Freya," Waverly wailed, practically falling into Kyle's arms.

"What do you mean you can't find her?"

"She ran down to the vending machine in the lobby, and now, no one can find her." Waverly buried her blonde hair in Kyle's chest. He looked at Maren, alarmed.

"Everyone back to your rooms! Now! We will go look for Freya." Maren's voice rose above the other voices, and within seconds, the group was moving off to their rooms. "And do *not* leave your room!"

The hallway was suddenly quiet with only Maren, Stephen, Kyle, and me standing in the center.

"What happened?" Kyle whispered to Maren.

"Freya was in Waverly and Everly's room with Izzy. They were watching a movie, and Freya wanted something from the machine downstairs. She went by herself and never came back."

"Someone had to have seen her," I said. "Did you ask the hotel staff?"

"Yes," Stephen said. "The manager is pulling the security videos. I'm heading back down now."

"I'll go with you," I volunteered. Freya was my only classmate friend on this trip, and I had a sick feeling in my gut that the Muladach were behind her disappearance.

"Should I stay here and look for the girl or go to Ashbury?" Kyle asked Maren.

Maren appeared as if tears were her next step. It was apparent she had never lost a student before on a trip. She was doing her best to maintain her perfect teacher's façade, but it was evident to those closest to her that she was crumbling inside.

Stephen patted Maren's arm. "Kyle, help me look for Freya by checking the other floors with Maren. Ashbury and Mr. Meadors will have to wait."

Stephen and I each took a stairwell to search while climbing down to the ground floor. Neither one of us turned up Freya. Once we hit the lobby, the manager rushed us into his office.

"Mr. Reeves, we're going to need to call the police." Beads of sweat dotted the manager's concerned face.

"Did you find something on the surveillance video?" Stephen asked.

"Yes. A man accosted her in the lobby in front of the elevator. It appears he drugged her with a syringe, then carried her out the side door into the parking garage. She's the fourth missing girl in the last few weeks in our town."

"Show me the video, and then we call the police."

The thin man pulled the video footage up on the giant color monitor. It showed the top of Freya's blonde head as she bounced around waiting for the elevator door to open, a can of soda pop in her hand. However, as soon as the doors opened, a white-haired man wearing a blue medical mask leaped from the elevator and grabbed her, forcing a syringe into her neck, the can crashing onto the marble floor and spewing its contents everywhere. I watched in silence as a black mist swirled around Freya and the man.

"Do you see that?" I whispered to Stephen.

"I think that is just shadows," the hotel manager answered.

Stephen and I exchanged glances. We knew better.

The man carried a limp Freya out of the frame. The manager changed camera angles, and we watched as the man hauled her out the side door to the garage. The garage's security camera followed the man as he carried Freya past the parked cars and trucks to a white van parked near the entrance. He opened the back door and tossed her into the back as if she was nothing more than a sack of potatoes.

I pulled on Stephen's shirt sleeve until he finally relented and followed me to the corner of the manager's office.

"I know that man."

"How? Who is it?"

"It's Harold Meadors - the son of the owners of Ashbury."

~ ~ ~

Although Stephen and I were aware of the identity of the man who had taken Freya, we both knew that if we told the authorities that I recognized the man, the police would descend on Ashbury. We would forfeit the chance to banish the demons.

Yet, with every passing minute, anxiety crept through me. What if Harold did something to Freya before we could help?

Over the next four hours, the police interviewed each of us, including Maren and the other students, about Freya. The police interviewed hotel guests who may have seen Freya during the short period of time when she wasn't in Waverly and Everly's room. The lead detective called Freya's father in Locklyn, and I could only imagine the frantic voices on the other end of the line. Maren was in tears.

Stephen, Kyle, and I met in Stephen's room after the police finished and left to begin their search somewhere other than the hotel. Stephen instructed Maren to stay with the students; it was more important that she was there for them. The three of us would have to handle Ashbury on our own.

"What's the plan?" Stephen asked Kyle.

"We go to the house and scope it out to see where Mr. Meadors and his son are holed up with Freya."

"What makes you think Mr. Meadors knows that Harold has taken Freya?" I asked, opening the adjoining door to my room and retrieving my backpack. I tossed in a couple of bottles of water.

Kyle shrugged. "He said there had been an accident with Harold. He thought the ghosts were responsible. I think he knows."

I closed the door behind me. "So is this a setup, or does he want us to stop Harold somehow? And why did he demand Alec be there?"

Neither man answered. Kyle frowned as he took a drink of water from a plastic bottle. Stephen didn't look at me as he removed his tee-shirt and put on a fresh one.

"I'm sure one of you has a theory."

Stephen pulled on his jacket. "Alec's grandfather is co-owner of the Ashbury. Maybe the Meadors want full ownership, or they want to force Edward Graham to do something by using Alec as leverage."

"Or, the demons want to move you out of the way," Kyle added. "They may have big plans to use Graham to break you."

I swallowed. "Okay, so we will just tell Alec not to come back to Mire Marsh, not to go anywhere near Ashbury." I pulled my cell from my back pocket. "He probably ignored my message anyway."

"*I'll* try calling him. The two of you head out to Ashbury in the rental car. I'll be right behind you," Stephen said, a mask of concern over his already dark features.

"I think we would be stronger together," I said, keeping my gaze level with Stephen's. I had a bad feeling about this.

Stephen blinked, then approached me and placed his hands on my shoulders. "Ainsley, your father never really needed me by his side to fight the supernatural. He needed a Protector. Kyle is going with you, and I won't be far behind. More importantly, God is walking ahead of you. He is not going to let Harold Meadors and the demons take you out. I'm sure of it."

"How can you be so sure?"

Stephen bit his lower lip before answering me. "I had a dream last night. Gerald was in it." He rubbed my shoulders with his thumbs as his eyes glazed over. "In the dream, he told me that a battle was coming and that you are so much stronger than you realize. He wanted me to remind you that even though your heart is breaking, you must stay strong and focused."

"That was a dream." I said the words, even though I really didn't believe it was just a dream.

Stephen smiled. "He said, 'Ains will say it was just a dream. Remind Baby Girl about the key and the box and the book.' I'm not sure what he was talkin' about, but I think you do."

My mouth dropped open. Kyle and I hadn't told Stephen or Maren about the safety deposit key or box yet. Dad *did* visit Stephen on my behalf. A tear ran down my face, and I quickly wiped it away. There wasn't time for tears. Freya needed us to stop whatever plans the Muladach had for her. I had the book Dad left for me. According to what Kyle and I had read, I had God's Spirit moving within me and about me like a fire. We could do this.

I could do this.

I nodded my head at Stephen. "Okay. I think I'm ready to face the Muladach. But what about Harold? I don't think I can physically fight him. I barely lived through the Artist's attack at Queens. If it hadn't been for Alec…"

Stephen patted my shoulder. "We will handle ol' Harold. You just work on banishing the demons."

~ ~ ~

The Ashbury was closed for visitors again today, and with Ravi still in the hospital, it seemed quieter than usual when Kyle and I entered. Stephen had had a couple of aluminum bats from his company softball team in the bed of his truck, so Kyle and I were armed to protect ourselves from creepy Harold. Kyle pinged the tip of the softball bat on the wooden floor, and the sound echoed through the house.

"Why is the door unlocked if Ashbury is closed today?"

"Mr. Meadors?" Kyle called from the foyer. There was no answer.

Kyle frowned, and I followed him into the main living room. "Mr. Meadors? Are you here?" he called again.

"Kyle, there's something I need to tell you."

"What?" Kyle continued looking around the room as if Palmer Meadors might be hiding behind the heavy velvet drapes.

"The other students were planning on coming to Ashbury tonight for the tour. Maren can't know I told you."

He shrugged. "No Ravi, no tour, no problem. With Freya gone, I doubt they will go anywhere."

"I don't think it's that simple. They seemed pretty dead set on seeing Ashbury."

He peered through the doorway to the stairwell. "Are you saying you think they would try to break into the house if it's closed? With their classmate missing?"

"I don't know. There's a couple that I wouldn't put it past them. Waverly and Ethan in particular."

Kyle shook his head. "I don't think any of them will do it now." He gave me a pointed look. "Can you feel Mattie's presence?"

"I never actually felt her presence. She just appeared."

"I can't feel her. It's like...she's gone." He narrowed his eyes at the doorway to the hall. "Come on." The two of us darted hurriedly through the house, looking in rooms and opening closets, adrenaline pumping through my body so quickly I felt jittery. I wondered if I really had the nerve to crack Harold Meadors in the head with the bat if he did jump out at me.

It took us an hour to search the entire house, every nook and cranny for Freya. We regretted bricking up the stairs in the upstairs sitting room where Mrs. Ashbury had met her grisly demise. At least with the stairwell sealed, Harold couldn't have hidden Freya in there. *Right?* I wasn't so sure anymore. The Muladach had a way of bending time and space. At least inside the Ashbury.

"Kyle? Ainsley?" We heard Stephen's voice calling us from somewhere on the stairs. Kyle and I emerged from the third floor and ran into Stephen armed with another bat on the stairs.

"Where have you been?" Kyle demanded.

"I called Alec, and he was on his way. He left Locklyn about an hour or so after Ainsley called him. I got him up to speed with Freya's disappearance, and he reviewed the security footage with the hotel manager."

"Where is he now?" I asked quietly.

Stephen took a deep breath as if preparing to give me bad news. "He was driving to the Meadors' house to speak with Helen Meadors in person. He spoke with her on the phone, and she was a nervous wreck. She said she couldn't reach her husband or her son on the phone." His gaze moved to Kyle. "I take it you haven't found anything?"

"Not yet," Kyle answered. "Neither one of us is feeling anything. I can't get a lock on any trapped spirits either."

"Could they be hiding? Perhaps because of the demons?"

"I'm not picking up on any vibrational energy from the demons," I said. "It's like we're the only ones here."

The three of us stood perplexed on the stairs. Had Harold taken Freya somewhere other than the Ashbury? Where were the demons? Mattie had been here since the forties, so where was her ghost now? "It was Mr. Meadors, Harold's father, who called us. Maybe we should try to call him?"

Kyle pulled his cell phone out and hit the last call on his phone. Suddenly a distant ringing sounded in the house. It sounded muffled. "I don't get it," Kyle said. "If this is Mr. Meadors' phone ringing, then why didn't we hear it before now if his wife has been blowing it up for hours?"

"The house didn't want you to hear it," Stephen said as he started down the stairs with the softball bat raised as if ready to hit the curveball out of the park from the second landing.

We followed the ringing down the stairs to the second floor, then on to the first floor. Kyle had to redial the number three times for us to keep following the sound as Mr. Meadors' voicemail kept answering.

We stopped at the hidden door under the stairs, the one where Kyle and I had moved through the portal into the other realm. "Can you sense any demons?" Kyle asked as he placed his hand on the door, listening for sounds from the other realm.

"Nothing is happening if that's what you mean. The rooms aren't rippling the way they usually do when I feel their vibrational energy. Everything is just…quiet."

"I know. It's weird." He ran his hand over the wallpapered door. Then as I watched in shock, he began pulling the wallpaper away from the edges of the door.

"What are you doing?"

"There are only so many places Harold Meadors could have taken Freya. My guess is that he has access to whatever is behind this door. If Palmer Meadors' cell is behind here, then maybe he is too."

"Or his body," Stephen added. "You aren't sensing anything at all? Even I feel like there is something otherwordly here." Stephen raised his bat again over his shoulder as he peered down the hall.

Kyle suddenly stopped pulling on the wallpaper and whirled around wide-eyed towards us. "Oh my God," he said. "No! No, no!" He retreated from the staircase and moved out to the front door, running his hands through his hair like a madman.

"Kyle! What is it?" He was scaring me.

He stopped moving at the front door, his back to us, and lowered his head, slumping his shoulders. He remained silent.

When Kyle dropped to his knees in front of the entrance, Stephen and I exchanged looks. *What was happening?* Had Ashbury's madness overtaken Kyle too?

"God, please," I heard Kyle breathe out the words in the silent house. "God, please don't take it away. I'm sorry I misused my gift for so long. Please, search my heart. Search Ainsley's heart. You know I am remorseful. I don't know if we can find the girl in time without discernment. Please!"

I took a step toward Kyle, but Stephen put his hand on my arm, and I halted. I watched the heavily-muscled young man on his knees crying out to God. I could hear the tears and remorse in his voice. Was this the consequence of breaking the rules? Had God taken away Kyle's gift? Had He taken away mine? I squeezed my eyes shut.

I remembered my father's words from the journal. *Talk to God like you would to your mom or me.* Silently, I prayed. *God, you know I didn't mean to break the rules. Please help Kyle and me find Freya. If you don't want me to expel demons, then I accept that. I'm probably more than fine with that. But, please, help us find Freya before it is too late.*

She doesn't deserve to die at the hands of some demonic maniac. Please. I'm trying to learn more about you and your Son, Jesus. Please, give us the gift just long enough to find Freya. Show me who I am in you, my true identity.

I felt Stephen's arm wrap around my shoulders. It was a simple gesture that reminded me of Dad, and tears began to spill down my face. Suddenly, a whistling sound started through the house. I'd never been in a storm with a tornado, but it reminded me of one. As if a strong wind was coming through the house. Kyle heard it too and stood, reaching for the handrail. Without thinking, I grabbed for the spindles on the stairs. Whatever it was, it sounded expansive...and hollow.

"What is it?" Stephen asked with his hand on my arm.

"You can't hear that?" I yelled over the sound. The invisible tornado seemed to be getting closer. Or maybe it was a train.

"Why are you yelling? The house is quiet."

I looked at Kyle, whose eyes were even wider than earlier. "He can't hear it. Brace yourselves."

Stephen grabbed the top of the railing, although he looked confused. I pressed my face against the wooden spindles, squeezing my eyes tight just as a blast of cold wind whipped through me, and I let out a shriek. The current passed through me taking its time to touch the morrow of my bones. The rushing sound filled my ears, and for a moment, I thought I might go deaf. Then just as suddenly as it had started, the wind stopped, and the roaring ceased.

I opened my eyes and let out a scream, forcing myself away from the wooden spindles and into the wall, slamming my head into the wallpapered plaster. Other people would have probably seen stars. I immediately saw a flash of lightning in my head.

Mattie stared at me, her face pressed against the wooden spindles as she sat on the stair – her dark hair still pulled up into its neat bun under her nurse's hat. She turned to Kyle, who by now was on the stairs leaning over her. "Mattie?"

The ghost smiled up at him.

"What is it?" Stephen asked.

I rubbed the back of my head as a large lump was forming under my hair. "The ghost of Mattie is here. I think God gave us back our gift."

"Thank God!" Kyle said.

"Well, it might only be for a little while, Kyle. We need to find Freya."

Kyle nodded as he sat down on the stair below Mattie. "Mattie, I'm sorry I couldn't see you earlier, but I'm not really supposed to talk to trapped spirits. This may be the last time I can talk to you."

Mattie's smile disappeared, and her eyes seemed to glaze over.

"Mattie, have you seen the owners of this house? Did they bring in a girl about Ainsley's age?"

Mattie nodded. I watched as Mattie slowly stood, moving closer to Kyle until he carefully backed down the stairs to let her pass. She gave me a sideways glance as she passed, headed down the hall.

"What is it?" Stephen asked, frustrated.

I kept forgetting that he couldn't see spirits or demons. Or hear invisible tornadoes and trains.

Or hear the breath of God. Wait, what? Where did that thought come from?

"Mattie is taking us to where she saw Freya, I think," I answered.

Mattie looked at me over her shoulder and nodded. She walked to the covered door under the stairs, glanced back at Kyle, and then walked through it. Immediately, Kyle was at the door, pulling the remaining wallpaper off. "This one isn't like the others. It must not be an original door. It's not thick." Kyle pushed on the door. The wood gave a bit. Unfortunately, it lacked a doorknob.

Kyle nodded at Stephen. "Decades-old wood."

The two men began punching holes with the softball bats into the thin wood paneling where a lock should have been. The noise echoed through the house. I kept a lookout for creepy Harold in case he would suddenly appear in the hall. I still didn't feel any demons.

"Freya, where are you?" I whispered.

~ ~ ~

With one mighty kick from Kyle, the door swung open. We peered into the darkness. It was a corridor that ran about eight feet in front of us, then veered sharply to the left.

"I wish we had the blueprints for this place," Stephen said. "Ravi said one of the paranormal investigators died under the house. The way he made it sound, the house has a crawl space, not a basement."

"Unless this is all on the first floor. Maybe when they rebuilt the house, they walled in secret passages," Kyle said.

"Maybe. Don't go in yet. Let me run out to the truck and grab some flashlights. Do you want anything from your equipment?"

Kyle thought for a second. "Yeah, grab a couple of the smaller cameras with the suction cups and my tablet."

"Do you smell that?" I whispered to Kyle after Stephen rushed out of the house.

"Like a cat died?"

I nodded my head. The scent was more potent than a dead cat, though. I rubbed the back of my head again.

Kyle studied me. "Sometimes you will smell something rancid or dead when there are a lot of demons moving in and out of the portals from the other realm. I guess it is all the energy. Are you all right?"

"I hit my head on the wall. It was spooky seeing Mattie's face right smack in front of mine when I opened my eyes."

Kyle laughed as he felt the growing lump on my head. "I bet so. The good news is that it's a lump and not a dent. I think you'll be okay. Just don't go to sleep anytime soon." He dropped his hand from my hair when he heard Stephen return.

I rubbed my head again. "Don't worry. I probably won't sleep for a while after this." The lump was beginning to make my head throb.

Stephen handed Kyle a duffle bag with the equipment thrown in, and I observed the wince on Kyle's face. I was sure the equipment was on the higher end of expensive, although his television show probably paid for most, if not all, of it. I waited as the two men crouched on the floor to check the batteries and turn on the cameras. The cameras were smaller than the ones he'd used during our investigations. These were in the shape of a cue ball, only a bit larger. Kyle powered on the tablet and made sure it was picking up the feed from the cameras.

"Okay, let's go find the girl," Stephen said as he stood, bat in hand.

Kyle handed me his bat before he slid forward into the corridor with Stephen shining a flashlight beam ahead of us. Kyle stopped at the corner and maneuvered the camera ball to the edge of the wall with one hand as he studied his tablet. He motioned with his head for us to come closer.

"There is a long, narrow corridor with a door at the end," he said in a low voice.

I started to nod, but the movement caused my head to throb more. As I stood wondering if I had a concussion or something worse, the walls and floor shifted out from under me. I grabbed Stephen for balance.

"Ainsley? Are you okay?" he asked, holding me up with one arm, the bat still raised with the other. The flashlight he carried dug into my back.

"She hit her head on the wall at the base of the stairs," I heard Kyle answer. I blinked. My vision was blurring even in the darkness.

I felt Stephen run his hand over my head. "She's got a goose egg, that's for sure. Maybe Ainsley should sit this one out."

"No," Kyle said. "We need the Seer."

"At what cost, Kyle?"

The narrow corridor shifted again, and suddenly it felt claustrophobic, more like a tomb than a hallway. A vibration started under my feet and slowly moved up my legs into my torso and finally to my arms. When it reached my head, for a moment, the vibration with the throbbing almost sent me over the edge. I gritted my teeth. This was more than just a bump on the head. The demons were here.

"It's okay," I finally managed. "I'm okay. I don't think it's my head. There's a demon nearby."

Kyle slid the camera around the corner again and checked the feed, then shook his head.

"I'm okay," I said as Stephen let go of me so he could follow Kyle around the corner; however, we'd only stepped around when the demonic little girl with the straggly black hair greeted us with a scream. We all three leaped back in horror, and the little demon laughed hysterically. With a wave of anger I hadn't felt for a long time, I pushed through Kyle and Stephen to confront the demon. Stephen shined the flashlight beam right into its reflective eyes. It didn't blink.

"To Hell with you, demon! You are no trapped spirit. You are a demon bound to the other realm. Be gone with you in Jesus' name!" The authoritative tone of my voice startled me, but the demon's image faltered. Its true form materialized before it gave a high-pitched bark, then vanished.

"Well, that's one down," Kyle said.

Stephen was still holding his hand to his chest. "I saw her! The ghost, I mean," he said breathlessly.

"She wasn't a real ghost," I said as I picked up the duffle bag he'd dropped. "She was a demon mimicking a child. It's how they tricked Mattie into staying at the Ashbury. Did you see her transform into the demon?"

Stephen shook his head. "No, the girl just disappeared."

"That's how they lure paranormal investigators here using the images and voices of children." Kyle took the duffle bag from me and slung it over his shoulder. "Come on."

We slowly made our way through the hall and stopped at the narrow door. "I wish we had a gun," I whispered.

"Can you shoot a gun?" Stephen asked.

"Yes, Alec taught me."

Neither man said anything as Stephen quietly tried the doorknob. It opened slightly. "Can we say trap?" Stephen sighed before raising the bat and opening the door further so Kyle could slide the camera ball through.

We huddled together, watching the camera feed as Kyle moved the ball in his hand. It was still in night vision mode. It was a room about the size of a small den with what looked like white paneled walls and a door on the opposite wall. It appeared that a wardrobe, an antique sofa, and a Queen Anne chair were the only items in the furnished room. When we were confident that Harold was not hiding in the dark den, we opened the door wider.

Stephen and Kyle went into the room first. I took my time on the narrow stepdown into this portion of the house. The knot on my head made my vision shaky, and the last thing I needed was to fall and break a leg in a haunted house. Thankfully, there was only one step I had to concern myself with at the moment.

"No windows," Kyle observed. "Do you see a light switch?"

"No," I answered, shining my flashlight around the walls.

"Why would they construct a secret room and hallway? This has to have been built in 1918 after the fire."

"Is this the only secret room?" I asked as I started for the door along the opposite wall. "This place is huge. Maybe there are more. Like the sealed-up servant stairs." I placed my hand on the wooden door, painted a slime green color. "I'm not picking up any demonic energy."

"No ghosts either," Kyle answered, still studying his camera feed.

"We heard that ringing. Try calling Mr. Meadors' cell again," Stephen said as he opened the wardrobe. But Kyle didn't need to call Mr. Meadors. The tall white-haired gentleman fell out of the cabinet with a thud and a moan.

"Mr. Meadors!" I ran over, but Stephen was already tending to the man's wound on his head.

"Harold…" the man groaned. "He's lost his mind." The man closed his eyes and became very still.

"Is he dead?" I whispered.

Stephen felt for Mr. Meadors' pulse. "No, but his pulse is weak. We need to get him to the hospital. It would take an ambulance too long to reach us out here."

Kyle and Stephen hoisted Mr. Meadors up between them and carried him out of the room and down the narrow corridor. We left the duffle bag and equipment in the secret room except for the bat I carried and Stephen's flashlight I'd picked up. It took several minutes to maneuver the man without dropping him around the sharp corner to get to the busted door that led into the downstairs foyer.

"Reynolds, stay here," Kyle ordered after I'd opened the front door for them and switched on the foyer and porch lights to push back the encroaching darkness. Thankfully, the power was still on. It did take away some of the Ashbury creepiness. I watched as the two men carried Mr. Meadors to Stephen's truck. Silently, I griped at Kyle that I should have at least gone to the truck to open the door for them, but they still managed somehow.

"Ainsley."

I spun around and peered up the stairs. "Freya?"

"Ainsley."

It was definitely Freya's voice floating down the stairs.

"Ainsley, hurry!" Her voice was more insistent. Had Harold left her alone upstairs, and this was the only chance she had to call for help?

With a glance back to the front door, I darted up the stairs. "Freya?"

"Up here! The third floor!" Freya sounded almost crazed now.

I sprinted up the stairs, and by the time I hit the third floor, I was so out of breath, I had to lean against the wall for a second. My head pounded louder in my ears, and the third-floor hall rippled. There were demons somewhere on this floor.

"Freya, where are you?" I called out as I held the back of my head and fumbled for a light switch. I couldn't figure out where to find the dimmers in the hallway.

"Here!" She sounded close but distant at the same time. She was on this floor, but where? I squinted at the closed doors. Kyle and I had just been up here and I could've sworn we'd left the doors open. Shining the flashlight in front of me, I carefully began to check each room. People no longer lived in the Ashbury, however the owners furnished the rooms with antiques to lend to the atmosphere. In these rooms, I checked under the beds and in the closets. After the third room, I called out from the hall again, "Freya, where are you?"

"This way."

I froze. The disembodied voice had come from right in front of me. I peered into the darkness and then shone my flashlight beam: nothing but air. I backed myself into the wall and slid to the next bedroom door, opening it as quietly as I could. I flipped on the bedroom light, and a thought occurred to me. I ran back out into the hall, and to the last three rooms I'd checked and turned on all the lights. Maybe I couldn't find a hallway light, but the light should illuminate the way if I left all the bedroom doors open. With the doors open, I didn't feel as afraid either. I went back to the room I'd been in last and resumed my search.

No Freya.

Leaving that door open, I peered down the hall. Only three rooms left, including a bathroom. Where was she? Somewhere in the distance inside the house, I could hear male voices. Kyle and who? Was Stephen back? Or was Kyle confronting Harold? I started for the stairs.

"No, Ainsley, please. I'm here," came Freya's pitiful voice again.

I spun around. "Where?" I wasn't sure what to do; help Kyle with creepy Harold or find Freya. I dashed to one of the bedrooms I hadn't checked and burst into the room, flipping the light on and dropping to my knees to look under the full-size bed. When I didn't see her, I started to stand, but I plunged into darkness instead.

CHAPTER SEVENTEEN

I blinked several times. The moonlight streaming through the window, and the beam from my Maglite was the only visible light. I hadn't lost my sight. I hadn't passed out. The power had gone off. *Freaking Harold.*

A creaking in the hall made me drop back down to my hands and knees by the bed. Someone was up here. I flattened myself out onto my belly then quietly slid under the bed, ignoring the dust that seemed attached to everything. With a deep breath, I pulled the bat closer to me and turned the flashlight off.

I waited as I listened to the creaking sounds. The old floorboards clued me in that whoever it was moved slowly in their search. Since the bedroom door was still open, I saw a flashlight beam sweep closer to the doorway. I inched further under the bed and turned onto my side, bringing the bat closer to my chest.

A pair of Timberland boots appeared at the door, and I covered my mouth. The flashlight swept through the room, then the person dropped to one knee and shined the light under the bed. I didn't take the time to identify the stranger but used the end of the bat to jab at them, hitting the flashlight, knocking it away. I scrambled out from the other side of the bed.

"Ainsley, stop. It's me." Alec came around the bed with the flashlight in one hand and his gun in the other.

I ran to him and wrapped my arms around his neck. "I thought you were creepy Harold."

"I get that a lot," he answered. When I let out a pent-up laugh, he continued, "I just got here. Drekr filled me in on Palmer. Stephen's with him at the hospital. But then Drekr said that when he came back into the house, you were gone. He's searching for you downstairs."

"I heard Freya. I think Harold has her hidden away up here somewhere, but then the lights went out."

"So you came up here by yourself? Why didn't you wait for Drekr?"

I shrank back. His tone revealed his aggravation with me. "I came up here because I thought that maybe this was the only chance Freya had to escape. Kyle would have wanted to grab the gear and check every floor."

"Yes, that would've been the cautious thing to do." He turned toward the door.

"This isn't about me wandering off to find Freya, is it?"

"What?"

"You're still angry with me."

"Not now, Ainsley." He moved to the door.

"I can't do this. I can't fight the supernatural and worry about Freya and theorize about our relationship. It's too much."

"Then don't worry about the latter. We have more pressing concerns," he said with a frown etched so deeply between his brows I could see it in the moonlight.

Against my wishes, hot tears spilled down my cheeks, causing the throbbing in the back of my head to intensify. This wasn't how it was supposed to be. I needed Alec on my side.

A creaking sound from the hallway caused Alec to stiffen, and he pulled me close. "Shh."

"Please, Alec. I'm so sorry. Nothing happened with Kyle," I sobbed softly into Alec's chest as he held one arm around my shoulder, his gun pointing to the floor in his other hand.

"Shh, not now," he whispered as he turned to look for danger.

I stared up at him. His clenched jaw held the tension as he peeked around the door frame. I pulled him back into the room and placed my hands on the sides of his face. If he would only look at me.

"Ainsley, stop it. We're in danger." He shook me off as he took his place by the door frame again.

I knew tears were running down my face and that I was acting like a spoiled child who'd lost her toy. No wonder he didn't want anything to do with me. I needed to get it together. I leaned into his shoulder, waiting for our next move. "I'm sorry I hurt you. But you made the wrong assumption about Kyle and me. I would never hurt you like that," I whispered.

He made eye contact with me for the briefest moment, and I saw something new in his eyes before he turned back to his post. Not anger or sadness, but perhaps resolution. Or determination.

"Please say something," I whispered.

He glanced down at me and exhaled. "Ainsley, I hurt you. I would rather die than ever hurt you, but I know deep in my soul that we aren't meant to be right now. Right now, we need to find Freya and get out of here."

"I know, but please tell me we still have a shot."

"Maybe one day," he whispered. "A long time from now."

I stood still watching Alec work his jaw. He was trying to strategize the best way to get us out of this situation alive. Yet, the pain in my chest wanted to fool me into believing that none of it mattered. It was a strange sensation, one of loss and grief, and also a growing numbness. I'd lost someone before, and I knew the familiar ache, but this was far deeper.

I placed my hand over my heart. Was it still beating? I didn't think so. Was this what people meant by having a broken heart?

"Okay, we're going to move out, quietly, down the hall. Stay behind me," Alec turned to confirm I'd heard him.

I blinked. "Okay," I answered so softly I wasn't sure if I'd spoken out loud.

Alec studied my face, then glanced back to the doorway. We were running out of time, but when he turned to face me a familiar fire lit up his green eyes. "Do you think this is easy for me? Do you think walking away from you was a spur-of-the-moment decision? I've agonized over this, Ainsley. One day, it will all make sense to you. Today, we need to concentrate on getting out of here alive and stopping Harold."

I blinked back the ever-forming tears from my eyes, but they silently came anyway. I grasped Alec's shirt when he moved closer to the door again. I could barely see him through the blurry haze of salty tears. He reached back with one hand to confirm I was close, and for a second, he squeezed my elbow without looking in my direction.

We began our trek to find Freya and escape Ashbury. As soon as my foot touched the top stair, the bedroom doors I'd left open all slammed at once. The silence was deafening with the exception of the heavy breathing coming from both Alec and me.

"Not Harold that time," I whispered.

We descended the third-floor stairs, but on the second floor landing, we heard a moaning. "It has to be Freya," I whispered.

Alec nodded, and we quietly followed the muffled groans. I prayed we weren't too late. The sound was coming from that dreaded sitting room. Alec braced his back against the wall near the doorframe and I followed suit. The wall was cold. Why was Ashbury so cold tonight? The moaning stopped.

I wanted to remind Alec that this sitting room was the one where I'd seen his great-great-grandfather murder Mrs. Ashbury. This was the sitting room we'd seen the demonic girl for the first time. On second thought, he probably remembered the story. Carefully, Alec peered around the door frame and then pulled back, a frown on his face. He motioned for me to stay put, then he took a deep breath and slid into the room.

The vibration began in the soles of my feet right through my Converse. I pushed myself against the wall as it continued to move through me. I counted silently to myself. The only sound coming from the room now was Alec's creaking footsteps. After I'd counted to fifty, I poked my head around the door frame. Alec was the only one in the room, and he was standing in front of the empty fireplace, his gun in one hand pointing to the floor. His other hand rested on the mantle near his flashlight.

"Alec?" I whispered as I entered the room, looking around. If there was a demon present, I couldn't see it yet.

Alec didn't move, only stood there staring into an invisible fire. "Alec?" I asked again. *What was wrong with him?*

I reached out and touched his back. He stiffened, and I jerked my hand away. Something was wrong.

Alec whirled around on me, anger and hatred in his eyes. "Mrs. Ashbury, that is not my intention at all. It's just that the tuberculosis is sweepin' through the poverty-laden part of town, and we don't have time to construct a separate buildin' for patients. Your house is the perfect size for a clinic." I took a step backward. This wasn't Alec. Sure, he was wearing Alec, but this wasn't *my* Alec.

"Alec?" My voice sounded even weaker than it had in my head.

Alec continued to advance towards me, encircling me so that now my back was to the cold fireplace. "Your family could easily live on this floor and allow the patients and medical staff the downstairs. You have multiple exits with the servants' stairs and all. Please, Mrs. Ashbury, our small town needs a place to house the sick ones."

This was Eugene Graham. Had he possessed Alec? Could ghosts do that? *Oh, Kyle, where are you? Oh God, Kyle is the only one who knows about trapped spirits.*

"Do you realize that some of these patients are mere children? The youngest we have is an innocent ten-year-old girl." Alec paused as if listening to Mrs. Ashbury's response. I replayed the scene in the upstairs sitting room in my head again. This was the part where the Muladach arrived and influenced Dr. Graham to kill the woman. Alec turned towards the only door to the hallway. I glanced around the room. Where could I hide? I so wished we hadn't bricked up that little servants' stairs. Instead, I turned to my left and ran into the bedroom, and slammed the door. However, the only lock on the door was a flimsy deadbolt probably older than the house.

Alec slammed his fist against the door, making me jump backward.

"And who would that someone be, Mrs. Ashbury? Your husband is dead, and your son is at work. You've only one housemaid left, and she's somewhere downstairs."

I backed up to the window, then tried to open it, but managed to cut my hand on one of the nails. It was nailed shut. *Who nails their windows shut on the third floor?* It wasn't like a burglar could scale the side of the house. I tried another window, then another. I tried the balcony doors. They were all nailed shut.

Alec slammed his fist into the door again, and a yelp escaped my throat. Suddenly an image of my father popped into my head. Rather it was as if he was standing right beside the door. I knew he wasn't there, but I practically ran to the door anyway. He was wearing the same pants and shirt he'd worn in my dream, yet the dark eyes following my movements seemed different somehow – somber. He was wearing his serious-Dad face.

He kept his eyes on mine as he placed the palm of his hand on the door at the same time that Alec slammed the door harder. I could only imagine that Alec was using his shoulder on the door. How much time did I have left until he started firing his gun through the wood?

Dad kept watching me. He wanted me to do something, but he wasn't saying anything. Apparently, this imagination-fueled version of my father was mute. I placed my hand on the door, and a voice entered my head, *"Talk to him. He's still in there. This is a ghost reliving a nightmare."*

I took a deep breath as I kept my eyes glued to my father's image. "Alec? Alec, can you hear me?"

Alec stopped pounding on the door.

"This isn't you. It's Eugene Graham using your body to relive his moments in this house. Memories he wishes he could forget. You have to fight him, Alec. You can't let him use you." I spoke through the door and could only hope he was still standing on the other side. The image of my father wavered.

"I know you're in my imagination," I whispered to Dad. "But I need you right now." The image wavered as it pointed to the floor. "*Go down to the furnace,*" the words echoed in my head. Then the image slowly dissipated. I was alone in the room again.

"Ainsley?" I heard Alec say my name with such anguish that I immediately threw the deadbolt back and swung open the door. But instead of grabbing me up into a hug, Alec's hand wrapped around my throat as he jerked me out of the bedroom, encircling me around his body and forcing me in front of him. His grip tightened around my throat as he stood behind me, the gun pressing so hard into my back I was afraid it might emerge through my chest at any moment.

Just like the fireplace poker through Mrs. Ashbury.

"Let go!" The words came out in a choked scream. "Dr. Graham, please don't! I'm not Mrs. Ashbury. Get out of your grandson's body!" I clawed at Alec's hand, my palm and fingers sliding in my own blood, but his grip was sure. I looked up to see Kyle running into the room with the bat raised to hit Alec.

"No!" I screamed in horror. "It's Dr. Graham!"

Kyle stopped short, rage contorting his face. He rocked on his heels as if ready to lunge at Alec at any second. He was struggling to sound calm. "Eugene Graham, hear me. Pass on from this realm to the next. Your memory holds no power over you anymore. Let your grandson go." Kyle's eyes shifted to me as Alec's grip tightened. "Or, I'll be forced to kill him."

A wheezing sound came from Alec's chest as he began to loosen his grip, putting some distance between his body and mine, the gun easing slightly from under my shoulder blade. When he'd let go just enough, Kyle grabbed my wrist and pulled me to him. Alec took two steps backward, still gasping for air. Kyle held me back as hot tears ran down my face again. I was afraid, not only for myself but for Alec. He still had the gun in his hand.

Eugene Graham stepped away from Alec, his body as solid as Mattie's had been. It was as if Dr. Graham's body was superimposed onto Alec's skeleton; one person became two. The senior Graham narrowed his eyes at us and then turned to Alec, who had dropped to one knee in front of the fireplace, the barrel of the gun scraping against the brick hearth as he struggled to breathe.

Then Eugene Graham vanished.

I shook Kyle's arms off me and ran to Alec, but it was a moment before he realized it was me. He wrapped his arms around me, pulling me onto the floor with him and burying his face in my neck. "I'm so sorry, Baby. I could see it happening, but I couldn't stop it. I could've killed you. Eugene thought he was holding the fireplace poker. If he'd realized he was holding my gun…" He pulled away and cupped my face in his hand. "I would never hurt you."

Then he looked up at Kyle, who still wore a menacing expression. "This can't happen again."

"I'm not the one you'll have to convince," Kyle said. "Pull yourself together, man. We need to find Freya. This ghost thing is a means to distract us."

Alec's gaze fell back to me, and he wiped my tears with his thumb, then stood and rolled his shoulders back, a look of determination finding its way into his eyes again as he studied my blood on his hand. "Well, the distraction worked."

After hearing the sudden coldness in his voice, I pushed my hands against my thighs and stood. Somehow I knew that when this was all over, I was going to lose Alec Graham. I swallowed. I had a job to do. "I know where Freya is hidden."

"Where?" Kyle asked.

"On the other side of the green door from the room where we found Mr. Palmer."

"How do you know?" Alec asked, rechecking his gun.

"A vision of my father told me."

Both men stared at me and then shrugged. *At this point, what did we have to lose taking clues from a vision?*

"We need to stay alert," Alec said. "After I visited Helen - Mrs. Meadors - I went to my grandfather's home to talk about his interest in Ashbury."

"He spoke to you about it?" I asked. The first and only time we'd visited Edward Graham, he'd accused me of insulting his dead brother's memory and accused his grandson of knocking me up. I was not a fan.

Alec gave me a half-grin. "Well, it took some physical coercion, but yes, he told me."

"You hit your grandfather?" Kyle asked, stunned.

"Not hit. My grandfather would call it a forceful show of affection. I held him against the wall and refused to let him go until he told me what was going on with Ashbury. It was how he always got me to tell the truth when I was growing up."

My eyes widened, picturing the towering Edward Graham being held against his will by his younger and equally powerful grandson. "What did he say?"

"He said Palmer came to him and wanted to buy Grandfather's share of the Ashbury Estate, but Grandfather couldn't see any reason to sell it to him. He said Palmer told him that the place was really haunted and that maybe they should shut it down for good. No tours, no investigations, no gift shop. Of course, Grandfather told him he'd invested too much into the place to lose his money by selling his half to Palmer. He said that before Palmer left the house, he said something cryptic."

"Like what?" Kyle asked.

"Palmer told Grandfather that the Ashbury Estate was making Harold's dreams come true...and that someone needed to stop him. I think it has something to do with those missing girls in the area, but we don't have time to contact the police and run through their case files. I do believe it is connected to the kidnappings in the 1930s. Tilda did tell me that her great aunt was Lorena Tarsey, one of the missing girls from the time when Mrs. Ashbury was killed. They never found the bodies. According to Tilda, Harold has always had a "fascination" with teenage girls. He got in trouble a few times in his twenties and thirties for stalking, but Palmer and Helen made the charges go away."

I nodded. "The kidnapper from back then was probably influenced by the same demon guiding Harold now."

Kyle frowned as he stared at the doorway leading to the second-floor hallway. "We need to find Freya and finish this."

~   ~   ~

Since Alec carried a gun, he led us down the stairs. I followed behind with Kyle bringing up the rear with the bat; the black duffle bag slung over his shoulder. Although we wanted to hurry down to the foyer, we took our time. None of us wanted to be caught off guard.

At the bottom of the stairs, a sharp pain shot through my head. I breathed through my clenched teeth. My hand trembled as I reached up to feel the knot.

"What's wrong?" Alec whispered.

"She slammed her head into the wall over there when Mattie appeared earlier tonight. She might have a concussion."

"Why didn't you tell me this sooner?" Alec's aggravated face softened as he approached me to feel the back of my head. His fingers pressed lightly on the area around the knot, and I involuntarily winced.

"Because we can't stop now. We have to find Freya." I kept my gaze level with him, but it was hard to do, and heat filled my cheeks. He was so close and yet so far from me.

Alec ignored my comments and my blushing cheeks and made me follow his finger with my eyes – side to side, up and down. "We good?" I asked, blinking from the movement. My head throbbed harder with every twitch.

"As soon as this is over, I'm taking you to the hospital." It wasn't a threat, but I could have sworn he made it sound like one.

"Through the door under the stairs is the small hall that leads to the room where we found Mr. Meadors tucked neatly into the wardrobe," Kyle said, pulling one of the cameras out of the bag.

"You think Freya is in another room off from that one?" Alec asked me.

I nodded and instantly regretted it. The sudden movement coupled with a vibration tucked under my feet sent waves of pain through me head to toe. Certainly, there had to be a Muladach using my body as a xylophone while he played a concert for his demon buddies. I closed my eyes.

"Maybe you should stay here, Ainsley."

At the sound of Alec's voice, I slowly opened my eyes. "No, I just need a second."

He frowned. I knew he was debating calling this off. Or locking me in Kyle's rental car while they searched the estate for Freya. The tremor shot through me again. "We are running out of time, Alec."

Against my better judgment, I started for the door under the stairs. Alec touched my forearm, making me pause so that he could move ahead of me with his gun drawn. When we reached the door to the room, Kyle slipped the camera through the doorway.

"Nothing. Not even a mouse," Kyle said.

Alec went in first, and I kept the flashlight beam low to the ground until I saw him motion for us to follow. I only glanced around the empty room before joining the two men at the green door.

"Reynolds," Kyle whispered. "Put your hand here and see if you can sense anything."

I did as I was told and closed my eyes. My head thanked me. Closing my eyes seemed to give me a reprieve from the pain. I tuned out the usual sounds - frogs, rustling, breathing.

Silence.

Listen for the sounds under the silence.

A whimpering began below the depths of the quiet. Maybe not a human whimpering, not demonic either. So much sadness. Then something else. The whimpering sounded hopeless.

"More than one," I whispered.

"More than one demon?" Alec asked.

I stared at him. "More than one girl. I think."

Alec nodded at Kyle, then grasped the doorknob and turned it.

There was another step down into this room, and Alec almost went running to Freya, but Kyle grabbed his arm and shook his head. Thankfully, Alec couldn't see what we could.

At least nine demons were surrounding Freya. She laid unconscious on the concrete floor in front of a massive antique coal-burning stove. The antique furnace's door was wide open and my skin grew moist from the blast of heat as I stood barely through the doorway. The stove was the size of a side-by-side modern-day washer and dryer, making it feel like we'd stumbled upon a boiler room. It set in the middle of the windowless room.

Along the right wall were four large iron dog crates. Three of the containers each held a girl – her hands and feet bound, a cloth wrapped tightly around her face covering her eyes, her mouth covered with duct tape. The fourth crate's door was open. It had probably been Freya's box. The room smelled of sweat and urine and feces. I forced myself to swallow to keep from vomiting. Lined along the same wall near the door sat four small fire extinguishers. *What did Harold plan to do to these girls?* Two words flitted through my mind as I observed the rest of the room.

Burn them.

Across the room was a narrow set of wooden stairs that led to an equally narrow door. This room was like a storm cellar, but where did the door lead? Was that how Harold had brought the girls down here?

The demons turned to face us, their necks swiveling strangely on their necks. The fire's light created more terrifying shadows in the room, making it difficult to see through the Muladach's skin. However, their sharp claws and teeth were quite visible. A demon larger than the others, close to Freya's head, leaned forward on all fours and let out a menacing growl.

Kyle slowly set down the bag and the equipment he carried. "Paul said, 'For I am convinced that neither death nor life, *neither angels nor demons*, neither the present nor the future, nor any powers, neither height nor depth, nor anything else in all creation, will be able to separate us from the love of God that is in Christ Jesus our Lord.'" His voice was low, but he kept his eyes fixed on the demons.

The demons watched him, and as he swayed, they did as well, mimicking his movements.

"The walls are soundproof. Look," Alec whispered.

The demons snarled in his direction as I glanced around at the white foam padded boards lining the room. This was why we couldn't hear the girls. But where was their kidnapper?

"Reynolds, send them away," Kyle whispered.

My first instinct was to ask how, but I knew how. I'd known it all along. I didn't need the Latin passages or the medallion around my neck. I needed to remember that my faith was bigger than what I could see.

I raised my arms. "Go back to Hell, demons! You have no place here, no home in this realm. You are banished!" The demons moved restlessly, pacing back and forth, increasing in frenzy so that it was impossible to see Freya through their legs. "Back to -"

Something heavy hit Alec from the side, knocking him into me. I flew forward toward the demons and the furnace with its wide-open door.

~   ~   ~

The demons parted as if they were the Red Sea, and I landed on Freya, my face only inches from the furnace door. The blast of heat sent me scurrying from the stove, falling over her body again and rolling us a few feet away;

the demons encircling us with their loud growls and barks. I struggled to see past them to Alec and Kyle.

Alec was on the ground, a fire extinguisher rolling on the floor near him. I thanked God as Alec slowly raised his hand to his face. He was still alive.

Kyle was hitting a crazed-looking Harold with the softball bat. The force should have broken Harold's arm in at least a few places, but he just kept coming towards Kyle. The demons became more feverish, jumping up and down like it was a school fight. The girls in the crates whimpered and cried through their blindfolds and tape.

My mind raced as my head throbbed. What could I do?

I drug myself up to my knees. My head hurt too much to stand completely. "Hear me, Beasts from Hell," I started, then had to take a deep breath as the pain surged from my head down my spine. "Hear me, Beasts from Hell! You have no dominion here. You have no right to take the lives of these girls, the life of this girl, Freya." I balanced my weight on Freya's hip to keep from toppling over while the largest of the Muladach advanced towards me, parting its lips so I could get a good view of its razor-sharp teeth. "You cannot hurt me, demon. You are banished back to Hell, and may our Lord judge you!"

One by one, the demons around the room began to retreat onto their haunches, letting out a shrill bark, then fading into nothingness. However, the bigger one seemed unbothered, saliva dripping from its open mouth onto the concrete floor, my reflection dancing in its eyes. Unlike its victims who became entranced with the reflection of some future self after the evil made their dreams come true, I could only see me.

"Ainsley!" Alec's voice rang out, and I looked to my right in time to see the end of a fire extinguisher flying toward my face like a missle. I threw my hand up to protect my face, and the cylinder collided with my wrist, snapping it back into my cheekbone. The force slammed my head against the concrete as I fell backward and lay on the hot stone near the roaring furnace as Alec wrestled with Harold not a few feet from me. I could feel nothing but the engulfing, all-consuming pain. I couldn't see Kyle at all.

However, I *could* see the large Muladach as it leaned down and sniffed my face and hair, blowing its hot breath over my eyes.

Pray, Baby Girl. Remember what I wrote to you.

I closed my eyes, wanting to embrace the darkness and the asylum from the pain. Instead, I forced words to form in my consciousness.

God, please. We can't do this. We can't save these girls on our own. I'm incredibly hurt. Alec has already been knocked out once. I have no idea what happened to Kyle. Please, I need You! I'm so tired.

A still voice entered my mind. It was the only way I could describe the sound. It wasn't an audible voice, but it wasn't my thoughts either. I opened my eyes and stared at the demon. It wasn't the whispers from the Muladach either.

I sought the Lord, and He answered me; He delivered me from all my fears.

All my fears.

My eyes widened, causing the pain to increase. In the journal, Dad told me to feel the fear and to push through it anyway. As if burning coal made up my spirit, I sat up, making the demon back away. It was still a struggle to get onto my knees and then to my feet, but the drive inside me was stronger than the fear that threatened to drown me if I continued to lay on the concrete.

I opened my mouth, and a voice sounding like a mixture of mine and my father on his best day came forward. "The Lord commands the armies of Heaven. He commands the realms. You have no authority here. Be gone!" I pointed to the demon with the index finger of my right hand and felt a hand cover the top of my left, intertwining fingers with mine.

Kyle stood to my left, one eye swollen almost completely shut. "Make him see, Lord!" Kyle shouted as the demon moved backward then faded away with a lingering growl. Once the Muladach disappeared, I could see past it to where Alec and Harold were still battling it out. A stream of blood had run down Alec's head from above his temple to below his jaw. Harold's arm hung limp at his side.

"Make him see, Lord!" Kyle repeated.

Harold suddenly stopped moving, and his eyes rolled up into the back of his head as his body began to seize.

"Make him see, Lord!" Kyle shouted a third time. Harold's body stiffened in his seizures, and he dropped back onto the floor, blood pouring from his mouth. Immediately, Alec was at Harold's side, forcing the man's mouth open and shoving in his leather wallet as he turned Harold over onto his side.

It was probably only a few minutes that Harold thrashed on the floor, but it felt like an eternity. Kyle let go of my hand and began checking Freya for a pulse. I watched as Alec pulled his phone out and began calling for emergency services. His gun laid several feet from him, apparently knocked away during the commotion.

Although my body screamed to give it rest, I managed to make my way over to the bound girls. One by one, I opened their crates and pulled the blindfolds and duct tape away. Kyle or Alec would have to get the plastic cinch ties from around their bloody wrists and ankles. I slid down the wall near the last crate as Alec rushed over to help the girls.

I closed my eyes and welcomed the silence.

~   ~   ~

After the events in the storm cellar – which I learned later opened out behind thick hedges that surrounded the back of the house, the windows sealed and covered on the inside but unsuspectingly intact on the outside of the house – an ambulance, police cars, and a fire truck arrived. A paramedic who I could've sworn was younger than me stitched up my hand and applied an ice pack to the back of my head and another one to the bruise across my cheekbone then rushed me to the hospital for a scan on my head and my wrist. However, once we returned to Locklyn the next day, Mom took me to our pediatrician, who prescribed bedrest for one week along with a prescription for painkillers. Thankfully, I wasn't behind in any of my classes.

I spent the first full day wrapped in a fleece blanket on my bed in a sweatshirt, a pair of blue shorts, and a pair of knee-high boot socks. I wasn't cold. I just thought my head and my heart would heal faster with a good ol' dose of cozy. The tight bandage wrapped around my wrist itched something terrible, but I did my best to ignore it. I was lucky that the fire extinguisher hadn't broken any bones.

I could hear Mom, Nick, and Ben in the living room laughing about something on the television. Mom had been frantic when Maren called and told her about Harold kidnapping Freya. But she went ballistic when Maren informed her that Kyle Drekr and I had gone searching for Freya at the Ashbury Estate and helped the police apprehend the kidnapper and find the missing girls. Of course, Maren didn't mention the organization's involvement or Stephen, Alec, and herself.

Mom was proud of me for being so brave – angry at me for acting impulsively, "just like your father" – and she made me swear I would not leave the house again until college. Stephen returned to West Virginia, and Maren was busy resuming her role as the responsible teacher. Kyle flew back to Los Angeles. Molly was still in the hospital, beginning her rehabilitation to strengthen her legs. Freya was home healing from the traumatic events at Ashbury, and I kind of doubted Waverly would ever visit me even if someone offered her a gold bar. The police were getting the other three girls back to their families. So, I lounged on my bed and watched the ceiling fan throw little pieces of dust around the room.

When the doorbell rang, I knew the time had come. I just knew. A couple of minutes later, my bedroom door slowly opened and a man dressed in cargo pants, a white thermal, and a black jacket, smelling like a sweet mixture of cinnamon and green apples, gave me a bittersweet half-smile. My heart dropped into the pit of my stomach.

"I came to see how you're feeling," Alec said as he set a bouquet of daisies of several different dyed colors on the dresser. His face had yet another bandage at the temple.

"I'll live. Thanks," I pushed myself up onto the stack of pillows Mom insisted I needed to help me recuperate, but I didn't smile. I didn't have the energy to pretend. I knew the real reason he was here. It was why Dad had told Stephen in his dream that I would need to stay strong even while my heart was breaking.

But I didn't have to agree to it.

Alec took a few steps closer to my bed but stopped when I pulled my blanket a little tighter around me. "I know you're angry with me, but I have to say this." Alec took a deep breath. "I did a lot of thinking while I was on my old stomping grounds – a lot of thinking about us and what's possible for us. Ainsley, we can't be together right now. There's too much of an age difference, and people won't leave that alone. And then there are your bruises." He pointed to the ring of fresh bruises around my throat. He couldn't see the ones under my sweatshirt, but he knew they were there – bruises from his own hand.

"This supernatural world you're a part of, it's dangerous, and coupled with my own issues, makes me dangerous to you. That's why I need to be the one to tell you that you'll get over this. You'll go to college and meet a guy there, and all of *this*," he waved his hand around, "will have been like a bad dream."

I blinked. "Did your grandfather say this to you?"

He didn't answer.

"Is this coming from Stephen?"

He took a deep breath.

"If this is about Kyle -"

"No. Edward's opinion of my life doesn't matter to me. As for Drekr, I know nothing happened between the two of you. I let him get to me. It's more than Kyle Drekr." Alec moved to stand beside me, and when my eyes started to well up with tears, he sat down on the edge of the bed and placed his hands on the blanket on either side of my lap, careful not to touch me, so he could look me dead in the eye.

"Other people have accused me of grooming you for myself."

"I don't know what that means."

"That I want you for myself. I'm not like that, Ainsley. I don't want people to think that about me. I want you to experience the world. Go out and have fun. No more hiding who you are. You've grown so much in the short time I've known you. When we met, you were the girl who always tried to blend in, staring down at the carpet. Now, I see you confronting monsters, and ghosts, and men three times your size. Yet, you're still this precious jewel that is learning how to shine. If I am in your life, I think you will always place a limit on what you can do, where you can go, who you can be around. I won't allow myself to hold you back."

I swallowed. The numbness in my chest grew. "I'm not going to beg you to stay. My newfound pride won't let me."

His eyes searched mine. "Good. Don't you dare beg anyone to be in your life."

"Then you should go. I understand."

Alec frowned and stared down at my blanket, but he didn't move. "I *have* to let you go, Ainsley, but I don't want to leave things like this." He raised his gaze to meet mine. "If you need help with anything in the future-"

"I'll call Maren or Stephen or Kyle. You should go now."

Alec softly exhaled. "Ainsley-"

"I need you to go now," I hardened my voice as I looked past Alec to the wall behind him and the reframed picture of my father and me at the fishing pier. *Baby Girl, hold it together for a little while longer.*

Alec nodded, then stood looking down at me for a moment, but I refused to meet his gaze again. He sucked in his breath. "This is going to be hard for both of us. I already think about you every day, every hour, every minute. But I promise you it will fade."

When he walked out of my bedroom, all of the air left my lungs. I heard him say goodbye to Mom and Nick, but he didn't stay to chat.

When I heard the door slam to his SUV, I allowed the first of many tears to fall. I prayed God would keep Alec safe and that maybe one day, when the timing was right, He would bring us together again. But for now, I gave in and felt the pain from my first heartbreak.

"Alec Edward Graham, I'm in love with you. I don't think that'll ever fade away," I whispered into the silence of my bedroom.

EPILOGUE

"Happy Birthday!" Mom and Ben burst into my room. Ben launched himself onto my small bed, and I barely managed to shield my torso from his knobby knee.

"Here's your breakfast now that you are officially eighteen," Mom said as she set the wooden breakfast tray that she usually used as a writing table across my lap. "Are you awake?"

"I am now. Look at all of this!" The tray held scrambled eggs, bacon, french toast, a slice of banana nut bread, and a small bowl of fruit.

"Oh! Let me grab your coffee. I'll be right back." Mom left the room while Ben snuggled up next to me.

"Are you feeling better, Ains?"

"Yes, don't worry, Ben. I'm much better."

"Mom said you got your heart broken."

I grimaced. "I did, I think. But I'm going to be okay."

Mom brought my coffee into the room. "You'll be happy to know that I picked you up a large bottle of chocolate caramel creamer, just for you."

I gratefully took the hot mug. "Thanks, Mom. That's the best gift you could have given me. I am so tired of cashew milk and stevia."

"I know, I know." She sat down at the foot of my bed. "By the way, Stephen Reeves, who used to work with your father at the plant, called this morning."

"Oh?" I tried to sound as calm as I could. I took a bite of bacon.

"Well, I called him several weeks ago, but he was out of town and didn't get my message until he was home. He lives in West Virginia."

"Why did you call him?"

"It's going to sound silly."

"No, it won't. I want to know."

"Several weeks ago, I had a dream about your father."

Ben perked up. "You dreamed about Dad too?"

Mom nodded. "I did. It was the first time I think I've dreamt of him. He was calling my name from the family room downstairs. When I walked in there, he was sitting on the sectional like he always did. Ainsley, he looked so real. He was wearing his favorite blue button-down, and his hair needed combed." Mom paused as she smiled to herself.

Neither Ben nor I spoke.

"He told me some personal things that I'm not going to share," she eyeballed us. "But he also told me some things about his faith, things I'd forgotten. You see, your father was a Christian, and he believed whole-heartedly in Jesus. But you guys know grandma and grandpa…they would never allow such talk. So, we raised you two only taking you to church on Easter. In my dream, Gerald begged me to find a church here and to start going every Sunday. He told me to call Stephen."

"Why?" Ben asked.

"Apparently, not only did your dad and Stephen work at the plant together but when Gerald would be on business trips to West Virginia, he would visit Stephen's church. I guess Stephen is also a preacher."

I shoveled the fruit in my mouth to keep from asking Mom questions. When I dreamt of Dad, he told me he wanted to visit Mom in a dream. He must've done it that night.

Mom continued, "Well, Stephen is going to drive down here and stay with us for the weekend. He's going to help us locate a church." She placed her hand on my foot. "And he said he wants to take us out to dinner tomorrow night to celebrate your birthday."

"My friend Freya goes to a church here. I could ask her which one. I'd like that, Mom. Stephen sounds nice," I said.

"From what I remember of meeting him before, he was."

~   ~   ~

Sure enough, Stephen arrived early the next morning. Of course, I had to pretend I was meeting him for the first time, which was a bit hard to do. Stephen made you feel comfortable from the moment you laid eyes on him, so it was too easy to treat him like an old friend.

We all dressed for dinner, and my breath stuck in my throat when I caught a glimpse of my mother emerging from her room wearing an emerald green dress that hugged her curves, black heels, and her thick blonde hair cascading in curls down her back.

"Wow," Stephen and I said in unison. I was surprised to see the expression on the single man's face.

"Is it too much?" Mom asked, and I could tell she was beginning to doubt her outfit choice for the evening. She was usually at home in jeans or yoga pants.

Before I could reassure her, Stephen jumped in, walking toward her.

"No, it's perfect. You look stunning."

Mom's face turned several shades of red which only made her look even more beautiful. For a moment, I wondered if this was part of Dad's wish too. Maybe he wanted Stephen not only to introduce Mom to a church here but perhaps he wanted Mom to spend time with the preacher. I wasn't sure where Nick Clendenin would fit into that picture, but things were a lot less awkward with Stephen here instead of my Vice-Principal.

I headed into the kitchen to grab a bottle of water to take with me when I heard Mom announce that she and Ben were going to the garage.

"Sounds good. Let me just run to your restroom real quick," Stephen said.

"Okay. Ainsley can wait for you."

A few minutes later, Stephen emerged looking quite dapper in jeans and an untucked button-down. I watched as he put on his coat. "Are you okay?" he asked me.

"I'm fine," I answered and gave him my best smile.

He stopped in front of me. "Alec called and told me what happened. I know it can't be easy."

I nodded. "It was his decision."

He studied my face until I couldn't take it anymore. No wonder people told pastors everything. He was good.

"I understand why he made that choice, but it still upsets me. He didn't even try to fight for us. He just decided that we were over before we even had a chance to start."

"It wasn't an easy decision for him, Ainsley. He struggled with it for days. He talked about it with me. Before we left South Carolina, he came to the Lord. Then he felt convicted that he wasn't doing right by you."

"Why didn't he tell me any of this?"

"I don't know. Alec is a private person. Maybe he's not ready to share that with anyone yet." Stephen placed his hand on my shoulder. "Give him time. If it's meant to be, then nothing can stop it. Okay?"

I nodded. "There's something else. On Kyle's video footage from the asylum investigation, Dad's disembodied voice told him to protect me from someone. I don't think he meant Harold. I think the name started with a J."

"Your father told me once that time works differently in the supernatural realm. The apostle Peter said that 'with the Lord one day is as a thousand years, and a thousand years as one day.' Gerald may have been referring to some time in the future."

"So I might have another enemy in my future?"

"As the Seer, you probably have more than one. But God is with you, and I'll help you. Not to mention Kyle and Maren. You're not alone. Come on, let's go eat."

I smiled. "I'm really glad you came, Stephen."

"Me too, Ainsley."

My phone softly beeped, and I glanced at it, hoping it was a Happy Birthday text from Alec, only to see one from Kyle:

Happy Birthday, Reynolds. Try to keep it together for one day. Ignore the voices, the ghosts, and the demons. And plan on your family spending Spring Break in LA with me. My treat. I'll call your mom. She can think of it as research for her next book.

I raised my gaze to the portrait of my parents hanging in the living room. Dad's image smiled back at me. I had a purpose, and I had God. I could do this.

One day, one hour, one minute at a time.

SNEAK PEEK

OF THE BEACON BOOK 3 OF THE
MULADACH SERIES

"**Y**ou have gotten his attention. He can see you now. He's coming for you – and your family."

It's been four years since Alec Graham walked away from Ainsley Reynolds. Four years that the blonde Seer has become confident and determined in her purpose, battling demons with the help of her Protector, Kyle Drekr. But with the return of Alec in Ainsley's life comes a new enemy – one so powerful that every Seer and Protector who has confronted him throughout history has died.

Each time Ainsley expels another demon back to Hell, her soul shines like a beacon, drawing the enemy ever closer. She can't hide from him. She can't protect her loved ones from him. But is the Seer ready to make the ultimate sacrifice to stop him?

FOUR YEARS AFTER THE EVENTS FROM THE MADDENING

"Good job, Ainsley," Stephen Reeves said as I picked up my gun and slid a new clip into it before switching on the safety and holstering it. The preacher watched me as I pulled my black leather jacket on, carefully concealing the weapon.

"Are you headed back to North Carolina tonight?" he asked.

"Yeah, I have midterms to finish up. As it stands now, I won't get any sleep before my next exam."

He patted me on the shoulder. "I know. I'm sorry. I wouldn't have called you if it wasn't urgent."

I smiled up at the dark-haired man with the tattoos and laid-back attitude. "That's why I came. Don't feel bad about that. How's the little boy?"

"He'll be fine now. The authorities will get him back to his parents."

I nodded. The demons, what we referred to as Muladach now, had led me to a ring of sex traffickers. Thank God, with Stephen's help, we'd found not only the two men kidnapping children, but I'd tracked the demons to the ring itself. Hopefully, these men would go to prison for a long time.

"Have you talked to Kyle lately?" Stephen asked.

"Just through text. He's working on his show in L.A., so I don't think he will be back around this way for a while." Kyle Drekr was the television host of a popular paranormal investigative show. The crew went all over the world, seeking out the unknown. Kyle had worked with my father a long time ago and knew without a doubt that demons and ghosts were real, and although he had *not* confirmed my suspicion, I believed his staff integrated a lot of the spooky things seen and heard on the show during post-production. I had no proof, but there was no way Kyle gathered evidence at every location. Plus, he made it a practice to ignore the dead as much as possible now.

With that being said, Kyle was still a powerful Protector, a sort-of guardian for the Seers.

I looked up at Stephen, the preacher from a small church in Charleston, West Virginia, who also worked with the organization Malus Navis expelling demons. Stephen always seemed laid back with his hard-parted black hair and stubbled beard, blue eyes, and distressed jeans. I'd always liked him, but I had come to love him now that he and my mom were officially engaged.

"Have you heard from Alec?"

"Alec? Alec Graham?" I asked as Stephen raised an eyebrow. We knew only one Alec.

"Of course not. Alec cut me out of his life four years ago and hasn't looked back since. My friend Bronwyn said she saw him once at the Locklyn Gym right before closing. She'd forgotten her purse and ran back in, and he was there working out. The owner, Henry, lets him work out after closing, so he doesn't have to run into other people."

"That's a lot of judging all at once, you think?" Stephen finished loading his gun case, locked it, and stood.

"I'm not judging him," I offered as I took a step back. "He made his decision. If he wanted to stay friends, he wouldn't have just left."

"Didn't *you* tell him to leave?"

"Yeah, maybe." I looked down at the ground for a moment. When Stephen didn't say anything else, I peered back up at him. "Why the sudden interest in my talking to Alec?"

It was Stephen's turn to appear uneasy. He dropped eye contact with me as he shrugged his shoulders. "No reason. He crossed my mind today."

"Then maybe you should pray for him," I quipped and then instantly regretted it. It was true that whenever someone crossed my mind out of the blue, eventually, I would hear something about them; an illness, a tragedy, or even death. Stephen had told me that when that happens to always stop and pray, it was God's way of bringing them to my attention. I certainly didn't want anything bad to happen to Alec.

"Yeah, well, maybe we should pray for him," Stephen said as he started towards the warehouse door. "Come on, let's get you back on the road for that exam."

~ ~ ~

I sat in the uncomfortable metal chair at the DMV with my registration card in my hand. It was time to renew my little Chevy Cruze, and I had procrastinated for too long, so instead of enjoying the perks of the online service, I got to enjoy the crowded DMV this morning. I'd known it was going to be a long morning when I noticed the broken kiosk.

I could so go for a cup of coffee right now, but that would require me to forfeit my number. There was no way I was going to leave after waiting forty minutes.

"Now serving 34-B at Window Number 12," the electronic voice announced.

I practically danced over to Window Number 12 and smiled at the short woman behind the counter wearing the Sophia nametag.

"Can I help you?" she asked in the most monotone of voices.

"I need to renew my registration, please," I answered.

I watched as she studied my paperwork and then typed something into the computer. I crossed my legs. I shouldn't have worn a short knit dress today. Why was it so cold in here? My dress only appeared warm, but my legs were freezing between my black ankle boots and the black material. I should've worn leggings. For the last four years, I'd come to love working out. Weights, Pilates, yoga, spin - I did it all. I took every class at the Locklyn Gym that the owner Henry's wife taught. Kickboxing was my favorite because it had resulted in very strong and defined legs, which I probably showed off a little too much now.

"That will be $54.30 if you are renewing for one year."

I slid my debit card into the machine and waited. "So, are you ready for Christmas?"

Sophia stopped and looked at me like I'd grown a third eye. "Why?"

"What?"

"Why do you want to know?" she asked as she narrowed her eyes.

"Just making conversation," I answered honestly.

The woman made an actual hmph sound and ordered me to withdraw my card. She handed me the receipt and new sticker.

"Have a nice day," she said, sounding like a robot.

I fought the urge to roll my eyes and instead answered loudly, "You too! Have a *fabulous* Christmas!" Then I turned on my heel to see someone standing in front of Window Number 14 staring at me. That was okay. I was sure everyone in the DMV was staring at me at this point. He could join the club. I didn't mind being the center of attention anymore.

It wasn't until I went to deliver the man a triumphant smile as I walked past that it registered with me who the man at Window Number 14 was and why he would stare so intently at me.

I walked a little faster out of the DMV building, fighting to breathe. There was no way I would fall apart out in public. As I hurried to my car in the parking lot, I heard him calling my name.

Girl, just get in the car. My mind yelled at my fingers to hurry and hit the unlock button on my keychain. However, my body as if having control of itself independently from the rest of me, slowed down and stopped at the driver's side door.

I felt his presence before I smelled his cologne. How could he stand so close to me after he'd walked away from me four years ago? I raised my gaze to meet Alec Graham's green eyes. He still had the stubble on his face, and his hair was cut a little closer to his scalp instead of the messy look he used to wear. He wore a black jacket that looked like it was tailor-made for him. Bronwyn said he was working out after the gym closed, and she wasn't wrong. Even covered by his jacket, I could see that his arms were larger, his chest broader.

I had to remind myself to breathe. I wasn't in high school anymore, and I was pretty sure I'd gotten over Alec. At that thought, the voice in my head laughed hysterically.

"Ainsley, I'd hoped it was you," he said. My, how I'd missed his voice.

"It's me," I said weakly and then caught myself. I stood up a little straighter. "I need to go. I have someplace to be," I lied as I threw my long blonde hair over my shoulder.

"Of course. Well, it was good seeing you again. You look…" Alec trailed off as I opened my car door and forced my body to obey me as I sat down, knowing my dress was hiking up a bit further than appropriate. I placed my hand on the inside of the door and looked up at Alec with every bit of coolness I could muster as if waiting for him to finish his sentence.

"You look beautiful," he finally said.

"Oh? Thank you.I thought you were going to say grown-up. Maybe I'll see you around."

The smile on his gorgeous face deflated a bit. I'd hit a nerve. He nodded and took a step back. "Goodbye, Ainsley."

I smiled as I shut my door and started the engine. As I drove back to my dorm, I never really saw the road. All I could see was Alec.

~   ~   ~

"Hey, Reynolds! Stephen told me about you saving that boy from those traffickers. Great job!" Kyle Drekr bellowed into the phone at me.

"Thanks, but that was all God. I had no clue that's what we would expose." Kyle and I had gone on a few adventures together with the organization, and we still rode each other a bit, but we got along now.

"Are you staying with your Mom for Christmas?"

"Yep. I'm going to try to spend some time with Ben." My little brother Benjamin was now a teenager and stood as tall as me at five-foot-six. "Between classes and work, I feel I've neglected him terribly."

"Well, let me know if you want to come out to California. I'm on hiatus from my show until spring."

"I might do that. I've only been there a few times." I remembered the investigation Kyle and I had performed outside of Los Angeles in some caves where a small cluster of demons hid near a portal. It was a gorgeous area, but I hadn't really had time to explore.

"You're more than welcome to stay. I have an extra bedroom."

"Thanks. I'll let you know. What about Maria?"

"Oh, we broke up. You know how it is. She wanted me to spend more time with her, but between the show, the shoots, and the investigations, I barely have any time for anyone else in my life. How about you?"

"What about me?"

"Are you seeing anyone?"

Telling Kyle about seeing Alec today was on the tip of my tongue. The men hadn't liked each other, and at one point in South Carolina, they'd come to blows over a misunderstanding. Technically, I'd *seen* Alec, but I wasn't *seeing* Alec.

"No. No one right now."

"Well, if you change your mind about California for the holidays, just call."

"I will, I promise," I said as I glanced around my dorm room. As much as I would love to hang out in Los Angeles, I felt Mom and Ben needed me home.

After I ended my call with Kyle, I text my best friend Molly to call me later. Now she, I could tell all about seeing Alec for the first time in four years. We'd been friends since grade school and were closer than sisters. We'd gone through a great deal a few years ago when we got too close to a serial killer influenced by demons, and, unfortunately, Molly had been stabbed and hovered in a coma for more than a week before she woke up. Even then, recovery was longer.

I started packing my bags to go home to Locklyn. Thank goodness that since I planned to return in the Spring, the school allowed me to keep my other items in my single dorm room. When I'd first arrived on campus as a Freshman, I was told I would be in a double room and that my father's GI bill covered quite a bit of my financial debt, however I would still need to pay more. I'd been heartbroken. I thought I would have to drop out because there was no way I was about to let Mom take money out of savings while she kept up with the house and utility bills.

However, right after I moved into the double room with a girl who I suspected was part demon by choice, I got a call from the Financial Aid office. They couldn't explain how or why but someone had paid all of my outstanding balances. Not only that, but I was registered for a single room with its own bathroom. *For all four years.* I made the woman check three times and then print me out a receipt showing this information just in case. I'd been able to keep the same room, and it almost seemed like home.

I hated to admit it, but part of me believed that maybe Alec was involved in my debt cancellation. While investigating a mansion in South Carolina, just minutes from Alec's childhood home, I'd learned that Alec came from a very wealthy family. He'd *chosen* police work over a luxury lifestyle.

But then again, it didn't make any sense. Why would the man pay for my schooling not covered by the GI bill for four years and then not so much as bother to call me? I stuffed my sweaters in my bag harder than necessary. I could've asked him. At the DMV, instead of getting in my car with my fake stuck-up attitude, I could've just asked Alec if he had paid the school.

And then what? What if he had said yes? I would feel obligated to pay him back. If he denied it, then I would have to admit to Alec that Mom and I were struggling to maintain the life we lived without Dad. Plus, I would still wonder who paid it.

The only other person I knew with that kind of money was Kyle Drekr. But Kyle was the type to *want* me to know that he paid it and that I was not obligated to pay him back – ever. He was always lecturing me about not allowing a man to take advantage. He lived in L.A., so I was sure he'd seen that a lot. It was one of his pinch points over Alec. No matter how loudly I defended him, Kyle believed Alec had taken advantage of a high school senior girl. We'd argued about it repeatedly when Alec first left.

"You don't need him. Let him get his life straightened out first," Kyle had said with a growl.

"We could have stayed friends, even if we waited to date." I'd sniffled out the words.

"He can't be friends with you, Reynolds. Some people can never be *just* friends. I don't think he can control himself around you for very long."

I'd glared at Kyle when he had said that, but secretly I wondered if it were true. I'd fantasized in class that Alec would burst into the room, tell me he loved me, and sweep me up into his arms. Instead, if it hadn't been for extra credit, I would have received a C in English my Freshman year for daydreaming and not participating.

Well, that was over now. Done. Alec had made his choice, and so what if I'd seen him today and already spent too much time dwelling on him? I would move on. My phone rang.

"Molly! You're never going to believe who I saw today."

THE BEACON, BOOK 3 IN THE MULADACH SERIES AVAILABLE SUMMER 2021!

ABOUT THE AUTHOR

Melissa **Plantz** is an author, Christian, and the founder of Fire and Grace Publishing. As the author of the spiritual warfare devotional series, *Take the Realm*, and of two Christian novels (*Fire and Grace*, *The Muladach*), Melissa is dedicated to equipping today's Christians with the tools for spiritual warfare through the power of storytelling. She believes that it's never been more important to spread the message of Christ, and that maintaining faith in the modern world is a powerful key to fulfillment and happiness.

When not writing, she enjoys spending time with her husband, children, and grandchildren. She currently lives in West Virginia, but she dreams of moving permanently to a beach off the coast of North Carolina. Connect with her at AuthorMelissaPlantz@fireandgracepublishing.com

For more information visit:

fireandgracepublishing.com

ALSO BY MELISSA PLANTZ

AND FIRE AND GRACE PUBLISHING

Take the Realm: 10 Days of Spiritual Battle Plans to Reignite the Weary Warrior

Fire and Grace

THE MULADACH SERIES

The Muladach

The Maddening

The Beacon (Available Summer 2021)